YVETTE

Of The

S.O.E

(SPECAL OPERATIONS EXECUTIVE)

By

KEVIN PAUL
WOODROW

YVETTE OFTHE S.O.E.

Copyright ©2023

Kevin Paul Woodrow
And
Woodrow Publishing
(www.woodrowpublishing.com/)

The right of Kevin Woodrow to be identified as author of this work has been asserted by him in accordance with section 77 and 78 of the Copyright, Designs and Patents Act 1988. - All rights reserved.

No part of this publication may be reproduced, stored in a retrieval system, or transmitted in any form or by any means, electronic, mechanical, photocopying, recording, or otherwise, without the prior permission of the author, Kevin Paul Woodrow, or publisher, Woodrow Books & Publishing.

(www.woodrowpublishing.com/)

Any person who commits any unauthorized act in relation to this publication may be liable to criminal prosecution and civil claims for damages.

ISBN: 9798386460297

**THIS BOOK IS
DEDICATED TO THE MEMORIES
Of**

**CRISTOBAL (CHRIS)
MELENDEZ**
(December 17th 1925 to January 15th 2022)

**JOSEPHINE
MELENDEZ-ZAYAS**
(July 17th 1933 to December 31st 2021)

**AND FINALLY, THIS BOOK
IS DEDICATED
To**

HEIDI

Who is sadly missed and
still loved by everyone who ever knew her
X

CONTENTS

YVETTE OF THE S.O.E	11
CHAPTER 1 – 'THE DEPARTMENT OF FISH & FISHERIES'	15
CHAPTER 2 - TRAINING CAMP	27
CHAPTER 3 - PREPARATION FOR ACTION	33
CHAPTER 4 - JOURNEY INTO THE UNKOWN	42
CHAPTER 5 - QUESTIONS WITHOUT ANSWERS	50
CHAPTER 6 - WELCOME TO THE WAR	59
CHAPTER 7 - GIRLIE FRILLS AND CYANIDE PILLS	67
CHAPTER 8 - A SUITCASE FULL OF GUNS	80
CHAPTER 9 - THE MASSACRE OF SAN EIELSON	87
CHAPTER 10 - LIBRAIRIE RIVEGAUCHE	96
CHAPTER 11 - PARIS	107
CHAPTER 12 - LE CAFÉ DUPONT	115
CHAPTER 13 - MESSAGES SENT	123
CHAPTER 14 - GRUBER OF THE GESTAPO	132

CHAPTER 15 – A PLAN IS HATCHED   141

CHAPTER 16 – WELCOME TO THE WAR - YVETTE   149

CHAPTER 17 – A NIGHT TO REMEMBER   157

CHAPTER 18 – A NEW DAY DAWNS   174

CHAPTER 19 – SIX DAYS AND SIX LONG NIGHTS 184

CHAPTER 20 = A FAREWELL TO PARIS   196

CHAPTER 21 – EMBRACE THE MUSIC OF THE WIND 207

CHAPTER 22 – THE END OF AN ERA   225

CHAPTER 23 – INTO THE UNKNOWN   230

CHAPTER 24 – THE SAVIOUR OF PARIS   235

CHAPTER 25 – LIFE GOES ON   242

YVETTE
OF THE S.O.E

From her position in the back of the truck, she could feel the turn as the vehicle banked to the left. She heard the change in sound and felt the difference in vibrations, as the wheels left the smooth tarmac of the road and entered the loose chipping stoned driveway of wherever it was she was being taken to.

Realizing that she was about to arrive at the destination she instinctively bent her knees and made her body as small as possible, braced herself and became extremely agitated when thinking about what was about to greet her.

When she heard the clunk-click of the back door being opened, she partially raised her head and attempted to sneak a peek at her new surroundings, but the hood being used as a blindfold, which had been placed upon her head, was preventing her from being able to see anything.

"Raus – Raus," she heard a man's voice demand as he grabbed her tightly by the arm and dragged her towards the entrance. "Schnell – Schnell," he angrily shouted as he pulled her roughly from the van, showing her no mercy.

As he gave her a final tug, she fell out of the compartment and dropped to the ground, landing on her knees. The pain she felt was excruciating as she landed on the pebble stoned surface, but then a far more intense pain followed as she felt her shoulders being almost ripped from their sockets, as both arms were grabbed firmly and she was lifted effortlessly and mercilessly from the ground.

"Komm mit mir," she heard the same man say.

Still wearing the blindfold, she was taken inside a building. She knew she was inside now as the temperature rose slightly, although this place still felt cold and also very damp and clammy.

'What the hell is this place?' she wondered, as all thoughts, as well as panic, now racked through her brain.

The two men holding an arm each dragged her along a long narrow corridor, where at the end they eventually stopped. She heard the sound of a lock being turned and a bolt being slid open. The next thing to happen was that she was thrown unceremoniously inside a room, landing in a heap upon the hard stone floor, with the sound of the door being slammed behind her. She stayed motionless, not moving for around fifteen minutes before daring to remove the blindfold.

As her eyes strained to adjust to the light, or lack of it, she found herself inside a small room with four stone walls, a stone floor and a stone ceiling, but with no window. In the middle of the ceiling was one small, low powered bulb for lighting, totally inefficient and continuously flickering. The light, which was constantly left turned on, was just enough for her to be able to see the water running down the walls from the dampness of the structure. This was definitely a room not fit for human habitation!

She eventually managed to drift off to sleep, but after what only seemed like a few seconds but may have been hours, she was disturbed by a man in a uniform which she'd not seen before.

"Komm," he demanded, gesturing for her to stand.

When upright, once again she was grabbed by the arm and marched along the corridor, where at the end she found a set of stone steps rising steeply to the level above. This corridor and staircase were lit no better than the room she was currently being incarcerated in Because of this, she was glad not to be wearing the blindfold any longer for fear of stumbling.

They finally reached the upper level and the beginning of another long corridor, but when only half way along this corridor, they came to a large oak door. The man dragging her behind him opened the door and pushed her inside, where she found herself inside a large room with a wooden chair in the center, with a bright spotlight illuminating the seat.

"Sit!" she heard a man command with a broad German accent. "What is your name?" he demanded, as she sat upon the very uncomfortable chair with the wonky leg.

Looking up to where the voice had come from, when she saw him, her knees began to buckle. Standing before her was a man dressed in full Nazi officer uniform.

This was not supposed to happen to her. She was a twenty year old medical student minding her own business when she was plucked from obscurity, literally half way through a lecture whilst she was studying at her university in Oxford.

Her only 'crime' was to be born with a French mother and an English father. Her only 'offence' was the fact that she could speak French fluently with no English accent, therefore making her invaluable to the British 'Special Operations Executive,' better known as the S.O.E by those in the know, although unknown to the vast majority of the population of the rest of Britain and certainly Europe!

Was this journey into occupied France going to be her first and possibly her last? Would she ever see her twenty-first birthday, or any other birthdays upon English soil ever again, or was she destined to die here, alone and desolate at the hands of these ruthless butchers?

"What is your name?" the Nazi officer demanded again.

"My name is Yvette Colbert," Yvette replied.

"But what is your real name?" he questioned again, sounding even more angry now.

"My name is Yvette Colbert," the young girl insisted.

"But surely that is your spy name given to you by the British," the Nazi claimed. "What is your real name?"

"My name is Yvette Colbert and I am not a spy!" she stated, trying to sound as truthful and strong as she possibly could. "I am a simple farm girl."

"HA!" the Nazi mocked sarcastically, then lowered his voice to sound more soothing and friendly, as he continued. "My dear girl, I will give you one more chance to do this the easy and most painless way," the interrogator said calmly, but still striking the fear of God into the young girl. "What is your name and where in England have you come from tonight?"

"My name is Yvette Colbert," she insisted, "and I have not come here from England tonight, I was merely going for an evening stroll in the countryside. As it is a pleasant evening, I was taking some exercise and minding my own business when I was apprehended by your men and dragged to this place, whatever it is."

"What it is my dear, is a place where you will not want to be, should you try to be clever with me." He looked at her sternly and then continued to say, "Okay my dear, we have tried it the nice way. You rest now and tomorrow we will begin the questioning in the not so nice way. You, young lady, have had your chance."

Yvette looked at the face of this man hoping to see any signs of kindness, but she could not see one ounce of compassion upon his features.

Guard," the officer shouted. "Take the prisoner away and back to her room."

'Back to my room,' she thought. 'Has this man seen my room? Does he think this is some kind of holiday camp?'

After being returned and thrown back into her cell, Yvette contemplated her situation and wondered what tomorrow might bring. She tried to sleep, but sleep evaded her.

CHAPTER 1
'THE DEPARTMENT OF FISH & FISHERIES'

It all began so innocuously when the head of the department, Mr. Greenstreet had entered the room mid-way through the lecture.

"Yvette Jackson," he called to gain her attention.

As she raised her hand and stood so he could see her, Mr. Greenstreet invited her to come and join him in his office.

"There's a man waiting to see you," he advised the young girl.

"There's a man here to see me? Who is he?" she questioned quite mystified.

"I have no idea as he didn't tell me his name, but he certainly looks official," Mr. Greenstreet confirmed. "Now Miss Jackson, please follow me."

Yvette did as was told and followed Mr. Greenstreet along the long, narrow, winding corridor towards his office. As she entered the room, she noticed a rather good looking gentleman sitting on a chair in the corner.

"Ah, Yvette, there you are," he announced upon her arrival.

He had the definite advantage on the young girl, as she had no clue as to who this man was, or what he wanted to speak to her about.

"I am known as Mister Black," the man announced, as though to confirm his identity. "May I call you Yvette, or would you prefer Miss Jackson?" he questioned, though as an afterthought.

"Yvette would be fine," she replied.

"Thank you," the good looking gentleman said.

"You are 'known' as Mister Black?" Yvette questioned suspiciously. "Why? Is this not really your name?"

"Forgive me," he smiled, "but where I come from, we do not use our real names."

This made Yvette feel even more uneasy than she already felt, although she felt even worse when the man said to Mr. Greenstreet, "Please Sir, would you mind leaving us alone? I have lots to talk about with this young lady today."

Yvette watched as Mr. Greenstreet did as was asked and left the room without a second glance.

Taking a good long look at the man now left alone with her, Yvette surmised he had the look of a businessman sitting there in his dark blue pinstripe suit, although in truth it was a little crumpled and definitely worse for wear. At least his shoes were highly polished and looked to be of good quality and very comfortable.

Yvette's mother had always advised her not to be stingy and to always spend good money on shoes and a bed, because as she said to her daughter, "If you're not in one, then you are in the other."

"Please sit down, Yvette," Mr. Black requested. "Are you sure you don't mind me calling you, Yvette?" he questioned again, as if needing complete confirmation.

"Of course," she replied. "It is my name after all," she told him sharply.

She immediately regretted the sarcasm in her voice, but then she was more than angry about being plucked from a lecture which was important for her medical studies. What did this man want of her, and more importantly, why her?

"Can I ask you a few personal questions?" Mr. Black continued.

"You may," Yvette replied, but with an air of suspicion.

"Can you please confirm that you are Yvette Jackson, daughter of Phillip and Claudette Jackson?" Black questioned.

"Yes," she answered, "but how do you know this?" This question was received simply with a smirk.

"Where I'm from, we know everything about everyone," Black observed.

"I don't like this," the girl expressed. "I don't like this at all!"

Please, Yvette, you are perfectly safe with me," he said, trying to reassure her as much as he possibly could. "You are also welcome to leave at any time." He looked at her to try to gauge her reaction at hearing this, before asking, "Would you like to leave?"

Yvette sat in silence for a few moments, but then muttered a resounding "No," as curiosity got the better of her.

"Is it true that your father is a British National born in England, but your mother is French?" the man questioned, but more like a statement than a query.

"Yes," the young girl replied slowly and with suspicion.

'What does this man want from me?' were the thoughts racing through her brain.

"Where in France was your mother born?" Black asked.

"Why, is she in any trouble?" Yvette retaliated, obviously stressed now.

"No, not at all," Black laughed. He could see the tension was getting the better of her so tried to ease her anxiety. "I am simply trying to get a sense of your background and upbringing."

"Is this some kind of job interview?" Yvette questioned, startling Black a little by her bluntness.

"I suppose in a way, it is," he answered, seemingly deep in thought. "So may I ask you again, where in France was your mother born?"

"She was born in Paris," Yvette confirmed.

This seemed to excite Black. "Excellent," he remarked with a beaming smile. "And is it true to say that you speak French fluently?"

"Yes, Sir, that is true," Yvette confirmed. "From the day I was born my father spoke to me in English, but my mother always spoke to me in French, and still does to this day."

"So it would be true to say that you speak French fluently and with no accent?" Black interrogated.

"No, Sir, that would not be true," Yvette replied.

"It's not true?" Black claimed, looking slightly perturbed.

"No it is not true that I speak French without an accent," Yvette stated. "I speak French fluently, but with a Parisian accent," she announced whilst smiling.

"Yvette, I think you, young lady, are a bit of a tease," Black smiled as he realised he'd not had a wasted journey after all. But then he became more serious.

"With what you're about to be offered," he proposed, "having a sense of humour could be a good thing, and could help you get through months of tough training."

"What is it you are offering," Yvette demanded to know now, but she was frustrated by Black's answer.

"Can you come to London next week for an interview?" he requested.

"But I thought this was my interview," she claimed. "Obviously not," she stated, after a few more seconds of total silence.

"If, and when you come, then all will be made known to you. I promise," Black revealed.

"I suppose if you put it like that, I will have to come," Yvette replied.

"Excellent," Mr. Black said again. "One final question, do you know your mother's maiden name?"

"Colbert," she replied. "It's spelled C-O-L-B-E-R-T, but the 'T' is silent, so pronounced as in, COAL-BEAR."

"Yvette Colbert," he said out loud. "Excellent," he said again, making the girl think this might be his favourite word. "Okay Yvette, we will see you at our offices in London."

"We?" she questioned, but by then Mr. Black had left the room with no elaboration.

Yvette sat alone for a few minutes, deep in thought and curious, wondering what the hell this meeting had all been about, but then she presumed it would all come out in the wash.

The following week, bright and early on the Wednesday morning, Yvette rose early and prepared herself for her journey from Oxford to Marylebone Station, situated in Central London and relatively close to the destination of her interview, curiously at the offices of a department known as, 'The Department of Fish & Fisheries,' situated at 5A Great Portland Street.

Dressed in a blue pleated skirt with a white blouse and wearing sensible brown shoes with just the hint of a Cuban heel, she considered which of her two overcoats she should wear.

"Which coat, Jen?" she asked her roommate, Jennifer Rumsey.

She'd met Jennifer on the first day at Uni, when they'd both arrived to study medicine. They instantly got on well together and seemed to share the same sense of humour, also both being as scatterbrained as each other. Not good qualities for a career in medical science, granted, but whilst attending lectures they were both dedicated students to the learning process, both taking it very seriously. They studied hard but also played hard. This is why they made the ideal roommates, which they'd been for several months by now.

"Wear the brown," Jennifer replied. "It will go well with your shoes."

"Makes sense," Yvette said nonchalantly, selecting her brown knee length tweed overcoat from the wardrobe, the coat which her parents had bought for her the previous Christmas. It was a little warm for what was an October day in the middle of an 'Indian Summer,' but the deep pockets she thought would come in handy. In fact, inside one of the inside pockets she placed the small, pocket sized 'London A to Z,' 'just in case I get lost,' she'd told herself that morning, even though Mr. Black had assured her there would be a black cab driver waiting for her upon her arrival at Marylebone Station, with a board with her name written on it.

She'd been pondering all week, since the strange meeting with Black, about whether or not to attend the interview. After all, what could this job offer be? What on earth did she know about fish? The only thing she did know about fish is that it tasted good with chips from the local chippy, covered of course with lashings of salt and vinegar and served wrapped in old newspaper.

Too late to back down now, she would have to go. Anyway, the train tickets and taxi had been provided free of charge, so it was costing her nothing. She told herself that whatever happened, she could always walk out midway through the interview and have a nice, free day out in London.

"Bye Jen, bye Atticus," she said, giving the white fluffy Ragdoll cat she shared with her roomy a tickle under the chin.

"See you later, Yvette, have a lovely day," Jennifer smiled. "Good luck with the interview," she added, almost as an afterthought.

Atticus just stared at her with a look of disdain. He was thinking, 'Why have you disturbed me from my busy day of relaxing and sleeping?' He yawned like only a cat could, exposed his claws, stretched out and adjusted himself on the chair. He was sleeping again in seconds, even before Yvette had reached the door.

Two hours later, Yvette stepped down from the train. It had pulled into Marylebone station right on time. As promised by Mr. Black, waiting there to greet her was a tiny man with craggy features, wearing a black cap and with an unlit, hand rolled cigarette seemingly stuck to his bottom lip. He was waiting patiently and standing beside a black London taxi. She saw him holding a board with her name on it, so walked towards him.

"Are you Miss Yvette Jackson?" he questioned, greeting her with a smile.

The man spoke in a strange accent that she'd not heard before, which Yvette later learned to be that of a genuine cockney, a person born within the sound of 'Bow Bells.'

"Yes, that's me," she told the jovial looking man. He opened the door of the cab and she climbed inside.

"Good journey, M'Lady?" he questioned, although she was sure it was only to make polite conversation. She smiled. No one had ever called her 'M'Lady' before.

"Yes thank you. Very pleasant," Yvette replied and then requested, "Can you please take me to………"

"I know exactly where you're going," he butted in, but again, politely.

"Well I'm glad you do," Yvette retaliated. "Because I have no idea of where I'm going, or why I am going there!"

They continued with the rest of the journey in silence and they soon entered Great Portland Street. Yvette spotted lots of grand buildings situated there, but when the driver dropped her at the destination, number 5A, she was taken aback, curious to see it was just a small door with a little silver plaque on the left hand side of the bell.

As she approached the entrance, sure enough it read, 'The Department of Fish & Fisheries.' She'd arrived at the correct place and was now even more curious to get inside and have her curiosity quenched.

Pushing the bell, she heard a woman's voice coming from a small speaker. "Yes?" the voice said.

"Yvette Jackson," she said in a sarcastic fashion, thinking she would show as much politeness and respect as the woman had shown to her.

She heard the sound of a buzzing noise and the entrance to the building clicked open. She pushed the heavy door and entered. Once inside she took a look around. The innocuous entrance outside disguised an enormous interior with a myriad of corridors, one to the left, one to the right, and one going straight ahead, as well as a wealth of offices scattered about the place, all with the clickety-clack sound of typewriters being struck at a rapid pace in the distance.

Just inside the reception area, Yvette was confronted by a large oak desk which a slightly older woman was sitting behind. The lady, who sported bright red lipstick, wore a blue and white polka dot dress, seemingly matched with a pair of thick black rimmed glasses. She was wearing a set of telephonist headphones and was positioned behind a telephone switchboard.

"Yes," she said, looking at Yvette with a total lack of interest. Instantly she recognised the voice as being that from the intercom.

"Is this The Department of Fish & Fisheries?" Yvette questioned. This question was answered with a smirk, so Yvette continued. "I have an appointment with Mister Black."

The receptionist, if that was what she was, pulled a plug from one hole on the switchboard and plugged it into another vacant opening. After a few seconds, Yvette heard the woman announce, "Mister Black, there is a young lady here to see you." She then looked at Yvette and questioned, "Did you say your name was Yvette Jackson?"

"Yes, that is my name," Yvette replied, thinking to herself that surely this woman should have asked her that before contacting Mr. Black.

"Yes, Mister Black," she heard the receptionist say before looking at her. "Mister Black will see you now," she announced.

Yvette was looking around and deciding which of the three corridors to take when a young man called her name.

"Yvette Jackson?" the man questioned.

"That's me," she confirmed.

"Please, follow me," the young man requested.

She followed the man, who she thought was about three

years older than her, along a corridor and up one flight of stairs. They came to a door and he knocked three times.

"Come," she heard a voice say from inside. The young man pushed the door and held it open for her to gain access.

When inside, she saw the man whom she recognised as Mr. Black, but this time he'd been joined by another gentleman. She didn't know why, but she thought this new man looked like he had more authority than Black, as well as looking a little scarier than his counterpart.

"Thank you, Jarvis," the 'scary' looking man said. Yvette watched as the young man accompanying her turned and left the room, closing the door firmly behind him.

"Hello Yvette. Lovely to see you again, and thank you for coming," Black announced.

"How could I refuse?" Yvette stated. "Also, I am curious to see what you're offering me. It's certainly nothing to do with fish!" This comment was not answered. In fact it was obviously ignored.

"Please sit down, Yvette," Black requested, whilst gesturing to a comfortable looking brown leather armchair, placed the opposite side of the desk which Black and his companion were sitting at. This desk was of far better quality and certainly larger than the one where the bored receptionist at the entrance was sitting.

"I hope you had a pleasant journey," the unknown man remarked, although Yvette knew he couldn't have cared less about her journey, good or bad.

"Very nice, thank you," she however answered the man, thinking that politeness would always be the best policy.

"My dear Yvette," Mr. Black began, "Please allow me to introduce my colleague to you. This is Mister Blue."

"Mister Blue?" Yvette queried suspiciously. 'Of course it is,' she thought sarcastically to herself.

"Yes, Mister Blue," Black confirmed. "As I told you last

week, we do not use real names for the reason that you will discover soon, depending on your actions today."

"Depending on my actions today?" Yvette was intrigued. "What actions? What do you mean?"

"My dear girl," Mr. Blue said taking up the conversation. "Would you be prepared to sign the official secrets act?"

"What the hell is that?" a by now frustrated Yvette questioned, beginning to get bored by all this mystery.

The two men spent the next fifteen minutes explaining the official secrets act to Yvette, taking particular care to point out that for her to break it could end in a prison sentence of up to fourteen years.

"Please take this outside with you and study it closely," Black instructed whilst handing her a small file of papers. "What we need to talk to you about today is a matter of utmost secrecy, but what we will be asking you to do would be vital to the war effort."

"What the hell?" was all that she could say in response to Black's statement.

"Yvette," Mr. Blue said, grabbing her attention and taking up the instruction. "Please read the papers you have in your hand. If you agree with what you read and want to know more about the reason why you're here, then please sign the papers and return here to the office. We will be waiting for you."

"But if you do not agree," Black took up the story, "then just hand the papers unsigned to the receptionist, and then return to Oxford. If you do this, you will never hear from us again."

Yvette returned to the reception area to ponder over her decision, all the time feeling the eyes of the receptionist glued to her.

"You have a difficult decision to make," the slightly older looking lady remarked.

"I certainly have," Yvette agreed. "Do you have any advice for me?"

"I'm very sorry, but I cannot possibly comment," the lady replied.

"Could I possibly ask you for your name?" the younger girl enquired.

"You can ask me but I cannot tell you," the receptionist answered with honesty. "I cannot tell you my name until you sign that paper."

"Oh I see," Yvette remarked. "So have you signed one of these 'Official Secrets Act' papers?" she asked.

"Of course I have," was the blunt reply. "How else do you think I am able to work here in these offices?"

"Do you ever regret signing the paper?" Yvette asked the pretty lady behind the desk.

"Never," was the short, sharp and honest reply.

Yvette stood from the bench seat where she was positioned and approached the lady. "Do you have a pen I can borrow?"

"Of course," the young woman said, passing her a pen.

She watched as the younger girl signed the official paper and then said, "My name is Jayne. It's very nice to meet you properly. Welcome to the company."

"It's very nice to also properly meet you, Jayne," Yvette smiled and then added, "My name is Yvette – Yvette Jackson."

"Yes – I know," Jayne replied, giving the younger girl an all knowing smile.

Yvette returned to the office where Messer's Black and Blue were waiting. As she knocked on the door she wondered if they would reveal their real names, now that she'd signed the all important document which she'd just filed with Jayne at the reception.

"Come," she heard a man's voice shout, although she couldn't yet identify which of the two men were calling her, as she didn't know them well enough as yet.

"Ah, Yvette, there you are. Welcome back," Mr. Black said

with a broad grin upon his face as she re-entered the room. "So you have signed the papers and decided to join us – Excellent."

"Yes I have, but I hope I've not signed my life away," she remarked with a degree of flippancy.

As she said this, she noticed Mr. Black and Mr. Blue giving each other a curious stare, a stare which slightly worried the girl, although she thought it better not to take this any further at this stage of proceedings.

Mr. Blue gazed at her with a look of admiration now apparent on his craggy features. "Welcome to the S-O-E," he said.

"The S-O-E," Yvette observed questioningly.

"Yes," Mr. Black said. "Welcome to the Special Operations Executive."

CHAPTER 2
TRAINING CAMP

"Come on, Jackson, punch me!" the instructor ordered.

"No! I don't want to punch you," Yvette retaliated.

"I order you to hit me," the man said. "Come on; punch me in the stomach as hard as you can."

"No!" Yvette screamed.

"Why? You cannot possibly hurt me," Mr. Green stated. "How can you hurt me? You're just a girlie." He said this in an attempt to get a reaction from the girl, wanting to make her angry enough to fight back.

"What is the point of all this?" Yvette questioned.

"What is the point of this?" Green repeated angrily. "My girl, I am trying to give you the skills to be able to save your life should you ever find yourself alone in a Parisian street, faced with a German soldier who wants to kill you! Do you think a member of the enemy will take pity on you because you are a pretty young lady?" he asked Yvette, but then answered his question himself by saying, "No, he will not. He will kill you because you are his enemy! Do you understand this?"

"But I'm just operating a radio," the defendant claimed. "How can I be a danger to any German soldier?"

"My God, woman," Green declared exasperated. "The messages you are sending back to Britain will be vital to both the resistance and the British troops. They will carry information of the best way to sabotage the German army's advance on Europe, hopefully to bring the war to an early close. The enemy will not want you doing this, and if they catch you, they will want to kill you and they will kill you!"

"But........" Yvette tried to make her point, but Green was having none of it.

"Don't think your beauty or femininity will save you," he

continued. "Your pretty face and curvaceous body will mean nothing to your German attacker. Don't think you can rip open your blouse and flash your boobs and the attacker will take pity on you. He will happily take out his bayonet and stick it between your tits and into your heart and wouldn't think twice about it! If he felt that way inclined, he could always have a little feel of your curves after you're dead!"

"You're sick!" Yvette shouted. "You, Sir, are one sick bastard!"

"Yes I am," Green remarked. "So come on, punch me!"

Mr. Green walked close to Yvette, undid his shirt and then removed it, revealing an extremely muscular, washboard like six-pack stomach, worthy of any serious body builder.

"Punch me in the guts," he demanded. "Come on, girlie."

"No," Yvette refused.

"Hit me!"

"No!"

"Hit me!"

"No!"

Green came even closer to Yvette and then slapped her around the face, not with his full power, but hard enough to make her face sting.

"Hit me! Punch me hard!" he screamed. "Come on, you silly little girlie!"

This was enough to spring the girl into action. Yvette gathered up all her pent up hatred of this man and put it all into her anger. She then clenched her right hand to make a fist and then punched this man as hard as she could. It felt good, but a split second later she felt the pain rising up her wrist and into her upper arm! It was as though she'd just punched a concrete wall! What made it worse was the fact that Mr. Green just stood there looking at her and laughing.

"I can see I'm going to have my work cut out with you," he chuckled.

"Piss off!" Yvette said angrily.

"What did you say?" Green queried.

"I said piss off," Yvette confirmed, but even more angrily.

"That should be, piss off – Sir," Mr. Green snapped back, reminding her of the 'Special Operations Executive' protocol.

"Piss off, Sir," Yvette said with attitude.

She spent the rest of the day in a really foul mood. Is this what she'd really signed up for that day back in mid October, when she'd walked back into that office after signing the 'Official Secrets Act' to be greeted once again by Messer's Black and Blue, and yes, the irony of these names had not escaped her.

"So you signed the paper. Excellent," Black had announced, as she sat at the chair opposite.

"Now we can tell you what you're here for," Blue revealed.

"But even if you do not agree to join us, you still cannot talk about this with anyone who has not also signed the Official Secrets Act," Black advised the girl.

"Do you agree with this?" said Blue, pointing out once again that to break the rules would mean a prison sentence of "Up to fourteen years."

"Do you agree, Yvette?" asked Black. "You have to say it verbally. Out loud please."

"Yes," Yvette replied, getting bored with all this secrecy.

"Excellent," Black said again.

"Okay, my dear," Mr. Blue began. "As you know, the German army invaded France earlier in this year and marched into Paris in June. This is where we want you to go."

"What, you want me to go to France?" Yvette questioned.

"Well yes, but we want you to go to France and live in Paris," Mr. Black confirmed.

"We want you to train as a radio operator and immerse yourself into Parisian life and culture," Mr. Blue said, continuing with the story. "Every night you will broadcast back to British Intelligence and reveal any secrets you have discovered, or been told about by the resistance."

"But I have no idea how to operate a radio," Yvette claimed.

"Don't worry about all that," Mr. Black revealed. "We will teach you how to operate a radio and how to use 'Morse Code.' All this will be done at the training camp."

"Training camp?" Yvette almost screamed. What HAD she let herself in for?

"Yes my dear, you will go to a training camp," Mr. Blue stated.

"Where is this camp?" Yvette queried.

"We cannot tell you exactly where the camp is," Blue answered vaguely, "but I will tell you that it's in a very nice area of Kent."

"All these secrets," Yvette sighed.

"I'm sorry about all this secrecy, my dear," Blue said apologetically.

"How long will I stay at this camp?" she asked the two men, with Mr. Black taking up the conversation.

"Three months," he said. "After this you will be ready to be parachuted into France and make your way to Paris." Hearing Black saying this, Yvette almost choked.

"What do you mean?" Yvette exasperated."Do you mean you want me to jump out of an aeroplane and land in France with a parachute?"

"It will be far easier than landing without a parachute," Blue quipped.

"Mister Blue, please," Black interrupted, reprimanding his colleague. "Don't worry, Yvette, you will receive full training from a member of the Parachute Regiment. As well as this, you will be fully trained in unarmed combat, just in case you should ever find yourself in, let's say, a sticky situation."

The two men looked at the young recruit and could see she was in a state of shock.

This meeting had taken place four weeks ago. During the time since, as Black and Blue had advised, Yvette had spoken with Mr. Greenstreet, her lecturer at the university in Oxford. He'd assured her that her place in the medical school would still be available upon her return, should she still require it. He didn't know what it was that she would be returning from, as she was not able to tell him anything about the meeting with the two men in London.

She'd then gone home to visit her parents in Dorchester, found in the county of Dorset. This was a lovely place for the young Yvette to grow up, as being very close to the seaside holiday resort of Weymouth; she spent many of her summer weekends lazing on one of the finest beaches in England.

Now of course, being situated on the south coast of England, the beach was now a no go area, being totally covered in barbed wire and converted into a minefield, with hundreds of landmines planted intermittently around the beach in case of enemy invasion.

Mr and Mrs Jackson were of course very pleased to receive the visit from Yvette, although rather concerned about the lack of information their daughter was able to give them about taking an early leave of absence from the university.

"Yvette, whatever it is you've gotten yourself involved with, just be careful my girl. Keep safe," her father, Phillip said.

As he said this, she could see he was not only worried, but also looked immensely proud. He thought that if it was a secret mission, so secret that Yvette couldn't tell them anything about it, then it must be extremely important for the war effort, and it was this which made him such a proud father.

Her mother, Claudette, didn't say much at all, she just looked constantly worried. Yvette wished she could tell her that she was going to Paris, the city of her mother's birth and a place where she still had many relatives living, but she knew that to do this would have been dangerous for both them and her.

One week ago she'd reported back at, 'The Department of Fish & Fisheries,' where along with two other young men, although not as young as she, climbed aboard a windowless van and were taken to a secret location, a camp previously described as being 'somewhere in Kent.'

The three had become friends during the journey from London to this camp in Kent, although at the time she didn't realise that whilst she was the pupil, Ben and Peter were the teachers. Ben was assigned to teach her how to jump from a plane, or rather, how to land on the ground safely after parachuting from a plane, whilst Peter had the unenviable and much tougher task of teaching Yvette Morse code, a task she was dreading!

"Don't worry, Yvette, you'll soon pick it up," Peter told her.

"But it's just all dot, dot, dot, and dash, dash, dash," she'd replied. "I mean, what the hell is that all about?"

As Mr. Green walked away laughing, he turned and called back to her, "You make sure you bring that attitude to my class tomorrow, my girl."

"What a prick!" Yvette said under her breath. "Piss off and die!"

"Don't let him get to you, Yvette," Ben Richards advised.

"Just try and calm yourself. He's not worth it," Pater Collins added.

"Hey Yvette, come to the pub with us tonight," Ben invited.

"Okay, that'll be nice," Yvette said accepting the offer. "I hope you two are buying?" she laughed, already feeling much calmer than she did five minutes earlier.

CHAPTER 3
PREPERATION FOR ACTION

"Wakey Wakey, Jackson," she heard a male voice bellow. "It's time to get up and at 'em!"

Prying her eyes open to see it was still pitch black, Yvette stirred from a wonderful dream to see Mr. Green standing at the end of her bed. He wore a demented and wicked expression on his face.

"What time is it?" she demanded to know, still very much bleary eyed and totally non compos mentis.

"What time is it, my girl?" Green repeated sarcastically. "Why, it's time for your five mile run!"

As he said this, he just about stopped himself from laughing at her misfortune, a misfortune of which he was very much the instigator.

"What are you talking about?" Yvette demanded.

"What are you talking about – Sir?" Mr. Green returned.

"It's too bloody early for all that shit!" Yvette said angrily. "What are you talking about, going for a run?"

"If you can take time from your training to go drinking with your friends, then you can get up bright and early and go for a five mile run with me," her tormentor instructed. "Come on, girlie, it will be fun."

"I can think of nothing which would be less fun than this," Yvette claimed before adding, "And stop calling me, girlie. My name is Yvette, or to you my name is Miss Jackson."

"I'll see you outside in ten minutes, Miss Jackson," Green said mockingly. "Don't keep me waiting."

Yvette pulled herself from under the covers and splashed her face with cold water in an attempt to ease the drowsiness.

Last night had been an enjoyable one getting to know Peter and Ben better, although in truth, she'd probably consumed far more port and lemons than was good for her, especially in the middle of the week and, "On a school night," as Ben had quipped.

After she'd dressed quickly in very unflattering loose fitting blue canvas trousers, with a white t-shirt covered by a thick blue woolly jumper which Yvette thought would keep her warm on this bitterly cold autumnal morning, she ventured outside to find Mr. Green waiting for her, performing stretches and running on the spot to warm himself. She looked at him doing all this, but made no attempt to join in and prepare herself in the same way.

"Come on," she demanded. "Let's get this shit over and done with!"

"Let's get this shit over and done with – Sir!" Green remarked.

"Yeah whatever," she replied, never much being one for authority.

"Come on, let's go," Green demanded.

Yvette ran off sprinting, leaving Green with some distance to catch her up.

"Come on, catch up old man," she taunted triumphantly.

As a fit twenty year old, she surprised her 'tormentor' with her fitness levels and athletic prowess. However, he gave chase and was soon only yards behind the girl.

"Not bad for an oldie," she quipped, laughing out loudly.

"Cheeky," Green retaliated, but not laughing.

The instructor however had the last laugh when last night's festivities finally got the better of Yvette, with the alcohol consumed during the previous evening deciding there and then to make a re-appearance. She quickly diverted her run towards the closest hedge and just about made it in time. In an eruption, she was sick like a water feature spewing its liquid all over the garden!

"That'll teach you for going out drinking in the middle of the week," Green laughed, sounding relatively normal for a momentary second.

As Yvette lifted her head from its downward position, whilst holding her wavy blonde hair clear of any spillage, she glanced over the hedgerow and was surprised by what she saw in the not too far distance.

"Is that the sea?" she questioned.

"Yes it is," Green confirmed and then pointed towards the horizon. "And just a few miles in that direction, our enemy are ruling Europe with a rod of iron. Come on, girlie, get ready to do your bit to defeat those bastards!"

"Okay – Catch me," she shouted, sprinting off and leaving him standing again.

"Why, you little........" was all he could say as he was out of breath from constantly chasing the much younger girl.

Now fifty yards ahead of him, Mr. Green watched as Yvette suddenly stopped and waited for him to catch up.

"Is that the......?" she began.

"The Feathers," Green replied. "Yes it is."

"But I was there last night, and I don't remember leaving the camp," Yvette claimed.

"That's because you didn't," Green observed. "The Feathers pub is all part of the camp, and everyone in there has signed the Official Secrets Act and all live within the camp."

"Even the landlord and the staff?" Yvette questioned.

"Especially the landlord and his staff," Green confirmed, astonishing the girl.

"What the hell is this place? And where the hell in the country are we?" she queried, demanding to know the answer to this question.

"Okay," Green began, almost surrendering to the girl. "You know you are now living on a training camp, and all I can tell you about the position of it is that it's in Kent," he conceded. "But we have to keep the exact location a secret, or the Luftwaffe will send their bombers over to destroy us."

"But why can't you tell me?" Yvette questioned.

"Because if you don't know where the camp is, should they capture you when in France, no matter how much the Gestapo torture you, you will not be able to tell them the camp location," Green said. Looking at Yvette, he hoped this revelation was sinking in.

"Torture me?" she questioned, with her facial expression changing to that of a far more serious nature. "They will torture me?"

"Yes they will, but only if they capture you. That is why you're here, so we can train you so you are not detected or captured," Green told her, speaking for the first time in a much friendlier manner.

"Crackerjacks, this is serious!" Yvette expressed at the thought of this.

"Crackerjacks indeed," Mr. Green couldn't help himself laughing as he said this. "Now come on, let's jog back to your dwelling and you can have a couple more hours sleep before breakfast. Your parachute training begins today."

"Parachute training," Yvette gasped. "Am I going up in an aeroplane today?"

"No!" Mr. Green belly laughed uncontrollably at the thought of it. "Not today, but you may be up there in the wild blue yonder very soon."

"Okay Yvette, be sure to land on the balls of your feet when you land on the surface," the instructor told her. "If you land on your heels there is a good chance you would do some damage to your spine, and that would not be good, not good at all!"

Yvette was standing on a gymnasium 'horse,' shoeless and in white ankle socks, about to leap from all of three feet and land on a thick blue rubber mat. She felt in no danger whatsoever, as Ben Richards, now in instructor mode, told her to land on the balls of her feet and then to roll onto one side, so as to break her fall.

"Are you ready?" she was questioned.

"Yes," she answered.

"Okay, jump!" Ben yelled loudly, trying to encourage her.

Although Yvette felt totally stupid launching herself from such a low height, she did as instructed.

"Not bad for a first attempt," Ben admitted. "Remember though, you may have to land on frozen ground when it comes to the real jump, so it's important to master this procedure."

"Yes, and I might be jumping from a height with a little more altitude than this," Yvette said sarcastically.

"Yes, okay," Ben admitted but then advised, "but you have to get this correct before we can go higher. Should you land badly in France and sprain your ankle, or worse, then you could well be a dead woman!"

"And what if they drop me in a minefield?" Yvette challenged. "What if I land on a landmine?"

"Should you actually land on a mine; the normal procedure would be to scream as loudly as possible whilst jumping high into the air and spreading your body over as much ground as you can!" Ben replied even more sarcastically than she'd asked the question. "Now come on you, this is important. Get back on the horse and please take it seriously."

"I'm sorry," Yvette replied softly and apologetically.

"Now jump again!" Ben demanded. This time the pupil obeyed without question.

She repeated this jump from the gymnasium horse several times during the next hour or so, until it became more than a little tedious and even boring. Ben could see her losing interest.

"Come with me please, Yvette," he politely requested, and the young girl followed him outside where he pointed to a system of pulleys, all set at different heights. Ben then told her, "Now you've reasonably mastered the toe and roll landing from three feet, you can start on these tomorrow."

Yvette looked up at the series of wires attached to pulleys, ranging from ten feet to more than fifty feet in the air.

"How do they work?" she asked her instructor.

"It's perfectly safe," Ben assured her. "We strap you in with a harness wrapped around you and you jump, more or less the same as from the three feet jump only higher. We can control the speed at which you hit the ground, making it more like that of jumping from a plane."

"I see," was all the girl could comment as she looked up to the highest of the platforms.

"First we will use the landing mat, but then we'll take it away and you can land straight on the grass," Ben continued to say.

"How high is the top jump?" Yvette asked, now feeling slightly more nervous.

"It's around fifty feet and is set so you will hit the ground at the exact speed as you would on the actual parachute jump when you arrive in France," Ben revealed. "If you land incorrectly from up there, you really will hurt yourself!"

This made the camp and all it stood for seem far more important to Yvette's wellbeing, so from that moment on she decided to take all the training far more seriously, and threw herself into everything with a greater vigour. This included Mr. Green's unarmed combat training, even the lesson where he taught her how to silently kill a man by creeping up from behind and sharply twisting his head and snapping his neck.

Although she hated the idea of actually performing this action and killing a man, or a woman, she knew that one day it really could save her life, or even the lives of the people she was with at the time.

"Okay, Yvette," Peter smiled, "Are you ready to learn Morse code?"

"I'm as ready as I will ever be. But it's a bit daunting," she admitted.

"It's actually quite easy," Peter revealed.

"If you say so," Yvette remarked.

"As you jokingly said before, it really is just dots and dashes," Peter stated. "Each letter is represented by its own series of dots and dashes, or just dots, or just dashes. The dots are the length of an on off flick of a light switch, whilst the dashes are the length of a beep. Are you with me so far?"

Peter stopped to look at the girl, but could see she was sporting a blank expression on her still pretty face, so he carried on with the lesson.

"What you need to do first is learn the alphabet. Once you've mastered this, then the words will come more easily," he informed her.

"Okay, so let's go," she said to Peter, genuinely now sounding interested.

Peter Collins laid a paper in front of her with not only the alphabet written down, but also the Morse code for numbers Zero to Nine.

"You see how easy it is?" he began. "The letter 'A' is simply dot dash. The letter 'B' is dash dot-dot-dot." Peter went through all the letters before beginning with the numbers. "Number One is dot dash-dash-dash-dash, with number Two being dot-dot dash-dash-dash, a variation on the number One."

"But on this paper it shows the numbers Zero to Nine, but how do you code the number Ten?" asked the student.

"Good question," Peter remarked.

"Thank you. I thought so too," she quipped.

"Well, as it says on this instruction paper, Morse code for the number Zero is a series of five dashes, with number One being a dot followed by four dashes," Peter began and then continued. "So the number ten would be a one plus Zero, hence it would be a dot followed by nine dashes."

"That's a lot of wrist action," she quipped. "I am never

going to get this," a frustrated and confused Yvette declared.

"You will, I promise you," Peter said confidently. "Trust me, Yvette; it's just like learning a foreign language. One day it will click and all fall into place. When that day comes, you will be able to write down the message you need to send and send each letter individually. It's then up to the receiver to decipher the message, so you have nothing to worry about."

"Of course I do," Yvette said angrily. "Peoples' lives will depend on the messages I send."

"You'll be fine," Peter advised, now immensely happy to see that his student was showing how much she cared about getting this right.

Two months later, Yvette was now confidently sending messages in Morse code, albeit in the classroom, and Peter was sure she was ready for her mission in France.

She was also now jumping from the fifty feet platform at least ten times every day, with Ben being happy with her progress.

Mr. Green was also now confident that he'd turned her from a moody and sometimes insolent little girl into a fighting machine capable of taking on any man in the training camp, including him!

She was in her sweats one afternoon, smacking hell out of the well worn punch bag when Green approached.

"My girl," he said gently, which was nothing like how he normally sounded. "We all think you are ready."

"Ready?" she questioned. "You think I'm ready for what?"

"You, my girl are ready for France," Green confirmed.

Hearing this, her legs quickly turned to jelly as she realised she was not the confident, brave young lady she thought she was.

"Are you sure?" she pleaded. "I don't feel ready!"

"Yes, my dear, it's time," Green smiled affectionately.

Yvette had never seen Mr. Green like this before and she

wasn't sure whether she liked it or not.

"Alright then, let's do it!" Yvette shouted. "France here I come!"

CHAPTER 4
JOURNEY INTO THE UNKNOWN

The plane taxied down the runway but then began gaining speed, slowly at first, but then it gathered momentum and was soon thundering along the tarmac until it reached the optimum speed for takeoff. As she felt the plane rise into the air, Yvette felt both an excitement, along with a strong feeling of nervousness, as she began this journey into unknown territory.

It was now a month since she'd been told of this mission, at the same time being given permission to go and visit her parents at their home in Dorchester, Dorset, close to the English Jurassic coast.

Even though she'd been at the training camp for more than four months by now, the 'company' still would not reveal its exact location to her. And so for the young girl to make the journey home to Dorchester; she first had to travel to London, once again in the back of the same windowless van which had been used to transport her to the training camp back in October.

She was then taken to the offices of 'The Department of Fish & Fisheries,' where she would be given a taxi ride to Waterloo Station, along with a first class return train ticket to travel on the South West line to Dorchester, all of course paid for by 'The Department of Fish & Fisheries.'

"Hello Yvette. I have heard nothing but good things about you," it was Mr. Black who'd come to greet her.

"Thank you, Sir," Yvette returned. "But you have the better of me," she continued. "I have received absolutely no information about the mission I am about to embark upon."

"And I'm sorry, but this is how it must stay until you return to base next week," Black confirmed.

"But why, do I not deserve to know?" she pleaded.

"Of course you do, my dear, but all in good time," Black

stressed. "The thing is, if you don't know what you are doing or where you're going, you won't be able to give away any secrets to your parents, thus worrying them for no reason."

"For no reason," Yvette repeated. Black could have cursed himself for making such a basic schoolboy error!

"You know what I mean, Yvette," he said, trying to backtrack and skate around his mistake.

One pleasant occurrence to the meeting was that she met Jayne in reception again. This time the meeting was far more relaxed and even a very friendly one. Jayne asked how the training was going, and Yvette could tell she was genuinely interested and not just trying to make polite conversation.

"Have you ever been to the camp, Jayne?" Yvette asked her now friend.

"Of course," Jayne replied, surprising Yvette. "Everyone who works here has been for training. We are all ready for action at the drop of a hat."

"Parlez vous Français?" Yvette asked the pretty receptionist.

"Mais oui, bien sur," Jayne replied, also with a perfect French accent.

"Touché Madam," Yvette joked, and then added, "The people in this place never cease to amaze me!"

One week later, Yvette returned to Waterloo Station and was collected by taxi and returned to number 5A Great Portland Street where she was again met and greeted, but this time by Mr. Blue.

"Have you had an enjoyable week, my dear," he questioned.

"No," she answered honestly.

Whilst it had been nice for Yvette to be able to see her parents again, at the same time it was also really frustrating for her to not be able to tell them anything. She felt slightly dishonest at not answering their questions, even though in all honesty, she couldn't answer them because she truthfully didn't know the answers.

When she expressed these feelings of frustration to Mr. Blue, he told her, "I'm sorry, Yvette, but all will be revealed when you get back to the camp. Mister Green will tell you everything about your mission."

"Thank you, Sir," Yvette responded respectfully.

"How are you getting along with Mister Green?" Mr. Blue questioned the girl.

"He is a total bastard! He's a right, royal pain in the ass!" Yvette replied, as she almost exploded with her anger. She immediately felt disrespectful for saying this to one of Green's colleagues and was just about to apologize when she noticed that Mr. Blue was also laughing almost uncontrollably.

"You hate the man, Yvette," he chuckled. "That means he is doing his job, and he's doing it correctly."

"Yes Sir," Yvette agreed.

"My dear girl, he's not there to be your friend. He is there to give you the skills to keep you alive," Blue stated.

"Yes I agree with you," Yvette responded, "but why? What will I be doing that could be so dangerous that I need to learn how to kill people?"

"Not people, enemy scum!" Blue said harshly. "Don't forget that. These are not normal people like you and I, they are evil Nazis!"

"No Sir, sorry Sir," Yvette said a little coyly.

"But in answer to your earlier comment, Mister Green will be telling you everything you need to know during the coming days," Blue confirmed.

There was a knock on the door and Jayne the receptionist quickly entered. "Excuse me, Mister Blue, but Yvette's transport is outside waiting for her," she instructed.

"Thank you, Jayne," Blue commented. He then turned to Yvette and spoke with sincerity.

"Well my dear, I wish you good luck for the future and thank you for everything you have done so far, along with everything you will do in the future for your country, a country which already owes you a great debt of gratitude. Give that bastard Hitler hell!" he said, extending his right hand forward to be shaken.

Although she was sure this speech was supposed to make her feel inspired, it did in fact have the opposite effect on the girl. In all honesty, hearing Mr. Blue saying these words out loud actually put the fear of God in her!

Outside, after shaking hands firmly with Mr. Blue and receiving a goodbye kiss on the cheek from Jayne, Yvette climbed into the back of the windowless van once again for her journey back to 'somewhere' in the county of Kent, where she arrived some two hours later.

The drone of the plane's engines was beginning to get on her nerves. It reminded her that with every passing second, she was getting closer and closer to her final destination. She was extremely nervous now, probably more nervous than she'd ever been before in her entire life, all twenty years of it.

She'd been extremely happy when Mr. Green had told her that both Ben Richards and Peter Collins were coming on the mission with her, and being able to look at them now during the flight made her tension ease a little, but not completely.

She noticed they were also looking nervous and were not speaking to each other, or indeed to her, and this also made her feel agitated. However, she was still happy that Ben and Peter were both here to hold her hand, so to speak.

It was one week earlier when Yvette had been summoned to his office, where Mr. Green, not like him at all, smiled at the girl and invited her to come inside and take a seat.

"Good news, Yvette," he began, really sounding quite excited. "You will be going to France next Wednesday, weather permitting."

"What does the weather have to do with anything," she asked, quite naively.

"Hopefully we will have a cloudy evening so the enemy cannot see your parachute as you descend," Green pointed out to the girl.

"What happens if they see me?" she questioned with the innocence only an inexperienced, twenty years of age girl can possess.

"Why, they will shoot you, Yvette," he said, harshly but truthfully. "You will be dead before you hit the ground!"

She pondered on the situation and decided that if this was supposed to be a confidence boosting conversation, then Mr. Green was certainly failing in his own side of the mission!

"So can you tell me now, what is my mission?" the girl questioned. Green scratched his chin and looked deep in thought as he looked at the girl now sitting patiently before him.

"Yes, my dear, it is time to reveal all," he said finally.

Yvette positioned herself closer, as though to better hear what he had to say. This did not go unnoticed by Mr. Green.

"Well, come on then, Mister Green, spill the beans!" an agitated and impatient Yvette blurted, finding it difficult now to control her feelings.

The youngster listened intently as Green told her that she would be dropped in a clearing in the French countryside around thirty miles from Paris. She would be met by members of the French Resistance, who would disguise her as best they could and do their best to give her safe passage to the nation's capital.

"When you arrive in Paris, you will be taken to a safe house close to Montmartre," Green instructed.

"And is that where I will be living?" Yvette questioned.

"No, my dear," Green replied. "You will be constantly moving. We cannot have you staying at, and broadcasting from the same place for more than three times in a row, so you will be moved every three days, if it's possible and safe to do so."

"And will they all be safe houses where I'll be going to?" she asked.

"They will all be run by the resistance, Yvette, but the words 'safe house' could be misleading. They are only safe if they remain undiscovered by the Nazis. If this happens, then they will be extremely unsafe! However, as I say, they are all owned and run by the resistance and they will fight until their last dying breath to protect you and keep you safe."

"Can I ask why Ben and Peter are coming with me?" Yvette queried.

"You can ask by all means" Green replied. "But I cannot tell you the reason why, as its top secret."

"Of course it is," a despairing Yvette exclaimed. "This place and its secrets are exhausting!"

The drone of the engine seemed to lower in tone as the plane was obviously slowing down.

"Five minutes," the pilot announced, turning round to face them so they could better hear him from the cockpit.

"Well, Yvette, there's no turning back now," Ben said trying to keep her spirits up, but in truth, failing miserably.

"Are you okay, Yvette?" Peter asked. "Are you nervous?"

"I'm not so much nervous about the mission," she admitted. "I am petrified about jumping out of this plane!"

"Don't worry," Ben Richards told her. "Just remember to do what you did in training and land on the balls of your feet and roll."

"Yeah, its okay when you're jumping from a plank of wood placed fifty feet in the air, but this is different. And I did not have people shooting at me in the camp!" she exasperated.

They were soon over the drop zone. The three stood in preparation for the jump and Ben attached the parachutes to the overhead bar by the clamps provided to ensure they opened upon leaping clear of the plane. They all had to jump within two seconds of each other or they would be landing too far apart.

Peter jumped first and then Ben surprised Yvette by unceremoniously pushing her out of the plane, thus allaying any final doubts in her mind about whether to jump or not. He heard her scream for a split second before launching himself into the atmosphere. Thirty seconds later, they were all safely on the ground.

"You Bastard," Yvette shouted at Ben, at the same time punching him hard on the shoulder.

"Sorry sweetheart, but I had to do it," Ben stated.

"Shush, be quiet, you two," Peter ordered forcibly, but as quietly as possible whilst holding a finger to his lips.

"Sorry," they both whispered in return.

"Now, gather up your parachutes and get them ready for hiding," Peter directed, seeming to have taken charge of the three.

As they were going through the process of stuffing the parachutes back into the bags they came in, Peter noticed something in the distance.

"Look," he said to the other two. "Over there."

The three looked towards the edge of the clearing where they could all see a flashlight signalling to them.

"Must be the resistance," Ben said.

"I bloody well hope so," Peter whispered. He looked at Yvette and could see she was shaking, so put his arms around her to offer comfort.

"Don't worry, darling," he said. "We'll take good care of you."

'He called me darling,' was the last thought in her head, as the three walked towards the direction of the flashlight.

They were getting closer now, but when they'd almost reached the edge of the forest, a volley of gunfire was heard to ring out into the air.

Suddenly Yvette heard Ben cry out in pain, followed quickly by Peter. She turned to look at the two but could see them both lying face down in the mud! With no time to mourn the loss of her friends, she turned back to face the direction of where the gunfire had come from. What was she to do now?

She froze on the spot where she stood, as she spotted a few men slowly walking towards her, all carrying guns which were trained in her direction. They were wearing a uniform she was not sure of, but the shape of the tin helmets was a bit of a giveaway.

'Germans,' she thought, ready for the inevitable.

The man in charge shouted something at her which the poor girl did not understand. Instinctively she threw her arms into the air in surrender. She was surrounded by the soldiers and marched into the forest. After a few minutes walking, they came to a road where she could see an army truck was parked.

"Werden," the man in charge ordered. Yvette, not understanding what it was he was saying, ignored the man. "Werden," he shouted again, this time louder and with a lot more authority.

Two of the other soldiers grabbed hold of her and after placing a hood over her head to use as a blindfold, roughly bundled her into the back of the vehicle and sat either side of her.

Yvette had to face the fact that she was now a prisoner of war!

CHAPTER 5
QUESTIONS WITHOUT ANSWERS

Yvette was abruptly and rudely awakened by the shrill sound of a terrifying, blood curdling scream. She listened to the silence which followed and felt the cold sweat on her forehead, even though the room she was incarcerated in could not have been much warmer than just above freezing. In fact she could not only see the steam coming from the heat of her breath as she exhaled, but it also strangely came from the dampness of the walls!

She heard the scream again and wondered what was happening to this poor man to make him shout out in pain like this. What the hell were they doing to him? She wondered if the same fate could be waiting for her in the morning. A few moments later, she heard the scream again. She put her arms around her head to cover her ears as best she could and attempted to get some sleep.

After losing all track of time she had no idea if, or how long she'd been sleeping, when the guard noisily entered the room.

"Aufstehen, get up!" he demanded, shouting angrily at the top of his voice.

Yvette shook herself from her slumber and looked at him, noticing how enraged he looked. He looked at her as though she were a lump of dog dirt which he'd just stood in, but what had she done to this man to make him feel this way?

"Kommen Sie," he ordered, which by the tone of his voice, Yvette thought must mean to follow him. She stood and walked towards the man and when she reached him, he grabbed her by the arm and dragged her from the cell.

Again they walked along the dimly lit corridor, but this time, instead of walking up the stone steps they turned to the right, seemingly going further into the building. At the end of this corridor there was a rusty old metal door which made an awful squeal as the guard pushed it open. Yvette thought it needed some oil on the hinges, but then thought how stupid it was for her to be having these observations when she was probably about to be tortured, or worse!

Again, positioned in the centre of the room, a large wooden chair awaited her. She was roughly pushed into it by the guard, but this time her wrists were strapped into the arms of the chair with metal chains. This act alone was painful, as the guard was no Florence Nightingale and his bedside manner was despicable! She couldn't see him, but she felt the presence of another man enter the room from behind her.

"Hello Yvette, or whatever your real name is," the man said. Yvette instantly recognised the voice as being that of the Nazi officer from the time before. "Are you ready to tell me the truth this time?" he questioned calmly.

"I have been telling you the truth," she said defiantly. "My name is Yvette Colbert and I am a simple farm girl. I was out for a walk when your men grabbed me and brought me to this terrible place."

"Oh dear, you are sticking to that story?" the Nazi asked, still sounding strangely calm and reassuring.

"I'm sticking to the story because it's true," Yvette remarked defiantly.

"Guard, fetch the tank," the Nazi ordered.

The guard left the room and a few minutes later, Yvette could hear the sound of small wheels being pushed along the outside corridor. The squealing sound became louder until she heard the wheels being pushed into the room. She could see nothing as all this was happening behind her, but as he came closer, she noticed out of the corner of her eye that a large tank of water had been placed by her side.

"Last chance," the Nazi officer announced whilst sill lurking behind her. "What is your name?" he demanded.

"My name is Yvette Colbert," she pleaded.

"Guard," he ordered.

The guard span her chair around and grabbed her by the hair. He then proceeded to push her head into the water and held it under the surface. After a few seconds, she felt her lungs starting to burn and thought they would burst. The guard had taken her by surprise and she'd not had the chance to take a deep breath before submersion. Just as she felt she would pass out, the guard pulled her painfully by the hair, but thankfully out of the water. This time she took a great gulp of air and waited to be placed back under the water.

"We can do this all day long, my dear," the officer stated, but then questioned, "Where in England did you come from last night?"

"I have not come from England. I am a French farm girl, and I was out walking and taking in the cool night air when your men apprehended me and brought me here," she said again, just like she'd been taught to say during all the months of training at the camp.

"Guard," she heard him say again, but this time she was ready and expected what was about to happen, so was able to take a huge gulp of air in preparation. Sure enough, she once again found her head shoved under the water.

With her ears now blocked with water she could hear practically nothing now, although she was just about able to hear the muffled sound of the Nazi officer shout, "Guard," and her head was dragged violently from the tank.

"What is your name?" he screamed. He was really insanely mad by now.

"Yvette."

"Again," he demanded.

Her head was back under the water, but this time for even longer. This time she felt like she was about to pass out, or maybe this was it, maybe she was about to die! She began to lose consciousness as the fluid began entering her nostrils, but then felt the sudden rush of water running over her shoulders as she was back in the room, gasping for breath.

"For the final time, what is your name?" the irate officer demanded.

"Yvette Colbert," the girl replied, trying hard not to show any fear of this monster.

"Guard, take her back to the cell," the Nazi ordered, now sounding quite deflated.

The guard did as was ordered and dragged her back along the corridor to her cell. However, this time when he threw her into the room he said, "Have a good sleep. Enjoy your last night on this earth." As he left the cell, Yvette could hear the sound of his laughter fading as he walked away.

'What did he mean, my last night on earth?' she questioned herself, fearing the worst and for good reason. She realised the situation she was in. If she gave them no information, what use was she to them? What was the point of them keeping her alive?

"My God," she shouted loudly. "They are going to kill me tomorrow! Somebody help me please," she shouted at the top of her voice, but no one heard her pleas and nobody came.

Yvette spent the next few hours sitting on the floor with her back to the wall, which felt cold from the damp, and wet from the condensation dripping down it.

Occasionally she heard the man screaming from the room further down the corridor. This made her think. What were they doing to this poor man to make him scream like this, and why were they not doing it to her? She surmised that he must have been a far more important prisoner than she.

Eventually the inevitable happened. The door opened, but this time there were two guards who greeted her.

"Kommen Sie," one of the guards ordered, and she stood and walked towards them. There was no point in struggling as this would only delay the inevitable fate which had already been dealt her, so she walked calmly towards the two.

This time, however, she was surprised when they put a hood over her head. She couldn't see a thing as they took her arm in arm along the corridor, but she was sure they were taking her in a different direction and away from the 'interrogation' room. Could this be good news?

Suddenly she heard another door being opened, but as she was pushed through it she could feel the change of temperature, which rose slightly as she felt the air and the sun on her still covered face. She was outside and the day was bright.

With the men directing and guiding her, they walked about twenty paces until the men stopped and span her around. Her arms were pulled behind her and were opened wide. The next thing was that she felt herself being placed against a thick piece of wood, maybe a tree trunk, with her arms being tied together behind it.

Yvette wondered what the hell was going on, but then she heard that voice once again and heard it say, "Are you ready now to tell me the truth? What is your name and where have you come from?"

"Go to Hell!" she answered defiantly. "You will kill me anyway no matter what I say, so you just go and do it and then fuck off and die!"

She was then chilled to the bone when she heard the Nazi officer say, "Firing squad, present arms." Yvette heard a small number of rifles being raised. "Ready – Aim – Last chance Yvette."

"Go fuck yourself," she remarked, content in the knowledge that if these were the last words she ever spoke, she was happy to be telling a Nazi officer to fuck off!

"Okay my dear, if that's what you want," the Nazi officer said and then continued, "Company – Ready – Aim – FIRE!"

Yvette heard the loud sound of gunshot ringing in her ears, but curiously felt no pain. Had they all missed her – surely not? Is this what death feels like? Had she passed over to the other side in the split second after the guns had been fired? Was she in fact now dead and resting with the angels above?

She then heard footsteps coming towards her. Was this really Saint Peter coming to greet her and invite her to pass through the pearly gates of heaven?

After another couple of seconds, she felt a slight tug on the hood covering her face and felt a pull as somebody yanked it off, uncovering her head. Her eyes clamped themselves closed tightly with the brightness of the day's dazzling sunshine, but as they slowly opened and adjusted to the light, she noticed a man standing before her.

"Congratulations Yvette, you passed the test with flying colours," the man announced.

She strained her eyes to see who was talking to her but was sure the voice belonged to the Nazi officer from before; although the foreign accent had now disappeared.

"What do you mean, I passed the test?" Yvette demanded.

As the ringing sound in her ears began to clear and her eyes became more adjusted to the daylight, she could clearly see the man in the Nazi uniform standing before her, but his demeanour had changed dramatically. Gone now was the scowl on his face and the anger in his voice, as she watched him taking off the cap and removing the uniform jacket. She studied his features as he began pulling on the moustache, realising it was fake. When the moustache was removed, she could just about make out the imposter.

"You bastard!" she shouted, for standing before her was Mr. Green.

"I'm sorry Yvette," he said, "but we test all our potential candidates. If it makes you feel any better, you are one of the best agents we've ever had."

"Are you telling me that all this was a test?" Yvette demanded.

"Sorry," was all Green could muster.

"You Bastard!" she roared. "You absolute, total Bastard! You absolute piece of shit! And what about Peter Collins and Ben Richards, I saw them both being shot dead?"

Mr. Green gave her a wry smile and indicated to the mock firing squad. "They're over there," he informed her.

Yvette, her eyes now clear and adjusted to the sunshine, looked at the five men still standing in the firing squad formation. True enough, there they stood, both men smiling, albeit apologetically.

"You bastard, Peter, you fucker, Ben" Yvette shouted angrily, although her face soon turned to relief as she realised her two friends were still alive and well and had not fallen at the hands of the enemy upon arrival in the so called, French countryside.

A few days later, life had returned to that of relative normality for the young Yvette. Mr. Green had given her a couple of days of freedom to calm herself down before revealing what really happened on the 'fake' mission into occupied France, and during these few days she'd also learned to forgive Ben Richards and Peter Collins for their part in the deceitfulness performed upon her.

After the fourth day, Mr. Green came to the billet to see her. "How are you, Yvette?" he questioned.

"My name is Yvette Colbert and I am a French farm girl," she replied, which brought a smile to Mr. Green's face.

"Am I forgiven, my dear?" he asked, almost pleading.

"I suppose so," she replied, "but did you need to be so rough and tough with me? I honestly thought I was going to drown!"

"Believe me my girl, should you be captured by the genuine Nazis in France, your treatment there will be a lot worse than you suffered here, and they will not be using blank bullets at your firing squad," Mr. Green remarked. He then went on to tell her the full story of what really happened that night.

When they'd left that evening, Peter and Ben, as instructors, were already in on the deceit. The three of them were driven to the airfield, put on the plane laden in full parachute regalia to supposedly be flown to a field very close to Paris, France.

What really happened was that when the plane took off, instead of carrying straight ahead towards the English Channel, it banked to the left and actually turned back and flew over the English countryside for an hour.

When the target area had been reached, now in total darkness, Yvette, Peter and Ben were told to prepare for the jump into no man's land. Yvette thought this was the French countryside and therefore riddled with danger, but the jump landing was actually taking place in a small clearing in the middle of a forest, less than ten miles from the training camp.

When they landed and hid their parachutes and helmets in the undergrowth, the men lurking in the trees, who were supposed to be the French resistance but were actually English dressed in German soldier uniforms, signalled to them.

When the three walked towards the torchlight, as they came closer, and as rehearsed many times before, when the fake German soldiers began firing their blanks, Peter and Ben both threw themselves to the floor, quickly rolling on their stomachs so Yvette could not see the lack of blood.

The imposters then came out from their hiding place, apprehended Yvette and threw her blindfolded into the back of a truck. They then took her back to the training camp, but to a secret area of the camp which she'd never seen before. Had she not had the blindfold placed upon her head, she would have seen that the driver of the truck was sitting on the right hand side of the vehicle and not the left.

The entire operation had been planned with military precision, and poor Yvette had been totally fooled. The poor girl had been living in fear for her life and petrified for three or four days and nights! She didn't know exactly how long, as she had no idea of whether it was day or night when incarcerated!

"Can you ever forgive me, Yvette?" Mr. Green questioned.

"My name is Yvette Colbert. I am a French farm girl and I am out for a walk in the French countryside," she replied. "This is my story and I'm sticking to it."

"Very good, Yvette," Mr. Green smiled whilst patting her affectionately on the back. He then laughed hysterically as he walked away.

CHAPTER 6
WELCOME TO THE WAR

As the coast of France came clearly into view, the nervous tension she'd felt since leaving terra firma after taking off in Kent, was now building into a mighty crescendo and throwing a party inside her stomach.

This time she knew this was the real deal, as since the fake fiasco, the situation for her had become a lot less secretive. This time she'd been driven to the temporary airport by Mr. Green himself, and she'd been allowed to sit alongside him in the front seat of the staff car.

"Good luck, Yvette," he'd said to the girl and meant it, as they'd shaken hands in farewell when parting company. "May God be with you," he also offered.

"Thank you," she replied with sincerity, with all the bad feelings seemingly melting away.

Two weeks after the fake firing squad episode she'd had a visit from Mr. Black, but this time at the camp, thus saving Yvette yet another trip to 'The Department of Fish & Fisheries,' at 5A Great Portland Street, London.

"I hear congratulations are in order, my dear," Black said after she'd entered the room.

"If you mean I survived the firing squad, congratulations are then very much in order," she replied sarcastically.

"Yes, my dear, I am sorry about that," Black said almost apologetically – almost! "We needed to find out whether you would crack under pressure or not."

"And?" she questioned.

"You passed with flying colours," Black revealed.

"Funny," the girl said. "Those are exactly the same words Mister Green said to me when he lifted my hood. Is this in the training manual?"

Black ignored this remark and continued to tell the girl of the forthcoming mission.

She was to be flown to France, where she would be met by members of the resistance. They would hide her the first night or two in one of the many safe houses scattered about the countryside. They would then move her by day until reaching the streets of Paris.

Once in the city, she would go from safe house to safe house, operating the radio and sending coded messages to Britain, whilst decoding messages received in France and sent from London. She was also assigned to send and receive messages from different pockets of the resistance and to pass them on to others. This was a very important job which she was undertaking, as well as being crucial to the war effort.

Because of the danger of this mission, Black informed her that she would never broadcast from the same house for more than three nights in a row, but would move every three days to a different location.

"I didn't realise there were so many radio sets in Paris," she said to Black, somewhat naively.

"Oh no my dear, you will carry the radio with you," he revealed.

"What the f..........!" She just about sopped herself from swearing when she heard this revelation. "How will I do this?"

"The radio is only small and portable. It will easily fit inside your bag," Black instructed.

"But if I'm caught carrying a radio, they will kill me," she claimed.

"Yes, they will kill you for sure," Black agreed. "This is why you must never be caught." He said this so 'matter of factly' that Yvette was taken aback.

He went on to tell her that she'd been chosen all those months ago not only for the fact she spoke French fluently, but also because of her size. She was quite small for her age, although perfectly formed. With her beautiful features, almost angelic in looks ad being quite short in stature, dressed correctly she could easily pass as a schoolgirl.

"We will do something with your hair, maybe put it in pigtails," Black told the girl. "We will dress you as a schoolgirl. Dressed in a white blouse, pleated skirt and with little white ankle socks, no one will suspect you of being a spy. You will ride a bicycle around the city and no one will ever suspect you are an S.O.E agent."

"There is one problem with this disguise," she said with honesty.

"Yes," said Black. "And what is that?"

"I have never ridden a bicycle in my life," she admitted.

Black almost choked on this information! "You mean to tell me that you can now parachute out of an airplane, use a radio to transmit and receive Morse code, and silently kill a man by using unarmed combat, yet you cannot ride a bike?" He despaired.

"Sorry," was all that Yvette could offer.

"For f......!" This time Mr. Black almost swore! "Give me one hour," was his parting comment.

She watched as he got into his car and drove off somewhere, but to where he was going, she had no idea. He returned less than an hour later with the boot of the car plainly opened and with the wheel of a bicycle poking out of it. Luckily the rest of the bike was intact and safely and securely trapped within it.

Leaving the car, Black walked away and returned a few moments later with both Peter Collins and Ben Richards.

"Okay, you two. Here is a bicycle and there is Yvette," Black announced to the two men who now looked confused. "Now teach her how to ride the bloody thing!" he ordered.

The two men, now both good friends of Yvette, simultaneously cracked up and laughed raucously.

"You cannot......." Ben laughed.

"You've never........." Peter mocked.

"Piss off you two!" was all Yvette could say, now both angry and also embarrassed.

For the rest of the afternoon, both men took it in turns to hold the saddle whilst the girl tried as best she could to balance. Finally, Peter let her go whilst she was pedalling down a slight incline. She was doing very well until she realised she was 'flying solo.' She then began panicking, but when both the lads shouted, "Keep going, Yvette, keep pedalling," the encouragement they gave her made her keep going and she cracked it. She was now officially a cyclist.

During the following weeks, Yvette practically lived on her bike and was seen riding it round and around the base as much as possible, because, all joking aside, as Mr. Black had told her, "The ability to be able to ride a bicycle with some proficiency could very well save your life when in Paris."

As she constantly pedalled as fast as she could around the training camp each day, she never forgot these wise words which Mr. Black had said to her, and they were now firmly implanted into her memory.

"Welcome to France," the pilot said to her as they crossed over the coastline. They were now flying over French soil. "Keep your fingers crossed," the young man added.

The pilot was only two years older than Yvette, and until nine months ago had never been inside an airplane, let alone flown one. He'd been part of an intensive training course to get young men airborne to help with the war effort.

"Keep my fingers crossed for what?" Yvette questioned.

"Keep them crossed for the enemy not to see us," Captain James replied. "If they attack, there will be nothing we can do."

"What do you mean," Yvette queried.

We are not armed," Captain James replied, an announcement that shocked Yvette.

They were flying in a specially adapted, 'Westland Lysander' aircraft, normally containing just the pilot flying solo. However, this one had had all the guns removed so as to accommodate one passenger, maybe two at a real squeeze, but possible if essential.

It had been adapted for missions just like this one, to take members of Winston Churchill's, Special Operations Executive and to drop them in the Loire Valley, some one hundred and fifty miles from Paris. Due to its small size, this was the furthest the Lysander could fly and return safely to Kent on a full tank of fuel.

This was the second attempt they'd made to get the girl to France, with the first failing due to it being a very cloudy evening. This night the conditions were perfect, as they were flying only by the light of the moon, and tonight the moon was both bright and full.

As they flew further inland and came closer to the destination, Captain James told Yvette to, "Keep your eyes peeled for lights."

"Lights?" she queried.

"Yes," James confirmed. "The resistance will place flashlights pointing upwards in a field to make a temporary landing strip for us."

"Wait – What! We're landing in a field?" Yvette gushed.

This was another reason why the Lysander was used for these missions, as with its small size, being only ten yards in length, it could take off and land in only one hundred and fifty yards on practically any surface, as long as it was reasonably flat.

"I'm sorry, Miss; did you think we'd be landing in a nice airport?" Captain James said sarcastically. "Maybe we could go for a pleasant cocktail in the bar after landing."

"No need for that!" Yvette retaliated, deciding she did not like this man.

Fifteen minutes later, now flying as low as was physically

possible by moonlight, Yvette spotted what maybe could be the temporary landing strip.

"Down there," she shouted, pointing in the direction of some lights.

"Well spotted," Captain James praised the girl. "Now brace yourself for impact!"

"What do you mean, impact?" Yvette questioned.

"We don't know what we are landing on," Captain James informed the girl. "If this field has recently been ploughed, we could be in for a bumpy landing, and this thing has no suspension. It's great in the air, but a bastard on the ground!"

The new S.O.E. agent did as was told and crouched herself down with her head almost between her knees and waited for impact, but none came. After bouncing a couple of times, Captain James had the plane down safely, securely and expertly.

"Here we are," the pilot announced triumphantly. "Home sweet home," he smiled.

"Thank you very much," Yvette said gratefully, almost forgiving him for his earlier sarcasm.

Captain James slid open the entrance to the plane and Yvette, after saying "Goodbye," clambered out over the wing and landed unceremoniously in a heap on the floor to be greeted by two men. They both had what could only be described as smirks on their faces, after witnessing the very unladylike disembarkation from the Lysander.

"Yvette Colbert?" one of the men asked, getting more serious again.

"Yes, I am Yvette Colbert," she replied. Even though responding to this false name sounded quite wrong to the girl, she knew she needed to get used to it, and fast!

"Welcome to France," the man said. "I am Jean Renoir."

"Like the artist," Yvette remarked.

Yes, like the artist," the man replied with yet another smirk. This made her think that this could also be a made up name.

Bloody Hell; was there anything real in this world?

The other man walked towards her and curiously kissed her on the cheek. "Good luck, my dear," he said with an unmistakably upper class English accent. "May God be with you and keep you safe."

After saying this, the man hugged her and continued to the plane, where Yvette watched as he climbed inside, much more elegantly than she had left it.

Captain James, after giving a wave of the hand, expertly turned the plane around in what looked like a very small turning circle and was soon gathering speed in the opposite direction to that of which they'd arrived, every second getting further away until she saw the Lysander leave the ground.

That was it, the moment she realised she was now stuck here in France and there was no going back.

"Come," Jean Renoir told her and she followed.

Over the coming days, Yvette would come to know that Jean Renoir, as the leader of this group of Resistance members was a man of few words. However, what he did say was always important.

They walked along a small country lane until reaching the edge of a village. The place was in total darkness and she was having a problem in seeing where she was going. Suddenly they saw a torchlight heading straight at them, but still around fifty yards away.

"Quick," Renoir demanded."Get into the hedge."

He immediately grabbed hold of her and dragged her by the arm and almost threw her into the bushes. "Germans," he whispered, putting his two fingers to his lips, making the international sign to keep quiet.

Yvette was struck with fear, totally petrified as the two men, both pushing bicycles, came closer. They were laughing and joking with each other and it was obvious to the girl that they were both very drunk. She could almost smell the beer on their breath as they passed her, less than five yards away. Thankfully these two men were oblivious to their presence in the bushes.

She looked at Jean and noticed the movement as he put his right arm inside his jacket and pulled out a pistol fitted with a silencer. The gun was trained on the two men and panned around on them as they passed and then went on their merry way. They waited in continued silence for five minutes until the two soldiers were well out of sight.

"Come," Jean said again, and they resumed their journey into the village.

"How did you know they were German soldiers?" Yvette questioned Jean.

"Simple," he returned. "Every night after eight o'clock there is a curfew. Anyone seen on the street after this will be shot on sight, no questions, just shot! When I saw the torchlight, I knew the only people on the streets after curfew would be the enemy, especially carrying a torch."

"What would have happened if they'd seen us?" Yvette questioned. "I could have coughed, or sneezed, or anything, so what would have happened then?"

"If that had happened," Jean began quite nonchalantly, "then we would have just buried two German soldiers and we would be riding along on their bicycles now."

Hearing Jean Renoir, the leader of the Resistance in this area saying this, really hit it home to the young girl. She realised she was no longer playing a game in the training camp. This was the real deal. This was deadly serious!

She was now in the war and one mistake could end her life, for real! Yvette had to admit that for the first time, she was now truly scared out of her wits!

CHAPTER 7
GIRLIE FRILLS AND CYANIDE PILLS

Yvette sensed the sunlight shining through the window as her body reverted from sleep to fully wide awake mode. Not sure if she was dreaming or not, she heard the voices of people all speaking together, and they were all surrounding her.

"Is this her?"

"It must be."

"She's very young."

"But she's also beautiful."

"Yes she is, very beautiful."

"She's stunning!"

"I think she will be great at the job."

"I hope so, for her sake."

"If not, she'll be dead within a month!"

Yvette listened to all these comments as she slowly came round from her slumber, but then she was shocked to hear a man speaking with a broad German accent. She instantly sat bolt upright from the sofa she'd been sleeping on, looked at Jean Renoir, and pointed at the foreigner.

"Don't you worry about him," Jean remarked almost laughing. "This is Gunter."

"But he's a German," Yvette declared.

"Yes he is," Jean Renoir confirmed.

"What the hell is he doing here?" Yvette demanded.

"Don't you be worrying about Gunter, I have known him for more than six years," Renoir stated. "He is sound, I promise you."

"But can we trust him?" the girl questioned.

"Your question should be, do 'I' trust him, and yes, I can honestly say that I trust him with my life," Jean replied. "I would lay down my own life and die for him, and I know he would do the same and die for me."

Jean Renoir then continued to tell Yvette the story of how Gunter the German came to be in their midst.

When Adolph Hitler came to power and took his place as the German Chancellor and Fuhrer in the early 30's, Gunter could foresee the future for the country he loved and didn't like what he saw. Three years later, in 1936 he predicted all the problems which were about to follow, especially Hitler's hatred and later persecution of the Jews, and so Gunter uprooted and moved from Köln to Paris, where he began working as a simple barista, even though he'd worked on a farm in Germany and was more used to manual labour.

All was good in his life until unbelievably, Hitler followed him and sent his men to invade the country, eventually reaching and entering Paris on June 14th 1940.

"I met Gunter when he first moved to Paris. I met him in the café where he worked, not long after he'd arrived from Germany," Jean began.

"You lived in Paris?" Yvette questioned.

"I was born there. I am a genuine native Parisian, my dear," he revealed. "I worked for a local newspaper until it became too dangerous for me to continue to do so."

"So what brought you here to....." she hesitated, "wherever this place is?" she questioned, realising that she had absolutely no idea of where in France she actually was, except for the fact that she knew it was somewhere in the Loire Valley.

"As I say, it became dangerous working on the newspapers because many men began publishing Anti-Nazi propaganda, converting it to posters and displaying them on the walls of Paris. A few of these men were found doing this and were in serious trouble."

"What happened to them?" Yvette queried, somewhat innocently.

"The German guards dragged them into the street and executed them. They shot them dead and made the Parisian residents watch as they did so," Jean Renoir informed the girl.

"Bastards!" she gushed.

"Exactly," Renoir agreed. "Bastards indeed."

"What about Gunter? What's his story?" Yvette asked, urging Renoir to continue.

"As I say, working in the news industry would have become dangerous had I stayed in Paris any longer," Jean said and then carried on with his story. "I knew Gunter shared the same hatred of Hitler and his Nazi Party as I did, and I also knew he was becoming scared of being discovered as a German hiding in plain sight, so during one conversation we were having in the café, I suggested we move to the countryside and look for alternative accommodation, along with a new type of employment."

"So you had no idea you would be joining the resistance?" the girl asked.

"No. At that time we had no idea whatsoever," Renoir confirmed. "Gunter and I wandered from town to town, village to village, working for food and lodgings on the various farms along the way."

"So why did you stop here?" Yvette asked, again not knowing where 'here' actually was.

"Again this was all caused by Adolph Hitler," Jean revealed. "In the summer of last year, when he began deporting all the Jews, including German people of Jewish descent to the various concentration camps, as well as forcing all the young German men to join his army, Hitler realised he'd made a mistake and had removed eighty percent of the workforce from the factories which were manufacturing the ammunition and armaments, including the Panzer tanks, and this was no good for his war effort."

"So wat did he do next?" an inquisitive Yvette questioned and Jean Renoir continued.

"He ordered that every French born man and woman between the ages of twenty and twenty-two should be taken to Germany and work in these factories, thus taking the place of the German workforce they'd already lost for one reason or the other.

What actually happened was that almost all of these people, not wanting to go to Germany, went instead to hide in the mountainside and forests and decided to fight against the German occupation of France, and so the French Resistance was formed. Gunter and I joined the resistance at the earliest opportunity."

"And here you are," Yvette stated.

"And here we are," Renoir agreed. "Anyway, my dear, you need to rest now and I will take you later to the house of Madame Chambourcey. She is the local dressmaker who will make adjustments to your clothes."

"But they fit perfectly, the girl claimed.

"Not those sorts of adjustments," Jean Renoir revealed.

Two hours later, after an ample breakfast feast of cheese and ham, along with thick crusty bread and served with more coffee than she could handle, Yvette and Jean Renoir were heading through the village en-route to the home of Madam Chambourcey, all the time with Yvette looking nervously over her shoulder.

"Relax my girl, you are perfectly safe in the village during daylight hours," Jean advised her.

"What about the German soldiers?" the young girl questioned the older man.

During the day they are polite. In fact they're really courteous with the local people, both men and women," Renoir revealed. "However, if these same young men, for that's what they are, young men, if they see you on the street after curfew, then it would be a different matter."

"What would happen then?" Yvette asked with the pure innocence of youth.

"They would shoot and kill any person breaking curfew, and would do it without a split second of hesitation," Jean instructed.

He looked at the girl to see a reaction, but none came, and this worried him. They sat on a wall enjoying the sunshine, and as they did so, he looked at the girl and asked her an important question.

"Yvette, I have to ask you something and I want you to give me an honest answer," he began. "Last night, when you saw those two drunken soldiers walking towards us, were you scared?"

"Are you serious!" she remarked. "No, I was not scared of them, I was petrified! I have never been more scared of anything or anyone in my life!"

"Good," Renoir remarked smiling.

"What do you mean by good?" she retaliated, beginning to get angry now.

"It's good because you answered my question honestly. This means that I can now trust you," he revealed.

"And if I'd said that I was not scared of the German soldiers?" she queried.

"Then I myself or none of my comrades would have trusted you and would not work with, or help you," he explained. "You would have been told to make your own way to Paris, or we would have hidden you in the village until the next plane was available to take you home."

As she listened to Jean Renoir spouting this speech, she thought, 'Shit! Why didn't I tell him I had no fear of the enemy? He would have sent me back home to the safety of England!'

However, it was only for a brief moment that she had this thought. In reality, she was proud to be here to offer her services and to do her very best to help defeat the enemy and drive them from this beautiful country which these people called home.

As they walked further along the narrow street towards the lady's house on the hill, Yvette almost froze when she saw three young Germans walking towards them, all in uniform.

"Keep calm," Jean whispered to the girl. "You are not in any danger, I promise you."

As the three young men came closer to the two, Jean looked at them and touched the peak of his cap.

"Guten Tag," he greeted.

"Hallo," the three returned in unison.

One of the guys also added, "Bonjour Monsieur," just to be even more polite. Monsieur Renoir gave the man a very nice smile. Yvette noted that as they exchanged pleasantries, they were all smiling in the direction of Renoir and her.

'What kind of weird and wonderful place have I landed in?' she questioned her inner self, as they calmly walked past the enemy.

Eventually they reached a little stone cottage with a bright blue painted entrance. Renoir knocked on the door and his calling was answered by an older white haired lady of small stature.

"Ah bonjour Jean," she greeted her companion, kissing him tenderly on both cheeks and then one more time for luck. "Please come in my friend. And who is this?" she asked, looking in Yvette's direction.

"Madame Chambourcey, it is my pleasure to introduce you to a new recruit. This is Yvette," he informed the lady.

"Enchanté," Madame Chambourcey remarked politely, also greeting the girl with a kiss on the cheek, but this time only once and with not so much passion.

Although she thought this lady was rather elderly, she was in fact a youngish and sprightly woman of just forty-nine years of age, but then, when you are a youngster of just twenty-one years of age, as Yvette was at the time, anyone over the age of thirty is considered as positively ancient!

"Please, come in my child," Madame Chambourcey invited, ushering Yvette inside and instructing her to take a seat. "Now, I hear you need some special clothes?"

Yvette did not know how to answer this question so she just kept quiet and said nothing, thinking this was probably the best strategy to follow. She did however offer the lady a smile in return.

"Please follow me," Madame Chambourcey instructed Yvette, and she followed her into a separate room. Inside the room she saw racks of shirts for the men, with blouses for the girls, all hanging immaculately on hangers and seemingly made of silk, albeit of a poorer quality silk.

Madame Chambourcey could see the look in her eyes and so revealed to the girl, "They are actually made from reclaimed parachutes, my dear."

"They are superb," Yvette admitted.

"Thank you my dear," Madame Chambourcey reacted. "Now, off with those clothes and try these on. You need to select three blouses and three pleated shirts."

"Why pleated?" Yvette queried.

"Because we need to make you look even younger than you are," the lady advised. "The younger you look, the less likely the enemy are to suspect you of anything and they'll leave you alone."

"That makes sense," Yvette agreed.

Before she understood what was going on she watched as Madame Chambourcey left the room, taking her clothes away with her and leaving the girl standing there wearing only her bra and panties. She began making a selection of the clothes and trying them on. Very soon she'd found some garments which fitted well, so she returned to the reception room and rejoined Jean Renoir and Madame Chambourcey.

"Oh there you are," Jean remarked.

"What do you think?" Yvette questioned, performing a

pirouette and making her green pleated skirt spin through the air.

"Very pretty," Madame Chambourcey told he girl. "You will do nicely."

"Thank you," Yvette replied.

"You remind me so much of when I was your age," the older lady remarked.

"Really," Yvette reacted sounding doubtful, but then realised the insult she might have just made. However, Madame Chambourcey seemed to either ignore it or hadn't heard it, but whatever the reason, she just brushed it aside.

"Yvette my dear, you have no idea who this lady is," Jean began. "During the last war, she was known by the enemy as 'The Silent Assassin,' because the victims never heard her arrive, and when she left them, they were all dead!"

The younger girl looked at the older lady and was shocked at what she'd just heard. She looked like anyone's granny or maybe older sister or even a mother, but whichever version, she looked like a really nice lady. But more than this, she looked normal, gentle and kind.

"So you were involved in the last war?" Yvette queried, really needing conformation that Renoir was telling the truth.

"Yes she was," Jean Renoir replied, appearing to speak for the lady.

"You may not believe it, my dear," Madame Chambourcey said, taking up the story, "but I was once considered to be very beautiful," she stressed.

"You still are very beautiful," Jean butted in.

"Oh you are too kind, Jean," the lady replied, flashing Renoir a beautiful smile before redirecting the conversation to the younger girl in the room.

"But it's true, my dear," she said. "Back then, in nineteen-sixteen when I was twenty-three years of age, I could walk into any room and everyone would stop their conversation and look at me." She stopped to look at the young girl, and when she knew she had her full attention, she continued. "I knew that every man in that room wanted me."

"They wanted you?" Yvette asked, again naively.

"Yes my dear, I mean that every man in the room wanted to have sex with me," she revealed, this time smiling at Yvette.

"Oh," was all the girl could offer.

"It didn't matter if they were with girlfriends, or even their wives, at that moment you could see it in their eyes that they were infatuated with me. I also believe that many of the ladies in the room also found me ravenous and would also have loved to have had sex with me," she laughed.

"And did you have sex with any of them, the men I mean?" Yvette questioned.

"Yvette!" Jean Renoir snapped.

"No its okay, Jean, it's a perfectly reasonable question," Madame Chambourcey said whilst looking at Renoir, who was still giving Yvette the stare.

"Sorry," the younger girl said apologetically.

"No need for apologies young lady, you need to know," the lady said turning to face Yvette. "I gave all the men in the room a certain look which made them feel like they were the only one for me," she continued. "I made them feel like I would lay under them as fast as they could get on top of me." She stopped to have a little chuckle again at the thought of this.

"And did any of them achieve this?" Yvette interrogated, still wanting her question to be answered.

Again, Jean Renoir was just about to protest at the girl's insolence when Madame Chambourcey raised her hand, gesturing for him to stop.

"Many of the men thought they'd seduced me," she smiled, "but the ones who did," she stopped speaking for dramatic effect, "well let's just say they were the unlucky ones."

"Unlucky, how so?" the girl asked, now thirsty for knowledge.

"These men thought they were walking me home, and they thought there would be a night of glorious love making at the end of it for them. However, what did actually happen was that I took them down a narrow lane where at the end of it, the man and I would begin to fool around. First a little kissing and hugging and then I even let them have a play with my boobs, but as they were enjoying themselves fondling my ample firm breasts, they didn't notice me taking out the long, thin, razor sharp edged knife from a concealed pocket in my coat. I liked to look them in the eyes as I struck them with the blade from behind.

I enjoyed seeing the look of surprise on their dying faces, as I watched the life drain from their bodies. As they looked at me lovingly, I enjoyed the way their facial expression changed when they felt the blade go in through their shoulder blades and straight into their heart.

I had to push them away quickly, so as not to get any blood on my clothes." Madame Chambourcey said nonchalantly, as she stopped and looked at Yvette.

"You have to remember this was during the last war," Jean reminded the girl, seeing how stunned she was at this revelation.

"I know, but she's such a lovely lady," Yvette almost whimpered.

"They were the enemy, my dear," Madame Chambourcey reminded her. "I did it then and I would do it again if I still had my looks and men still desired me. You must make the most of your looks my child. Believe me, they do not last forever."

"Madame," Jean butted into the conversation. "You 'do' still have your looks. You are still a very beautiful and desirable lady, and of course men still desire you," he stressed.

The two smiled at each other, but not the smile of friends, there was more to it than that.

The thought suddenly occurred to Yvette that these two were more involved than they were letting on. She even wondered if, had she not been there today, these two might even have been jumping the bones off each other in lust! If alone, would they be doing something far more strenuous and enjoyable than partaking in polite conversation, along with afternoon tea?

"Yvette, have you found the tiny compartments in the shirt sleeves?" Madame Chambourcey questioned.

"I noticed a tiny pocket in each of them, but have no idea of what they are for," Yvette admitted. Hearing this, Jean Renoir looked at the older lady in the room and she looked at him.

"You tell her, Jean" the older lady said.

Yvette looked at the two of them, now standing together in silence. "Well, somebody tell me. You're scaring me now," she demanded. However, when the reason for the pocket was revealed, the girl could not believe what she was hearing.

"The small pocket is the place for you to keep your cyanide pill," Renoir informed her.

"What!" Yvette choked.

"Do not worry, my child," Madame Chambourcey said, trying to reassure the girl. "Yes it's true the cyanide pill is for you to take should the worst come to the worst and it's your only way out, a way of dying, a painless release, but it is also there for you should you find yourself in a sticky situation."

"What sort of sticky situation," Yvette demanded to know.

"Well, let's say a Nazi has taken you back to his lodgings and is expecting to have his wicked way with you," the elder lady said.

"His wicked way," Yvette sounded confused.

"Sex," Jean Renoir offered.

"Oh," Yvette said, now understanding.

"As I was saying," Madame Chambourcey continued, a little angry now for the interruptions. "Should you find yourself in a sticky situation as this, you can offer to pour the officer a glass of wine to get him even more into the mood. While you do this, you can unscrew the cap of the cyanide pill and put it into his glass.

When he drinks it, depending on his size you will have

about three seconds for him to die," the lady instructed the girl.

"The bigger the man the longer it will take, but four seconds would be the longest," Renoir joined in.

"But the reason we're telling you this," Chambourcey continued, "is that you must make sure he is nowhere near his gun, or he will have the time to kill you before dying."

"Oh shit!" the younger girl muttered. "I really am now involved in this war."

"I am sure you will be okay my dear," Madame Chambourcey told her, with her smile lighting up the room.

"Thank you," Yvette said, and her response was genuine.

"You are more than welcome my dear, and thank you for helping us French to win this war," the Madame smiled again.

"Can I ask you, why did you take my clothes away?" Yvette questioned.

I had to check them to make sure there was nothing on them associated with England," Jean told her. "No British maker marks or the like."

"And, were there?" Yvette asked.

"They were clear," Jean replied.

"But we burned them anyway," Madame Chambourcey revealed.

"But why did you do that?" Yvette exasperated.

"Because they made you look too old. We need you to look like a young girl of school age and looking like an angel," the older lady stated.

"And now you do," Jean Renoir smiled, making the young girl feel a little uneasy.

Half an hour later, after leaving the comfortable home of Madame Chambourcey, as they walked back to the village 'safe house,' the home of Jean Renoir and Gunter the German, Yvette dared to ask the question she'd wanted to ask before.

"Monsieur Renoir, Jean, you and Madame Chambourcey,

are you more than just good friends?" she asked the man.

"What do you mean? What are you asking?" the man teased.

"I'm asking if you and the lady are lovers?" she questioned.

Renoir looked at the girl and again put his finger to his lips.

"Shush, my child," he whispered smiling. "A gentleman never tells!"

"I think you just did," Yvette replied, trying her best but failing miserably to stifle a little laugh.

CHAPTER 8
A SUITCASE FULL OF GUNS

Yvette stood on the platform and looked down suspiciously at the brown leather suitcase positioned on her right hand side. Although the case contained the new clothes which had been provided by Madame Chambourcey, she'd also been told, to her absolute horror, that there were also four pistols wrapped inside the garments. These weapons had been requested by the member of the resistance who'd be waiting for her upon arrival in Paris a few hours later. Even looking at this case was making her feel almost numb and extremely nervous.

She'd quite enjoyed the last few days staying at the home of Jean Renoir. She'd even begun to enjoy the company of Gunter, a man whom she now could not believe she didn't trust when she first heard his voice talking in that accent.

Speaking of Gunter, the man of German nationality, it soon became apparent to Yvette that he hated Hitler and the Nazis' just as much as any man, woman, or child living in Britain. She was now very sure in her mind that she could rust him, and no longer felt any fear or suspicion when in his company.

She'd asked Jean Renoir to tell her the name of the village several times, but every time he replied, "My girl, if you don't know the name of this place, then you cannot give us away."

How Yvette was beginning to hate all this secrecy, but she supposed it was all part of being a spy and working for Winston Churchill's 'Special Operations Executive,' better known as the S.O.E. Renoir did however answer another question she had for him.

"Why is the atmosphere of the village so different at night compared to the daylight hours?" she'd asked Renoir.

"What do you mean?" Jean had questioned.

"I mean that during the day the occupying soldiers are all so very well behaved, even being pleasant and polite with the locals. Yet during the night, they would shoot them on sight without hesitation. Why is this?" she asked of Renoir.

"That's easy," he replied. "They have no idea that we are all resistance members. This is a sleepy place where nothing ever happens and we are not involved in any local skirmishes, or at least, they don't think we are," he laughed as he said this.

"And a good thing too," the girl commented.

"Also," Renoir continued, "during the daylight hours we never carry weapons of any kind. They kept searching us when they first arrived, but soon realised, incorrectly, that we were just normal men and women going about our daily business and keeping ourselves to ourselves."

"If only they knew the truth," Yvette remarked, with a slight smirk on her pretty face. "But you carried a gun the night when I arrived."

"Of course," Jean confirmed. "But that was because I was on the streets after curfew. If those nice young lads had seen me that night they would have used me for target practise because I would have been breaking curfew rules, and the only people breaking curfew rules would be members of the resistance, which of course we are not," he laughed.

"Nice young lads?" Yvette queried.

"What?" Jean said, confused by her question, or lack of one.

"You called them nice young lads," Yvette said again. "But they are the enemy."

"Yes, they are the enemy," Jean Renoir began, "but these lads do not want to be here. They don't want to be involved in this war, and being here in this village is probably the best, and definitely the safest place they could possibly be spending this time."

"How so," Yvette interrogated, popping up with another question.

"When and if the British or American troops land on French

soil, we are about fifty miles away from anywhere en-route from Normandy to where the action would take place. These boys know this, so if they keep their heads down and don't antagonise the locals, there is a very good chance they might survive this war without having a shot fired in anger in their direction."

"So this is why they are so polite to the locals?" Yvette asked, but not really a question.

"Exactly," Renoir confirmed.

"Can I ask you another question?" Yvette pleaded.

"Of course, my dear," Renoir replied. "Ask away, my dear."

"The night I arrived and you met me from the plane," she looked at Jean and could see she had his full attention so continued. "Who was that man, the man who kissed me on the cheek, wished me good luck and then climbed aboard the plane to fly back to England with Captain James?"

"He was a very brave man," Renoir revealed. "He'd been in hiding here in the village for almost two months until now. He is an extremely heroic fighter pilot who has been involved in several confrontations with the enemy, but his last fight was an unlucky one for him."

"What happened?" questioned an impatient Yvette, butting in again.

"He was shot down. His plane was hit by a pilot flying a Focke-Wulf and his gunner bailed out and parachuted into enemy territory, never to be seen again," Jean revealed.

"What was his name? The man I met, I mean," the girl queried.

"Well," Jean said, looking deep in thought. "Let's just call him John,"

"Oh for f...." Yvette cursed, "More secrets?"

"No my dear, not this time," Renoir confirmed. "I cannot tell you his name because I never knew it."

"Did he not stay with you in the safe house?" the girl asked.

"No, in fact I didn't even know he was British until a week

ago, when yours and his flights were arranged."

"So what's his story?" Yvette begged the question.

"If you shut up and stop interrupting, I can tell you," Jean exasperated.

"Sorry," Yvette said, interrupting Renoir yet again.

Jean went on to tell the girl how 'John' had been hit in battle. It was obvious to him that the plane was going down, but at the time he was flying over a small town with thousands of innocent people living below. Not wanting to put these people in danger, he refused to leave the plane and attempted to fly it away from the town and headed towards the surrounding countryside.

The amazing thing was that the German pilot who'd shot his plane could see what he was doing, so completely left him alone. He had so much respect for the British pilot that he escorted him safely away from the town and then banked his own plane and flew away, leaving him to survive - possibly.

'John' crash landed the plane in a field about twenty miles from here and spent three days wandering aimlessly through the countryside until he finally found himself entering this village.

He was a really lucky man for the second time in the story. First he survived the crash, and secondly he was not seen by any of the Germans as he walked through the village. He was seen instead by the local priest, Father Michael, and he hid him in the church for all the duration of the time he was here.

Father Michael even dressed 'John' in robes and a Cassock, in case anyone ever spotted him through the stained windows of the church.

"Obviously no one did," Yvette said.

"I think one or two of the local people spotted him, but none of them said anything to give him away," Jean revealed.

"And if they had?" Yvette asked. Renoir answered this question with a smile.

It was a lovely sunny day and very warm, as Yvette waited

for her transport to arrive and take her to her destination of Paris. The sun was now almost overhead and she studied the shadow of her figure on the floor, but also the shadow of the brown suitcase standing next to her. This shadow was making her feel sick with worry.

When the train pulled into the station, Yvette took a last look at her shadow, but it was gone. There was now a much larger shadow dwarfing hers, as the people moved forward to step off the platform and onto the train.

She leaned to her right and went to pick the case up from the floor, but as she did so, she let out a slight groan.

"Here, let me carry that for you," the man standing behind her, and the owner of the shadow, said in perfect French.

Yvette turned to face the man and nearly died, for standing there behind her was a huge man in full German Officers' uniform.

"No, that's okay," Yvette pleaded, but the man in uniform was having none of it.

"Nonsense, here, please allow me," he said again. "It looks far too heavy for you. Please allow me to take it onboard the train for you."

As he said this, he gave the girl no opportunity to protest as he grabbed the case from her side and plucked it from the ground.

"My word," he said. "This bag is so heavy. What on earth do you have inside it?"

Yvette almost froze with fear as he said this. Should she make a grab for her cyanide pill? Surely not! 'Let's just see how this plays out,' she thought.

"I am a second year medical student," Yvette revealed, thinking on her feet. "I've been visiting my grandmother for a few days and I brought my books with me so I could continue with my studies whilst holidaying with Granny."

The officer seemed to believe this explanation and Yvette

felt a lot more happy and relaxed, but the feeling was not a long lasting one, for as the officer picked the case up and attempted to place it in the overhead luggage rack, both Yvette and he heard the distinct clanging sound of two metal objects hitting each other.

"And what is that?" he asked, a little more suspiciously now.

Yvette racked her brains for an explanation. "Ice skates," she replied.

"Ice skates?" the officer almost choked. "Why are you carrying ice skates on a warm day like today?"

Again she racked her brain for an answer. "They are very old ice skates," she said. "They belonged to my granny when she was a girl, and now she wants me to have them. I'm taking them back home to Paris with me in the hope that we have a cold winter. Hopefully some of the small ponds in the Parisian parks will freeze over so we can all go ice skating."

As she said this, she looked at the officer and realised what she'd said about living in Paris and hoped he didn't ask her for the address of where she was staying. Luckily he did not.

"Have a pleasant trip, my dear," he said instead, and left her alone as he walked towards the front of the train, Yvette thought to the more comfortable section where there might be a bar or a restaurant carriage. She decided that wherever he'd gone on the train, she hoped he would not be returning to her carriage, or the bag!

After an hour or so into the journey, Yvette began feeling safe again and began to relax, although she constantly kept looking up at the case above her head, at the same time lightly fondling and stroking the cyanide pill which had been sown into the cuff of her shirt sleeve. She wondered if she'd ever have the nerve, or bravery to use it, should the guns inside the case be discovered.

"When you arrive in Paris, you will arrive at the station

named, 'Gare du Nord.' You must find the exit which takes you to the Rue de Maubeuge," Jean Renoir had instructed the girl at the breakfast table that morning. "When you leave the station, there will be a young boy named Philippe Barstrom waiting for you."

"You mean a young man dressed as a boy?" Yvette had queried.

"No my dear, not this time," Renoir stated. "He really is a young boy, either fourteen or fifteen years of age. Not even he knows how old he is for sure, but one thing's for certain; he's the bravest boy I have ever met."

"So how come a boy so young would be involved in the resistance?" Yvette questioned.

"Because he's also a cold blooded killer," Renoir replied, shocking the girl.

"And what makes a young boy like that become a cold blooded killer in the French resistance?" she queried.

"You'd better sit down and make yourself comfortable," Renoir said seriously. "I have one hell of a story to tell you."

Yvette did as instructed, and Jean Renoir began telling her a story of unbelievable cruelty.

CHAPTER 9
THE MASSACRE OF SAN EIELSON

Jean Renoir began speaking about Paris during the April of the previous year of 942. The Nazis had been in control of the place for almost two years by then and they had almost rid the city of any Jews who'd been living there before the occupation. Those people of the Jewish persuasion still left in the city were either relying on good friends to hide them in secret compartments within their houses, hiding in plain site by using false papers, or as the majority were, living and working underground with the brave men and women of the 'Parisian Underground Resistance Movement.' However, by this time, life in Paris had returned to some sort of normality, or as normal as it could be with the Nazis in charge.

Adolph Hitler had visited the city the year before and had fallen in love with the place, so much so that he'd ordered that no damage or destruction should take place to any historic buildings. He also proclaimed that all non-Jewish Parisians, as long as they did not break Nazi laws, should be treated with respect by his troops.

The Fuhrer also ordered that whenever members of his army visited shops, bars and cafés, be they lowly soldiers or high ranking officers, they should always pay for everything they eat, drink, smoke or wear.

Problems on the streets began when the underground resistance members started printing anti-propaganda posters and pasting them on the walls of the centre of the city.

These posters encouraged the local French to fight against the occupation by Germany. They contained slogans like, "Fight the Bosch," – "Hate the Enemy," and "Do Your Duty and Kill a German!" This last slogan was the worst insult to the occupiers and they made it their duty to find the people who were printing and displaying these posters and then 'deal' with them!

The German authorities counteracted these posters by printing and displaying posters of their own. One of these posters showed a German soldier helping an old lady across the street. The slogan upon it simply read, "Trust the Germans." These posters were torn down almost as quickly as they were put up, and when they were replaced, they were torn down again!

The real trouble began when posters began appearing in the streets with a picture of the Fuhrer holding a very happy looking child in his arms. He was looking at the child with a great deal of love in his eyes, whilst the child was laughing and smiling broadly, obviously having no fear of the man holding him. It was later discovered that the child was a genuine relation of his, and the photo had been taken at Hitler's home in Munich. The slogan on this poster incensed the locals because it read:-

"Trust Adolph Hitler - The Fuhrer is your friend."

Not content with just ripping these posters from the walls, suddenly they appeared with huge red crosses painted on them with bright red paint, one was painted with the words, "Hitler is a Monster" emblazoned upon it

This was the final straw for the Nazis and the hunt was intensified to find the culprit, or culprits. The unlucky man was a member of the resistance who owned his own printing business. In fact his company had been responsible for most of the propaganda posters seen in the city a few months before. His name was, Claude Proust.

Monsieur Proust went out almost every evening in search of these Hitler posters, with the sole purpose of destroying them. This was a task he'd completed regularly and successfully, until one evening when his luck ran out. He was caught with his small pot of red paint and paintbrush whilst defacing one of the insulting posters in the aptly renamed street, now called, Rue de Berlin.

Caught literally red handed by the guards, he was bundled into the back of a truck and taken to the Gestapo Headquarters, situated close to Notre-Dame Cathedral.

"We know you are not acting alone," his interrogator accused him the next day. "Tell us the names of the people, no, tell me the names of the scum who are doing this act of vandalism with you."

"I was working alone. I am always alone," Proust claimed, although he was not believed by his tormentor, who gave him a sharp slap around the face with the back of his hand, which made him flinch. It stung, but Proust had felt much worse.

For three long days and even longer nights the prisoner was tortured, along with lack of sleep, food and water. He was beaten and kicked until black and blue, but he never gave up the names of the colleagues who'd been working with him and destroying the Nazi propaganda.

As he was sitting there, tied into the chair whilst alone in the room, he could hear two men arguing outside in the corridor.

"Sir, he is never going to give up the names of these traitors. I say we should just take him outside and shoot him now," he heard one say.

Claude Proust recognised the voice as being that of the Gestapo interrogator that had been inflicting the pain upon him for all this time.

"No, that would be too easy. I have a better idea," he heard the other man remark. "I will fetch the map."

As he heard the footsteps of the two men walking away, he wondered what the hell was going on. What was this map the second man was going to collect? His question was soon answered when the two men entered the room, but he went weak at the knees when he saw that one of the men was a Nazi officer, curiously carrying a rolled up paper under his left arm.

"I commend you, Sir," the Nazi said to Proust as he approached. "You are indeed a very brave, but stubborn man."

"Thank you," Proust admitted sarcastically.

"My name is Herbert Schlesinger of the SS," the officer announced.

"Very pleased to meet you," Claude Proust smiled at the man, again extremely sarcastically. In his mind he knew he was about to die, so why should he cower down to these monsters.

Schlesinger ignored the sarcastic remarks as he unrolled the paper, which had been lodged inside his left armpit, and laid it face down on the table. He then pulled it closer to the prisoner.

"What is this?" Claude demanded to know.

Looking at the paper on the table, all Proust could see was a large blank sheet of paper, but with a circle drawn in the middle and taking up most of it.

The German removed his pistol from its holster, "For my safety and security," he said as he also pulled out a knife and handed it to Claude.

"What's this for?" Proust asked with curiosity, considering if this could be an excuse for the Nazi to shoot him in 'self defence.'

"Stab the point of this knife into the paper, anywhere outside of the circle," Schlesinger demanded.

"There," Proust shouted defiantly, as he not only pierced the paper but also put a hole in the table, leaving the knife jutting out of it.

The Nazi pulled the knife from the table and gave it to the member of the Gestapo standing beside him. He then picked the paper from the desk, turned it over and laid it back down on the table the correct way up, with the map now clearly on display.

"Congratulations," Schlesinger sneered in Proust's direction. "You have made a good decision."

"What the f.....?" Claude Proust was shocked to see the table now contained a map of Paris and its surrounding areas, all positioned within thirty miles of the Eiffel Tower. In one small section there was a small hole where he'd placed the point of the knife.

"Ah, good choice," Schlesinger remarked picking up the map to scrutinise it closer. "You have chosen a small village called San Eielson," he chuckled.

"Chosen it for what?" Proust demanded.

"You have chosen it to be the victim of a nightmare of monumental proportions," Herbert Schlesinger announced as he walked out of the room, quietly chuckling to himself.

San Eielson was a pretty little village of only two hundred houses, which until that day had not been affected by this war or the German occupation of France, which had taken place a little more than two years previously.

It was a picture postcard location with stunning looking cottages and little houses surrounding a village green, where the older residents passed their time by using the green to enjoy playing the much loved French game of 'Pétanque,' a similar game to the British game of 'Bowls,' only played on a smaller playing area but with equally heavy Pétanque balls.

The village green in San Eielson also surrounded a picturesque duck pond, where on a sunny day many local people came to feed the ducks, whilst younger children also used the pond to sail their small wooden sailing boats. The green was a place where many older children came to play football, or just spend time relaxing with their friends.

Whatever it was used for by the locals who frequented it regularly, it was a place of friendship, peace, serenity and tranquillity, but all that changed one beautifully sunny day in May of 1942, a day which started like any other day but soon disintegrated into a nightmare in a catastrophic scale!

As midday approached, they could hear the footsteps. They

heard the terrifying sound of the marching army long before they could see the invading troops, but they then watched in horror as more than one hundred soldiers marched into San Eielson. As they entered the village, people old and young looked on and wondered why their peace had been shattered. Why had they been brought into this terrible war?

Behind the marauding troops, people could see a black open topped Mercedes-Benz carrying what looked like a high ranking Nazi officer, and behind this magnificent looking car was a rather tatty looking truck. Once they'd halted the parade, the officer left the vehicle and shouted to his men in the truck behind. The local people looked on as the figure of man was pulled from the following truck and dragged towards the Nazi officer.

"This is your last chance," the officer was heard to say.

"Go to Hell!" the man, who had obviously been tortured and beaten, was heard to reply. He was in a real mess, and probably in a lot of danger.

"String him up!" the officer ordered.

The poor prisoner was dragged unceremoniously to the once peaceful and tranquil village green. A small three legged stool was produced from the back of the truck, along with a long piece of rope. He was made to stand on the stool whilst the rope was placed and tied around his neck, with the other end of the noose thrown around and attached to the branch of the tree he'd been placed under.

"My God, they're going to hang that poor man," one of the older villagers whispered to his elderly wife, who in turn squeezed her husband's hand in an effort to comfort him.

"Don't get involved," his wife pleaded, knowing her husband had been a decorated soldier in the last campaign, but was now too old to make any difference.

When the task of tying the prisoner to the tree had been completed, the officer turned to face his troops and spoke quietly to them, or at least so quietly that the locals couldn't hear what he was saying. Suddenly the troops scampered away towards the cottages and houses and a few seconds later, through loud halers, the sound of loud and angry shouting was heard all over the village which only consisted of three streets.

"Everybody out of your homes," an angry voice was heard to bellow. "Out of your homes and stand in the street. Anyone found inside their house five minutes after this will be shot!"

The locals began emerging from their homes to do as ordered. They were all soon standing outside in the street, whilst the troops went inside each house to check they were empty. The people all looked terrified, wondering what the hell was about to happen.

As they all stood petrified, the black Mercedes-Benz containing the Nazi officer slowly made its way along each of the streets at a snail's pace, all the time with the officer scrutinizing the faces of all who stood before him.

"That one," he shouted, pointing to one of the men.

Immediately the man was taken away by two solders, one on each arm, leaving behind a wife and children in tears, the wife sobbing uncontrollably and the children shouting for their daddy!

"That one," the officer shouted again a little further down the road. Again the selected man was taken away.

This process was to be repeated a further eight times, with a total of ten men all being dragged away by the German troops, an enemy who until that day had been no threat to man or beast in San Eielson. This day however, they were taken to the village green and made to stand next to the prisoner perched precariously upon the stool.

"Good afternoon, everyone," the Nazi shouted, as though he was their best friend in the world. "We are sorry to disturb you on this beautiful sunny day, but it is the fault of this man." He stopped speaking and pointed to Claude Proust, the man standing on the stool with the rope around his neck. "Are you ready to give me the names now?" he questioned the man.

"Go to Hell!" Proust returned again.

The ten selected men were made to all form a line, whilst the officer paraded in front of them.

"What is your name?" questioned the Nazi of the first man.

"My name is Thomas, Sir," the scared man responded.

"Prisoner, say sorry to Thomas," the Nazi ordered Proust. "Apologise now," he demanded.

"I'm sorry," Proust said sadly, realizing what he'd brought to these innocent people.

Sorry Thomas," the Nazi corrected. "Say it!"

"Sorry Thomas," Proust announced.

With that said the Nazi drew his pistol from its holster and shot Thomas clean in the head. As the body fell to the ground, a loud gasp was heard to come from the watching villagers, who could not believe what was unfolding before them.

"What is your name?" the Nazi questioned the second man, who just stood there defiantly saying nothing, although he did piss himself with fear! The officer immediately also shot this man in the head.

"You see what you're making me do, Prisoner?" he demanded, like the insane man he really was!

"Oh I'm bored with all this," the officer announced. He raised the pistol again and shot the other eight men in quick succession, leaving them all lying in a heap on the ground.

Screams were heard from all across the village green as the local residents looked at the pile of bodies, bodies of friends, sons, husbands and fathers, all good men who only a few minutes earlier had been enjoying their sedentary lifestyles in the beautiful village of San Eielson.

"I will leave this man's fate in your hands," the officer offered as a final parting gift. "If you want him to die, then kick the stool. If you want him to live, then cut him down. But remember, he is the reason why these men were executed here in your village today."

Suddenly, as quickly as they'd arrived, they departed. Within fifteen minutes there was no evidence of the German army ever being there, except for the ten dead men lying on the ground and the one man left standing on the stool. Oh yes, what to do with the man on the stool.

"Why should we let you live?" the young boy demanded of Proust, a few minutes after the soldiers had left. As the tears streamed down his face, he made the accusation, "You just killed my father."

"No," Proust retaliated. "I didn't kill your dad. That Nazi, Herr Herbert Schlesinger of the SS killed him."

"You know this man?" a slightly older boy asked.

Yes, I know him." Proust revealed. "I also know where you can find him."

After the two lads were involved in a couple of minutes of conversation, the younger of the two boys climbed upon the back of the elder and loosened the knot holding the hangman's noose around Proust's neck.

"My name is Philippe Barstrom and this is my older brother, René," the younger of the two said, introducing the two brothers to the now very relieved man, as he happily stepped down from the stool and could stretch his legs and breathe properly again.

"My name is Claude Proust," he told the boys. "So one of those men that Schlesinger shot dead was your father?"

"Yes, and he will die for it!" René stated. "I will make sure of that! Can you help us, Monsieur Proust?"

"Of course I'll help you," Proust said without hesitation. He then added, "And please, my name is Claude."

The younger of the brothers, Philippe, had just turned fourteen years of age, whilst his brother, René was almost sixteen. However, for both these lads, their childhoods ended that day and they became men, but men still encased in young boys bodies.

CHAPTER 10
LIBRAIRIE RIVEGAUCHE

Two weeks later, after allowing Claude Proust a few days to convalesce, recover and grow stronger at the home of the boys and their mother, the three arrived in Paris.

Having travelled by day so as not to draw suspicion, and then resting by night, it had taken them four days to make the twenty-eight mile journey to Paris on foot. They'd not taken the train or any public transport in case there was a security check at the station, as they were not sure whether Claude was still on any watch lists.

Having nowhere else to go they took the risk of staying in Proust's Parisian, city centre apartment, hoping that this was also not being watched. But then, why should it be watched? As far as the Nazis were concerned, Proust had been hanged that day after one of the locals had kicked that stool and hung him in revenge of their murdered friends and loved ones.

"So Claude, where is this place where that monster goes every day?" Philippe asked, reminding Proust that he would show them the building where Schlesinger and other Nazis met every day to play cards and consume many brandies.

"It's very close to here, less than half a mile," Proust confirmed.

"What is it, and what's it called?" questioned René.

"It's an old book store that was named the 'Librairie Rivegauche,'" Claude confirmed. He then gave the two a brief history of the shop.

When Germany invaded France in 1940 and occupied Paris on June 14th 1940 they soon went about destroying all the Jewish shops and businesses, one of these being the Librairie Rivegauche, which at the time was the biggest library and book shop in an area mainly made up of book stores and libraries.

All the other shops were left alone, but the Librairie Rivegauche had been owned and run for generations by the same Jewish family. Therefore it had been confiscated and rumour had it that the owners were eventually sent to Auschwitz, the death camp in southern Poland, but to be honest, their fate was never truly known.

The Librairie Rivegauche was not only the biggest bookstore and library in the street, it was also the biggest in the entirety of the city, so rather than destroy it, as they'd done with all other Jewish owned shops, they decided that this one would make a great meeting place for officers of the SS, where they could meet up and relax away from their busy days of terrorising and murdering people!

"And Schlesinger goes there every day?" Philippe questioned.

"Yes, I'm sure, or at least he goes there most days, usually in the afternoons," Proust replied.

"So how are we going to do this?" René asked the other two.

"We will need the help of the local resistance," Proust informed the boys.

"Do you know any of them?" asked Philippe.

"Of course I do," Claude confirmed. "My company printed the propaganda posters for the resistance, and that is one of the reasons why you found me standing on that stool that day in your village."

"What can you get from them?" René queried.

"Anything you want," Claude responded. "What do you want? I mean, what do you want to do to Schlesinger?"

"Kill him and anyone with him," the boys reacted simultaneously.

"So you want explosives," Proust stated.

"Can you get dynamite?" the older boy asked.

"Of course," Proust smiled.

"Can you take us there so we can see the place?" Philippe questioned.

"Okay, but you must not get angry," Claude insisted. "If you see Schlesinger, you cannot attack him without weapons!"

The boys agreed to this, so Claude went into the bathroom and freshened up before taking them to the store. This was not a case of vanity, the reason for this act of cleanliness being that the last time any soldiers had seen him walking the streets, he was in dirty clothes and covered in red paint. He thought that if clean, he would not be so recognisable to any occupying troops on the Paris streets today who may have seen him on that fateful night of his capture.

Twenty minutes later, the three were standing on the corner of a street aptly named, 'Rue de Livres,' or 'Street of Books,' and studying the Librairie Rivegauche on the opposite corner of the road.

It had been true what Proust had said when he informed to the boys that the bookstore was within half a mile of his apartment, and they'd been surprised at how close it was, being only a matter of five streets from where they were staying.

The Rue de Livres was a long and wide street, literally three streets back from the Champs-Elysées, an area now mainly frequented by German soldiers enjoying the bar and café culture of the city.

As he looked at his young companions, Proust could see the anger on their faces, especially on the elder boys features.

"Keep your control, René," he ordered, whispering through gritted teeth.

"I can't help it. I want to go inside and kill them all," the youngster replied, his face becoming red with anger.

"Control yourself and be patient," Claude ordered again.

Over the coming days, the boys stood on this same spot on a

daily basis to spy on the bookstore, gauging the comings and goings of the SS officers who frequented the place. Although he was not a daily visitor, when they first saw Schlesinger, Philippe, although the younger of the two, had to become the man and control his elder brother, René and attempt to cool his temper.

"You cannot do anything, or achieve anything brother," he told him. "Just bide your time, be patient and wait for Claude to get the explosives."

"You're right, Philippe," René agreed, although he froze with sheer hatred each and every time he spotted Schlesinger's open topped Mercedes-Benz arriving at, or parked outside the bookstore.

The plan was to buy two books and stick all the pages together. They could then make a hollow within these pages, where one stick of dynamite could be hidden inside each. The boys would then creep inside the bookstore and take these 'books' with them, hiding them on the shelves alongside the normal books.

"But what do we do then?" Philippe questioned his brother.

"Then we light the fuse and run like bloody hell!" René instructed. The plan was basic, but they couldn't think of a better one.

One problem they had was that to carry out their plan they first had to get inside the store and look at the layout.

"You stay here, little brother," René said to a worried Philippe. "I'll go inside and take a look. It doesn't need the two of us."

"But what if Schlesinger sees you?" the younger of the siblings questioned.

"I could wait until he's not inside," René suggested. "We know that if he's in attendance, his staff car is always parked outside, so we'll wait until we're sure."

"But what if he arrives when you're inside and he sees you," questioned Philippe, always the pessimist.

"Look brother, when he shot our father in the head," René waivered slightly as he said this, but then composed himself enough to continue. "When he shot our father in the head, we were only two faces in a crowd of more than two hundred people. Okay, we were at the front, so we could better see what was going on, but I believe that monster was too busy killing people and enjoying himself to notice two boys in a sea of hatred!"

"But he might remember you," Philippe pointed out.

"That is a risk we have to take little brother," René stated, and this was his last word on the subject.

Two days later the opportunity arose when they arrived at the Rue de Livres and there was no black Mercedes in sight.

"Wait here," René ordered the younger one.

"What? Wait, I'm coming with you," Philippe protested.

"No brother." René demanded. "If I am caught, then it will be up to you to continue with our mission. If we're both captured, then our quest will be over and our father will never get his revenge."

The ideology of this made great sense, so reluctantly, Philippe agreed with the plan and watched as his brother left him and walked across the street towards the Librairie Rivegauche. His heart skipped a beat when he saw him enter the building and go inside the bookstore. He wondered if he would ever see his brother alive again.

Once inside, René's heart also skipped a beat when he realised the size of the place. From the outside, the doorway made it look quite small, just like most of the other shops in the area. But as he looked around now, he could see this place was huge!

As you walk inside the entrance, the width inside the store was at least double to that of the outside, but the length was three times the width, if not more. All the bookshelves from the original layout of the store, from floor to ceiling, were still there at the entrance, but at the far end, the end where the officers played cards and drank, this area had been cleared of all books and stripped of the shelves, which had been ripped out to be replaced with a bar area.

A member of staff was now standing behind this bar, dressed in white shirt, black trousers and a waistcoat. He was busy dispensing drinks to the officers in attendance, of which René counted ten. These ten men were sitting around a huge oak table, big enough to seat at least twenty SS officers comfortably and with ease.

The young man felt deflated. He realised that to do any real damage he would need to get much closer to the table than the safety these bookshelves offered.

He wouldn't tell his brother, but in his mind he'd already changed the plan. There was no way that Philippe would agree to it, but it had to be done. Herr Herbert Schlesinger of the SS must die at all costs, even if that cost included his own life!

He put his hand inside his pocket and felt a soothing feeling as he stroked the 'Zippo' lighter which had belonged to his father. His dad had been given this gift of a Zippo by an American tourist whom he'd met in the village back in the early thirties. It was an early model and quite rare, in fact it was one of the first lighters manufactured by the company in America during 1932.

It was the one thing René had brought from their old house when they'd left that day with Claude to venture to Paris to search for, and kill Schlesinger. It gave the lad great comfort to think that his dad's old Zippo lighter would be used to light the fuse of the dynamite which would kill that Nazi bastard!

"So how is it in there? How is the layout?" Philippe questioned upon his brother's return.

"It'll be no problem," René lied.

Three days later, all three stood in the Rue de Livres on the opposite corner to the bookstore. René looked at Claude Proust and smiled as he saw the two specially made fake hardback books he was holding tightly in his arms, both with the required stick of dynamite in each.

So far the plan had worked beautifully. Claude had been in discussion with his friends in the resistance and they'd provided him with the two sticks of dynamite, along with two fifteen second fuses attached.

"Once lit, the boy will have fifteen seconds to get the hell out of that place," Claude had been instructed by his good friend, Patrice Bauton of the resistance.

"Thank you, my friend," Claude had replied. "And please thank your friends for permission and the dynamite."

Claude had to ask the resistance for their permission to use explosives inside the bookstore, just in case they had anything planned in the area themselves, but he'd been given the explosives along with the permission and their seal of approval, along with their good wishes.

"Let's hope the boy succeeds in his task and kills that bastard, Schlesinger," Patrice said to Claude, after hearing the full reason for René and Philippe wanting revenge.

So here they were. Everyone was here except for Schlesinger, who was nowhere to be seen.

"Don't worry, he'll be here," Claude told the boys. He could already see that René was becoming more and more agitated by each passing second.

Suddenly, there it was, the big, black, open topped Mercedes-Benz arrived and parked outside the store. The driver left his seat and came around to the opposite side to open the door for Schlesinger.

"Lazy bastard," Philippe proclaimed.

"Soon to be a lazy 'dead' bastard," René stressed.

They gave the Nazi a good few minutes to get himself settled, and then Claude looked at the older boy.

"Are you ready, Son?" he questioned René.

"Yes," he replied. "I have never been more ready in my life!"

Claude Proust and Philippe Barstrom watched as the brave young man walked slowly across the road, but then began to worry as he stopped outside the entrance to the bookstore.

"What's he doing, Claude?" the boy queried.

"I don't know," Proust replied with honesty. "I have absolutely no idea, but I have a bad feeling about this."

They watched as René stopped outside Librairie Rivegauche, and panicked as they saw him ripping the fake books apart. Proust's heart almost left his stomach as he watched the lad take a knife from his pocket and cut the fuses to make them shorter.

"He'll never get out alive!" Claude stressed.

"Do something," Philippe demanded.

"What the feck can I do?" Proust despaired.

He could see the young lad thinking about running after his brother, so he held him tightly by his jacket.

"There's nothing you can do either," he stressed.

They watched in horror as René, on the other side of the street, took out his Zippo and walked slowly into the store. A few more seconds passed by, with each second seeming like a minute! They then heard the start of utter pandemonium.

"This is for my father!" they heard the lad shout loudly.

"What the........." Philippe started to say, but was stopped by the sight of his brother in the shop doorway. A single gunshot was heard to ring out and René was seen to fall to the floor. A split second after the bullet struck the attacker, a huge explosion was heard and smoke spilled out into the street.

"Quick, let's........" Philippe began.

"Wait!" Proust ordered the lad, now taking full control of the situation.

They watched as René, obviously badly wounded, crawled towards the exit of the bookstore, but then they saw another badly wounded man standing over him. The man pulled a gun from its holster and pointed it at the young boy's head.

"And this is from me," the huge man taunted. He then took aim, and with the poor lad still trying to crawl away from the danger, he pulled the trigger and shot René in the back the head.

"Herbert Schlesinger," Proust proclaimed, for the man standing over the body of his young friend and the brother of Philippe, was none other than Schlesinger himself. Out of fifteen officers inside, although very badly wounded, that day he was the only survivor.

Proust looked at Philippe, expecting the boy to be in tears, but no, there were no tears coming from the boy, and there never would be. All he had was even more hatred of the man who'd killed both his father, and now his brother.

"And is that the end of the story?" Yvette asked Jean Renoir, as he stopped to light his pipe.

"Sadly not, my dear," Renoir revealed, and he continued.

Unbeknown to everyone, Herr Herbert Schlesinger of the SS was a personal friend of Adolph Hitler, and when the Fuhrer heard about these events, he came to Paris to visit his friend in the hospital. He was so incensed at what his friend told him, he sent the army back to the village of San Eielson.

"Everyone out of your homes," the officer was heard to shout through the loud haler. "Out of your homes and stand outside."

A few minutes later, all the village residents were outside their homes, although not curious like the last visit, this time they knew nothing good would become of it.

Every villager had a gun pointed at them and they were made to watch as gasoline was poured on and inside their homes. Minutes later, the entire village was ablaze and the streets were filled with angry men, with women and children crying their hearts out as they watched all their possessions literally going up in smoke, but worse was to come.

"Men, this way, "the officer shouted again, "Women and children that way," he announced, pointing for the women and children to walk towards the church.

All the men were forced at gunpoint to walk to the village green, where they were made to stand on the grass in a large circle.

The women and sobbing children were marched, also at gunpoint, to the church, where they were ordered inside the building and the door was locked firmly behind them.

The women began screaming when they realised what was about to happen to them, when they heard the noise of machine gun fire coming from the village green in the distance. This time, there were not ten men executed, this time every man was executed. After a barrage of bullets was fired, there were at least seventy dead bodies strewn about the grass.

If the women thought they and the children might be spared, their hopes were dashed when they smelt smoke and realised the church they were entombed inside had now been set on fire.

The screams could be heard for more than twenty-four hours, before the Nazis finally unlocked the church and entered to check for any signs of life. Any victims still found alive were extinguished with a strategically placed bullet.

Every inhabitant of San Eielson was now dead, murdered by the Nazis, whilst the village had been destroyed, wiped from the face of the earth! Sadly, the dead women of the village included Philippe's mother.

"In only a few weeks, the poor lad had lost everything," Renoir proclaimed. "He'd lost his mother, father and his brother. He now had nothing, not even a home to return to."

"And he has been a member of the Paris resistance ever since?" Yvette questioned.

"Yes," Jean confirmed. "And believe me when I say, he is a killing machine! He has no fear of death. In fact, I believe he looks forward to it."

"Well as long as he doesn't get me killed alongside him," Yvette stressed, now understanding why a now fifteen year old boy could be a valued member of the resistance.

"What happened to that officer they wanted to kill?" the girl questioned.

"Schlesinger?" Jean said.

"Yes, Schlesinger," Yvette confirmed.

"After a few weeks convalescing in hospital, he was up and about again," Renoir informed her. "He soon returned to his wicked ways. I'll tell you, Yvette, Philippe Barstrom will never stop until Schlesinger is dead!"

CHAPTER 11
PARIS

She'd been sitting in the carriage now for what seemed to her like hours. Strangely, Yvette was finding the clickety-clack, clickety-clack, clickety-clack sound of the train wheels as they rotated on the railway tracks below, both annoying but also quite soothing and hypnotic. In fact it had almost taken away the nervousness she felt as she thought constantly about the unwanted cargo she was carrying in the brown leather suitcase perched above her head.

Looking through the window at the rolling countryside as it passed by, as she looked further into the distance and saw the mountainous regions and the vast forest areas in the faraway expanse of land, Yvette thought about something which Jean Renoir had told her.

"When, during your travels you see the mountains and forests on the horizon, this is where the resistance group known as the Maquis are living. It's a great place for them to hide from the enemy," he'd told her. "And they really need to hide, as they are made up of men and women from France, Spain and even Germany."

"Germany!" she'd almost choked. "You mean there are many German people fighting against Germany?"

"Yes, of course," Renoir confirmed. "But they are not fighting against Germany, they are fighting against Adolph Hitler and his Nazi values."

"So how was it they ended up fighting for the resistance, here on French soil?" Yvette questioned.

"As I said, these men are fighting against Hitler's Nazi policies and hatred of the Jewish race," Renoir reminded her. "So as soon as they'd arrived here in France, at the very first opportunity they deserted from the German army and joined the

French Freedom Fighters, known in that region as the Maquis."

As she looked now at the distant forest and beautiful cloud covered mountain areas from the comfort of the train, Yvette wondered if any fighting was taking place at this moment. Even as she looked to this faraway land, were there young men and women dying right now in that area which looked so peaceful and tranquil from the comfort of her carriage seat on this train?

A little further along the journey, she eventually caught her first glimpse of Paris when she spotted the Eiffel Tower, although it was some way off in the distance.

As a youngster, she'd always dreamed of visiting this magnificent city and seeing this landmark, but today it made her feel sad. She'd always imagined she would come to this romantic city with a boyfriend or a husband by her side. Before the war it had been eternally known as the 'City of Love,' but when she thought about the place now, the only thoughts she had during these years of Nazi occupation were those of fear, danger, hopelessness and despair!

As the train was now slowly approaching Paris Gare du Nord, Yvette hoped and prayed that the German officer would not come back to offer his help with the case. However, her prayers were not answered, as just before the train slowed down and prepared to come to a complete stop at 'Platform Nine,' the door to her carriage slid open and Yvette turned to see the huge figure of the officer completely filling the frame of the door.

"Hello, my dear. I trust you've had a pleasant journey?" he asked politely, but without waiting for her to reply, he added, "I thought I'd better come back and give you a hand with your heavy case."

"Thank you very much, but I think I'll be okay," Yvette replied coyly, trying to remain calm as she thought about the contents of the case, desperately hoping they would not be discovered.

"Nonsense my dear, the very least I can do is to help a

damsel in distress," the officer insisted whilst smiling.

She felt really worried as he sat beside her, whilst thy waited for the train to come to a complete stop. When it did so, he stood and reached for the brown leather suitcase in the overhead compartment. As he grabbed the handle and pulled it down, he let out an exaggerated groan.

"Are you sure your granny is not still in the bag and wearing the ice skates my dear," he joked.

Yvette fake laughed as best she could, hoping to God that he could not see the nervous tension inside of her as he picked the case from the floor of the carriage and carried it from the train and onto the platform.

"In which direction are you headed," he questioned.

"I have to get to the exit to the Rue de Maubeuge," she replied. "Someone is waiting for me there."

"A boyfriend?" he joked.

"No," she blushed.

"You need the exit to the Rue de Maubeuge?" he said, looking deep in thought. "Oh, that's in that direction," he finally said, pointing down the station platform to the exit she required. "That's the opposite way to me. Wait here for one moment," he told her.

Yvette watched as the German officer approached a young man wearing a railway porter's uniform. As they spoke, she noticed him putting money into the young man's hand. The porter left the officer for a few seconds while he went to fetch a trolley. After this, the two men walked back towards her.

"This young man will assist you to the exit, my dear," the German instructed. The porter lifted Yvette's suitcase, also letting out a groan as he did so, and placed the bag into the trolley.

"Thank you," she said to both, but mainly looking at the officer.

"Don't mention it," he smiled. Then just as Yvette turned to walk away, he said, "Enjoy the summer. Let's hope it's a hot one," but curiously, he said this in perfect English.

She almost froze to the spot, but without flinching, she kept walking and ignored him and his comment.

"Enjoy the summer. Let's hope it's a hot one," he repeated, but this time in perfect French. Yvette now stopped, turned around and smiled at him.

"Thank you very much," she replied, also in French. She then also dared to say, "Danke schön," to which he smiled in return.

As she walked with the porter, she considered what had just happened. Was the German officer testing her? What would have happened had she responded to his use of English?

One thing she did know for certain was that this was no longer a training camp exercise, neither was it a game to win or lose. Losing was not an option. In this scenario losing meant death, and probably a violent one!

Once outside after leaving the station at the Rue de Maubeuge exit, she spotted a young boy standing on the pavement and holding a bicycle with a large basket over the front wheel. The bicycle was painted all in black and was obviously used for deliveries, but Yvette wondered what kinds of deliveries it was used for.

Reaching the lad, she turned to the porter. "Thank you," she said, but he just stood there and put his hand out. "You have already been paid," she reminded him. "I saw that officer putting money into your hand," she insisted.

The young porter ignored her and remained standing there with his hand out, waiting for remuneration.

"Just give him some money," the boy with the bike said.

"He's already been paid for his trouble," Yvette stated.

"It doesn't matter," the boy said. "It would not be wise to cause a scene and attract attention to us with all these soldiers milling about the streets. Just give him a couple of francs."

"Okay," she said, angrily handing over a couple of coins and watching the porter walk away. This was not the best way for her to arrive in Paris!

"Give me your case," the boy demanded.

"Wait, I don't even know who you are yet," Yvette stated, still angry with the confrontation with the young porter. "Are you......?"

"Yes, I am Philippe Barstrom and you are Yvette Colbert," he snapped, confirming his identity, along with hers. "Now that we've been introduced, hand over the case."

Although she'd only know him a couple of minutes, she'd already decided that she did not like this boy. Yes, she was sorry for the way that he'd lost his family, but there was no excuse for the way he was treating her today, treating her with absolutely no politeness or respect. Nevertheless she did as requested and handed the suitcase to the boy, but was horrified by what he did next.

In the middle of a street full of German soldiers, and even a few officers, he opened the bag in full view of all and sundry and began rummaging through its contents, with the case laid on the pavement for all to see.

"What the hell are you doing?" Yvette demanded. "Are you trying to get us shot?"

"I'm making it lighter for you, so it'll be easier for you to carry," he replied, astounding her.

"What the hell?" she gasped, as she looked down at her clothes in the case in fear for her life. But as she scrutinised the contents, she could clearly see there were no guns but there were four, bright shiny, metallic silver Pétanque balls, and it was these which had been supplying the weight. She picked up one ball from the bag and felt how heavy it was.

Suddenly it dawned on her what had happened. "Don't tell me this was another bloody test?" she demanded of the boy angrily.

"Yes it was," he replied. "We wanted to make sure you had the courage to carry certain things for the resistance, and now we know that you do."

"I am sick to death of all this secrecy and deceit," Yvette exasperated. "Don't tell me," she began to say whilst rubbing her sleeve. "This cyanide pill is also a fake!"

"No, that's genuine," the lad admitted to her, although somewhat matter of factly.

"So one bite of this and I'd be dead?" she queried.

"Yes," he simply replied.

She told the boy about the German officer aboard the train and how he'd helped carry the case on and off the train for her.

"So if I had panicked and reached for the pill, I'd be dead by now?" she questioned.

"Yes," the boy said nonchalantly.

"What the shite!" Yvette yelled.

"But if you had taken the pill and committed suicide because of that German, it would have been bad for you, but good for us," he advised.

"How so?" she demanded to know.

"Because if you had become so agitated by that confrontation that you felt the need to kill yourself, you would have saved us all a lot of wasted time," the youngster revealed. "There will be far more dangerous events happening to you over the coming months when you might actually need to take that pill." Yvette was so angry at hearing this.

What the hell was she doing here in this place with these people? She was a second year medical student training to save lives, not to be here about to be used to help kill them!

"Come," the boy said after placing the Pétanque balls inside the bicycle basket. She picked up the now much lighter suitcase and followed him.

Although she knew there would be a large German presence before she'd arrived, she did not expect it to be this prevalent. In every direction she looked, the city appeared to be wall to wall with the occupying troops, although to be honest, the troops she could see now did not seem like much of a threat as they basked in the sunshine whilst sitting outside the various cafés, making sexist comments to the pretty girls as they walked by. This included Yvette, who felt sick when finding herself the centre of their attention.

"Just ignore them," Philippe advised.

As she walked further with the boy, seeing these young men spilling out of bars and sprawling onto the pavement in a drunken stupor, Yvette was stunned to think that these soldiers were part of Hitler's 'Master Race' and members of the 'Third Reich,' an organisation supposed to be well disciplined, and to last for one thousand years!

"I cannot believe what I'm hearing and seeing," she commented, still angry at the sexual taunts she'd received, along with the disgusting scenes she'd witnessed within only fifteen minutes of her arrival.

"This is supposed to be Hitler's army?" she despaired.

"They are pure scum! They are worse than pigs!" Philippe observed. "Ignore them," he said again. This was probably the nicest thing he'd said to her so far, although he'd said it with absolutely no emotion on his face.

After walking for another half an hour or so, the streets seemed to become narrower and also less busy. This made Yvette feel much happier as they made their way along the Parisian walkways.

One thing she did notice however was the fact that as they ventured deeper into the less busy part of the city, the drunken, beer guzzling troops she'd seen outside the bars and cafés in the area of the Gare du Nord train station had now been replaced by coffee drinking officers in full Nazi uniforms. These men looked far more sinister to the young Yvette than those drunken louts did earlier.

"Just look straight ahead and not at them," Philippe advised in a whisper, trying his best not to attract any unwanted attention.

Yvette looked at the youngster walking beside her, and as she did so she noted that he had absolutely no fear of these soldiers or the officers of the occupying army. He didn't seem to feel anything at all, no emotion, and this worried her.

She thought that Philippe could possibly be inclined to take unnecessary risks, which could be dangerous not only to him but to whomever he was accompanying at the time. For this reason, she decided there and then to spend as little time with this boy as possible.

As they rounded the final corner en-route to the unknown destination, she noticed a pleasant looking establishment with a large sign outside announcing, 'Café DuPont.'

"Here we are, this is it," Philippe announced, but then walked past the entrance. "We need to go to the rear entrance, the door into the bakery. The café will be full of Germans at this time of the day," he explained.

'Full of Germans,' Yvette thought to herself. 'Jeees, what the bloody hell have I come to?' she thought again, and not for the last time during her stay in this beautiful, but highly dangerous city.

CHAPTER 12
LE CAFĔ DUPONT

Philippe led Yvette along a narrow muddy lane and into a small garden. This area appeared to be used mainly as a rubbish tip, being almost totally full of refuse bins. Philippe tapped his knuckles three times on the back door as quietly as possible, although loud enough to be heard. Eventually the door was opened by a lady who stood before them.

"Madame DuPont, this is Yvette Colbert," young Barstrom announced to the lady, who instantly smiled at the girl.

"Come inside, child," she ordered politely, although with more than a hint of authority as she ushered the girl to join her. Yvette duly obliged and stepped inside the doorway, where she instantly felt the intense heat of the ovens currently baking bread, cakes and delicious pastries.

"Very good to meet you, Madame DuPont," Yvette smiled.

"The honour is all mine, my dear," the lady replied, "but please, call me Nicole," she added, as she greeted the girl with the customary kiss on each cheek, as favoured by the French.

"Philippe, fetch Yvette's bag," Nicole instructed the boy. He immediately did as he was told, thus making the 'new girl' believe that Madame DuPont was a lady of whom everyone had a great respect for.

"Come girl, follow me," Nicole requested. "Let me show you to your room."

'Oh, so I must be staying here,' Yvette thought in her mind, although she had no idea what the plans were or her, or for how long this was to be her place of abode.

They slowly climbed the six levels of creaky wooden steps up towards the attic room situated on the third floor of the building. When they finally reached the summit, Yvette looked more closely at Nicole DuPont, whose age she guessed to be mid to late forties. Although she was still a strikingly good looking woman, Yvette imagined her to have been extremely beautiful, even stunning in her younger years, although it was painfully obvious that the endless fear of impending danger and the stress caused by the war, as well as the constant pressure of this German occupation of France, had not been kind to her.

"Here you are, my dear," Nicole said gently, trying to make her new guest feel as welcome as she could. "Please, make yourself comfortable."

Thank you Madame," Yvette replied politely.

Thank you Philippe," Madame DuPont said, gesturing for the young man to leave.

The boy sauntered away, returning back down the stairs after first acknowledging Yvette by touching his forehead with his middle finger, as if in salute.

She took a look around her new room, her home for the foreseeable future. Comfortable was not the first word which sprang into her mind. The room was basic to say the least. There were bare, untreated wooden floorboards, covered in part by a piece of tiny carpet. A small wardrobe stood in the corner of the room, which already had a few clothes inside but still contained enough space for the sparse amount of clothing contained within her suitcase. Then, unexpectedly she noticed there were two small single beds.

"You're sharing with another girl," Nicole explained, after seeing the confusion etched upon her face. "She's a lovely young lady called Luisa."

"Is she a lovely young girl or an older lady dressed as a young girl?" Yvette questioned somewhat sarcastically.

Madame DuPont either ignored her comment or didn't hear the question. Either way there was no reply forthcoming, with Yvette's slightly sarcastic comment being met with just a blank expression on Nicole's face.

"I'll leave you to it," Madame DuPont said softly as she left the room, with her footsteps on the wooden staircase becoming quieter and quieter as she exited down them.

Yvette found herself alone and in solitude. She took a better look at her new home, the attic room where she would be for she didn't know how long. It looked bleak, even more unwelcoming than her first impression suggested.

One good thing was that there was a window positioned in the slant of the sloping roof. It was high enough to let plenty of light into the room, but also low enough for her to be able to look out at the spectacular views over the rooftops of Paris, after standing on one of the two wooden chairs left in the room. She noticed that if she craned her neck enough, she could just see the top of the Eiffel Tower in the distance.

The tower was maybe a mile or two away, but she didn't really know how far it was as he'd never seen it up close, so did not know the real size of it. What she did know, however, was that as she looked at the top of the tower now, she couldn't stop thinking about Peter Collins and Ben Richards, her two friends from the training camp in Kent.

She had to admit to herself that she really missed both of them. Was it really only a week or so since she'd been with them at the camp, with the two saying their goodbyes and wishing her good luck?

"Keep your head down, darling, and don't take any chances," Peter had offered.

"Don't do anything stupid and get yourself killed," Ben had also chipped in.

Was she now beginning to get romantic feelings about these two? If so, what a ridiculous time to be getting them, surrounded as she now was by all this death, destruction and misery!

Her thoughts and memories were disturbed when she heard someone enter the room. Her attention was drawn to a girl in a long, light brown trench coat, wearing a floppy hat and white ankle socks with polished brown shoes.

"You must be the new girl?" the visitor questioned.

"Yvette Colbert at your service," Yvette replied, not really knowing whether she should be using her real name or the 'S.O.E' name as allocated to her by 'The Department of Fish & Fisheries.' She decided using her 'agent' name might be the better option.

"Pleased to meet you," the girl said in a friendly manner. "My name is Luisa," she declared and then added, "Luisa Silva."

"Good to meet you too, Luisa," Yvette remarked. She extended her arm to shake the other girl's hand but Luisa bypassed the offering and, after placing both her hands on Yvette's shoulders, she went in for the double kiss on both cheeks.

"Silva, that's a strange name. Is it French?" Yvette asked.

"Spanish," Luisa replied. "I was born here in Paris, but my mother is French and my father's from Spain," she confirmed.

"Why are you living here in the bakery? Where are your parents?" Yvette questioned, although she immediately regretted doing so in case it was too personal a question for the girl. "Please do not answer if you don't want to," she quickly added.

"Not at all," Luisa replied. "I am very proud to tell you about them. When Paris was invaded, both Mum and Dad joined the French Resistance here in the city and immediately began making nuisances of each other."

"Are they still living here in the city?" Yvette questioned with genuine interest.

"No, they left when it became too dangerous to stay here," her new friend confided. "In the early months, they didn't know who they could trust or who not to. In the early days the German occupiers made it very worthwhile for the Parisian residents to inform on those people who, let's say, might not be so compliant towards the invaders."

"So where are they now?" Yvette asked, again tentatively.

"You would have seen them on your train journey here,"

Luisa stated, confusing her new friend. "They are living within a group of the resistance who live in the hills and forest regions."

"The Maquis," Yvette stated.

"Yes," Luisa replied, appearing to be deep in thought. "But how do you know that?" she questioned.

"I was told all about them by the people I met during the past three days. Have you heard of Jean Renoir?" Yvette queried.

"Of course," the beautiful girl replied. "Whenever he's in Paris, he always comes to visit us here."

"So you know him?" Yvette interrogated.

"Yes, he's a lovely man," Luisa said. "But he is also a dangerous man to be on the wrong side of."

"I can imagine," Yvette remarked.

Luisa began to undress, surprising Yvette by her lack of modesty. First she removed the long coat, revealing the clothes she was wearing, which were obviously designed to be worn by a much younger girl.

"Madame Chambourcey?" Yvette asked. Her question was replied simply by a smile.

She was very surprised, if not shocked when Luisa removed the blouse to reveal bandages wrapped tightly around her breasts.

Noticing the new girl's full attention, Luisa announced, "They make my breasts look smaller and flatter, thus making me look younger. Now, please help me to take it off, it's bloody killing me!"

This made Yvette smile. First impressions suggested that she really liked this girl and thought they would become good friends.

She began to chuckle when she was reminded of her roommate at the medical university in Oxford. Every night when her friend Jennifer Rumsey returned from lectures, she let out a loud, exaggerated gasp and ripped off her bra.

"Bloody torture," Jennifer would exclaim. "Why do we do it?" she questioned on a nightly basis, as the relief from removing the item was etched on her face.

I say let the buggers swing," Yvette always joked, and the two friends would laugh uncontrollably together.

How she now missed those happy times when life seemed so much simpler, which of course, they were. It was unbelievable to think this was only a few months ago.

A few seconds later Yvette was shocked to see Luisa standing before her as naked as the day she was born, with not a hint of shyness or embarrassment.

She couldn't help but study the girl. She was beautiful, simply stunning, with lovely long legs and well developed breasts. She now understood the need for using the bandages to make her look younger. Her breasts were magnificent, in fact her entire body was magnificent, although a little on the thin side, which was strange as she lived above a bakery!

"You like what you see?" Luisa teased with a wicked smile.

"Sorry," Yvette replied shyly, realising that she'd been caught staring at the girl.

"I'm only joking," Luisa laughed, easing the tension. "We are two girls living together in a small room in occupied Paris and sharing this small box together. It will be much easier if we can get undressed in front of each other without any bashfulness."

"You are correct, of course," Yvette agreed, "but it might take a few days before I can do this."

"Promise I won't look," Luisa laughed.

Yvette knew she was going to like this girl, but was surprised when a few moments later she noticed Luisa was wearing a black evening dress and highly polished black high heeled shoes.

"I'll see you later," Luisa said.

"Are you going out for the evening?" Yvette questioned.

"No, I will go to the café to begin my evening shift," the girl explained, but when she saw the confused look on Yvette's face, she continued. "Beginning tomorrow, you will also be working as a waitress in the café. This is how we learn the enemy's secrets, secrets which you will then broadcast to the people who need to know them, when you send the messages later."

"No one has told me any of this," Yvette said somewhat angrily. She felt like she'd been thrown into the lion's den without any protection. "Why tomorrow, why not tonight?" she questioned.

"Henri and Nicole will talk to you in the morning about it and bring you up to speed," Luisa told her new friend. "Don't worry, Yvette; believe me when I tell you that we will have fun working together in the café."

"I hope so," the confused girl announced.

Just relax tonight and get some rest on your last night of freedom," Luisa offered.

"I might go for a walk and discover my surroundings," Yvette said naively.

"You cannot do that," Luisa stressed.

"Why?" the new girl quizzed.

"Because there is a nightly curfew here in Paris, and you will be arrested if caught on the streets between nine in the evening and five in the morning, unless you are accompanied by a German soldier," Luisa revealed.

"And who would do that?"

"Who would do what?"

"Who would be accompanied by a German soldier," Yvette queried.

"You'd be surprised at how many French women are giving themselves to the enemy to give themselves a more comfortable life during this occupation!" Luisa stated angrily.

"Bitches," Yvette stressed.

"Bitches indeed," Luisa agreed, and then stated sinisterly, "but they will be severely dealt with when this is all over!"

"I hope so," Yvette agreed.

"They will be, for sure," Luisa confirmed. Then changing the atmosphere quite dramatically she said, "Okay, we close at ten so I'll see you later. Have a nice, relaxing evening."

After Luisa left to go down the wooden staircase to who knows where, Yvette placed her head upon the bed designated to her by the beautiful Luisa. Instantly she gasped. It really was very lumpy. She positioned herself to find the most comfortable position, or at least the least uncomfortable position on the mattress, and very soon she drifted off into a much deserved deep sleep.

She was woken sometime later by the sound of music and raucous singing coming from the café below. She had no idea what the time was, but the room was in darkness.

Stumbling towards, and making her way to the window, she looked out to see that it was not only her room but the entire city was now cloaked in darkness caused by the curfew.

She did the only thing she could and found her way back to the bed, laid her head on the pillow, and drifted back into a deep sleep.

CHAPTER 13
MESSAGE SENT

The Hotel Paradiso loomed ever closer, as Yvette and Luisa rode their bikes slowly towards it. She became more and more nervous with each revolution of the bicycle pedals, as well as feeling sick and extremely agitated, with an uneasy feeling in the pit of her stomach as she approached.

Even though during the past two weeks since she'd arrived in Paris she had come to this hotel at least four or five times each week, today was the first time she would be operating the radio and sending messages back to Army Intelligence at their base in London.

Monsieur DuPont had instructed Luisa to do the 'bread delivery' at the hotel with Yvette every time she went there, so whatever soldiers were milling around the place would get used to seeing her and wouldn't take any great notice of the girl carrying the basket of bread and cakes to the kitchen, positioned on the third floor of the hotel.

The same reasoning applied to Yvette when on the street, whilst riding her bike alongside Luisa. The more the authorities saw the two of them in the open air, the less chance of her being stopped and searched there would be. Anyway, if they did stop and search her, all they would find would be a few freshly baked baguettes and the odd sweet or savoury pastry, as she carried nothing more incriminating for the first two weeks of this Parisian adventure, so as to give her a little time to build up her confidence.

"Don't forget, Yvette, one hundred and twenty seconds maximum," Henri had instructed quite sternly on that first morning. "One hundred and thirty seconds is ten seconds too long, and those ten seconds could be the difference between you being caught, so those ten seconds could be the difference between life and death!"

As Yvette thought about these words of wisdom, she put her hand inside the coat pocket and placed her hand around the pocket watch which Henri DuPont had given her. She felt a great comfort with the feel of it in her hand.

"Begin your broadcast when the seconds hand reaches the twelve and stop before it reaches one minute and fifty-nine seconds," Henri warned. "Do this even if you have not finished sending the message. This is important, and the people in England will know why you have done this and they will understand."

Monsieur DuPont went on to explain that when broadcasting, if the German radio detectors are in the area it takes them roughly one hundred and thirty seconds to pinpoint exactly where the broadcasting signal is, or at least it gives them a vague idea of where the broadcast might be coming from. Although he also said that sending the messages from the Hotel Paradiso should be a very safe place to transmit from, as it's full of German soldiers and so it would be the last place they would suspect the resistance of using for their enterprises.

This had stunned Yvette when she'd first heard it, but the first time she visited the hotel last week, she understood what he meant. For although the soldiers sleep there at night, with around fifty rooms and three soldiers to each room, during the daytime it was almost empty, with only a few of the enemy wandering about the place.

The radio room had been set up on the third floor in the laundry room and the only people who ever went there would be the hotel staff, but they only ever visited the room very early in the morning, with Yvette broadcasting in the late afternoon, so as long as she was very careful she should always be safe.

Even though she knew all this, as she approached the hotel now with her beautiful friend by her side, she still felt as though her insides were about to explode!

Luisa had gently shaken Yvette awake on the first morning after she had first arrived at the Café DuPont with Philippe Barstrom. "Wake up, lazy bones," Luisa said.
"What time is it?" Yvette questioned sleepily.
"It's after six o'clock," Luisa informed her.
"Six o'clock?" Yvette complained. "It's still very early."
"Not at the Café DuPont," Luisa stressed
Looking through the window and seeing it was not dark, but also not quite light, was confusing to the still sleepy girl and she begged the question, "Is that six o'clock at night, or six o'clock in the morning?"
"Morning, silly," Luisa laughed. "You are funny. Now, up you get. Henri is waiting to meet you."
"You mean I have been sleeping all night?" she questioned, whilst wiping the sleepy dust from her eyes.
"Yes. I came back around ten last night but you were sleeping soundly and you didn't wake," Luisa smiled.
"I must have been exhausted," Yvette offered.
"I guessed you needed it after your time with Jean Renoir and Madame Chambourcey, so I left you alone and just climbed into bed and slept myself. However, Yvette, now you must get up as Henri is waiting," Luisa repeated, although with a little more urgency this time.

As the two girls walked together down the creaky wooden staircase, the aroma of freshly brewed coffee, along the wonderful smell of croissants taken straight from the oven greeting her nostrils, gave Yvette quite a feeling of calm as they entered the café.

"Ah, there you are girls," a rather large man said as they entered. "You must be Yvette. Welcome my dear. Come in and sit yourself down."

"Yvette," Luisa said taking over the conversation. "This is

Monsieur DuPont."

"Henri, please," the big man pleaded.

"Henri," Yvette agreed, as she smiled in his direction.

Henri DuPont was indeed a big man, although he was full of muscle and without an ounce of fat on his body. He was almost as wide as Yvette was tall, but as Luisa advised her, he was a soft and gentle pussycat to the people he either loved or had no problems with. To the German occupiers however, he could be ruthless and dangerous, with no problems in killing an enemy soldier if he had to do so.

Henri was born just after the turn of the century in the year 1902, which made him just about too young to take part in the last war, the war to end 'all wars,' and too old to be in the regular army for this one. This was one major reason for his joining the Resistance in Paris when given the opportunity to do so by none other than Jean Renoir, but all this had happened by total accident.

As a young man of twenty-three years of age, in 1925 Henri moved to Germany to live and explore the country. He only intended going for an extended holiday and maybe staying for a few months or so, six at most, but when reaching the city of Munich he fell in love with the place, ending up residing in this beautiful city for more than seven years.

During this time he made many friends and fell in love with the culture, as well as falling in love with many of the pretty girls who resided there. (He was a strikingly handsome young man in his early years, and still a good-looking man now.)

Henri had heard the rumours going around the city about a certain man named, Adolph Hitler, and the hate speak he was sprouting in and around the drinking bars of Munich. Because of this, young Henri could feel the gradual change in the atmosphere of the place and felt it growing more and more hostile.

He decided to leave Munich, and Germany, when he had doubts in his mind that the city had become too dangerous for a non-German to reside, making up his mind to return to Paris and back to the family bakery in late 1933, when the rise of the Nazis' in Munich became just too dangerous and impossible for him to bare.

One of the very good things about his time in Munich was that Henri had been working in the hospitality business, working in hotels, bars and nightclubs found mainly around the area known as Marienplatz. However, his favourite job was working in a high-class café close to the main train station. Here he became friendly with the baker who taught him how to bake Munich style bread, croissants and cakes, along with real German treats such as pretzels. He also learned how to make real bratwurst sausage from scratch, which would become invaluable during his life in the resistance. He put this training to good use upon his return to the Café DuPont.

Henri DuPont became good friends with a certain newspaper worker, when Jean Renoir began coming into the café for coffee and a filled baguette on most days of the week during his lunch breaks, returning again often in the evening for a nice glass of red wine.

One day in 1938, Jean met a man in a bar who had migrated from Koln in Germany, and he brought him into the Café DuPont for a bite to eat and to meet Monsieur DuPont.

"Henri, I would like to introduce you to a new friend of mine," Jean began. "This is my friend, Gunter. He has come here from Germany."

"Very pleased to meet you," Henri had said, greeting the man. He then surprised both Jean Renoir and Gunter when he began speaking to the foreigner in his native language, fluent German!

"Henri," Renoir gushed. "How long have I known you?"

"About three, maybe four years," DuPont replied.

"I had no idea that you could speak German," a surprised Jean Renoir commented.

"Well, I should be able to, because I lived in Munich for more than seven years, and they don't speak a lot of French there," he laughed.

Over the coming years, the three men became very good friends, and when the rumours of the German invasion and occupation began, a plan was hatched.

Henri spoke to his mother and father about his worries for them, should the invasion happen. They agreed to hand the business over to their son and move close to the French Alps in the Vichy region of France, about as far away as they could possibly get away from the occupation. Henri agreed to send them money each month for expenses. They also had relations living in the area so they would not be on their own.

"You can bake your German goodies each day and attract the occupiers to this place," Jen Renoir advised.

"You can put up a massive sign outside saying, 'Bratwurst for Sale' and they will flock here," Gunter offered.

"As long as they don't know you can speak the German language, they will begin to trust you and will talk freely in front of you," Renoir continued. "This way you can discover many secrets about this occupation, and we can pass them back to the authorities who will be helped by them," Jean had suggested, and this is exactly what happened after the invasion.

Every morning and every evening the café was now filled with German officers, with a few of their collaborating French girlfriends along for the ride, but officers only, because once they'd found the place they wanted to make it their own, and so banned all the lower ranked soldiers from coming to the café.

Over the months, it had become an unofficial officers club, and the secrets they unknowingly revealed to Henri were plentiful!

Luisa and Yvette leaned their two bicycles against the black wrought iron fence outside the entrance to the Hotel Paradiso, situated at the Rue de Maubeuge. The nerves inside her stomach were by now dancing a merry jig, even worse than the first time when she'd visited last week.

The girls collected the baguettes from the bicycle baskets and walked up the five stone stepped entrance to the door. Once inside, Yvette was happy to see there were not so many soldiers milling about the place today, as she and Luisa made their way to the elevator which would take them to the third floor laundry room.

The hotel was constructed with a strange configuration where there were seven floors, but only five of them had guest rooms available. The ground floor was the reception area and restaurant, although neither of these had been in use since the occupation. Floors one and two, and four and five, were formerly guest rooms but were now occupied by the lower ranked German soldiers.

Floor three however, was the staff quarters where the hotel staff rooms were contained, along with the staff kitchen and laundry room where the fresh sheets and blankets were kept. Also kept in this room, and probably far more importantly, was the radio which Yvette would use to send her coded messages to whoever was listening.

When the German authorities commandeered the hotel, they insisted on all the staff remaining and 'living in' to take care of the men, making beds and keeping them fresh for the soldiers.

The staff all still lived in the hotel, which was a problem at first, as a few of the younger men had molested a few of the younger girls, and two of the girls claimed rape!

In fairness to the German authorities, these men were hunted down and punished for their crime by being sent from the relative safety and luxury of Paris and sent back to fight on the front line, where there was a good chance they would be dead within a few weeks, if not days!

Since this punishment was dished out, there had been no further incidences. The girls were now treated with the utmost respect.

"Bonjour Luisa," a girl said as the two approached.

"Merci beaucoup," another said, as they handed the bread over to the girls in the staff kitchen. Although this was just a cover to get Yvette inside the hotel and to the third floor it was greatly appreciated by the girls, as it really did keep them from going hungry.

Leaving the kitchen, they kept a close look out for anyone considered as non-friendly as they walked along the corridor. When reaching the laundry room, after another close search scanning the surrounding area, Yvette opened the door and cautiously entered, leaving Luisa waiting outside and 'on guard.'

"I will tap on the door three times if anyone comes," Luisa told the now very nervous radio operator.

"What will I do if that happens," Yvette questioned.

"Pull the sheets over you with the radio and hide under them," Luisa advised.

This suggestion sounded more than a little bit stupid, but what better idea was there than this extremely dangerous game of hide and seek?

Inside now and the nerves were building into a crescendo. Yvette found the radio in the place where she'd been told to look. It looked like such an innocent piece of equipment, but it could be a life saver for those on the receiving end of the messages, or in the case of Yvette, if discovered it would be a life ender!

She connected the radio, pulled out the pocket watch and waited for the second hand to reach twelve.

Dot-dot-dot-dot-dot-dot she tapped.

This was her signing on signal so those receiving knew it was her sending the message. She then began –

Dash = T

Dot-dot-dot-dot = H
Dot = E
Dot-dot-dot = S

She did this, all the time keeping one eye on the clock until she'd 'Morse Coded' the entire message, which she had been supplied with by a strange man who'd passed the message to Monsieur DuPont at the back door to the bakery.

T-H-E-S-H-E-E-P-H-A-V-E-R-E-T-U-R-E-D-
T-O-T-H-E-V-A-L-L-E-Y
(The sheep have returned to the valley)

She had no idea what the message meant, nor did she want to know, she was just happy that her first ever transmission had been sent successfully.

As she once again tapped dot-dot-dot-dot-dot-dot to sign off, she looked at the watch again and smiled when she saw there were still twelve seconds of relative safely remaining.

"Come on, let's get out of here," Luisa offered, after Yvette had rejoined her in the corridor. She could see the girl was trembling but didn't know if it was from fear, or excitement.

Outside, back on the bicycles and riding through the streets of Paris, the air seemed fresher, the streets smelled sweeter, and the bicycle wheels seemed to be revolving more freely, travelling faster than ever as Yvette and Luisa made their way back to the Café DuPont to first rest, and then to make themselves ready for the evening shift.

CHAPTER 14
GRUBER OF THE GESTAPO

It had now been a few weeks since Yvette had arrived at le Café DuPont and she seemed to be fitting in rather well. She'd even been to the Hotel Paradiso a couple of times on her own to send messages from the laundry room on floor three, although she still preferred to have Luisa with her, both as company, and for the extra security offered by her being on lookout duties.

Her life working in the café also felt quite 'matter of fact' now with her no longer feeling in danger when surrounded by Nazi officers all day every day. This was not always the case, especially during her first week.

On her third or fourth day, whilst waitressing on the breakfast shift, the door opened and a large man entered the building. Even the other officers fell into a hush as they noticed the man who'd come into the room.

"Heil Hitler," the men all shouted in unison, whilst standing and giving the outstretched straight arm Nazi salute. This gesture alone almost chilled Yvette to the bone, as it was the first time she'd ever seen this motion in action.

"Yes, yes, yes," the newcomer replied with disdain. "Sit down," he ordered sternly. The men all did as he commanded without a second of hesitation.

"Be careful, Yvette," Nicole DuPont had time to whisper in her ear. "This man is dangerous!"

"Boujour Madame DuPont," he said to Nicole. "Where is Henri?"

"He is in the bakery, Herr Gruber," she smiled. "Please, make yourself comfortable and I will fetch him for you."

As she said this, Nicole disappeared for a few moments, but soon returned with her husband. Yvette was very pleased to see them both emerging from the bakery, as every second Nicole was gone, she could feel the cold, steely eyes of Herr Gruber drilling holes into her head!

"Ah there you are. Bonjour Henri," Gruber announced at the appearance of Monsieur DuPont, all the time without taking his eyes from Yvette.

"Bonjour Herr Gruber," Henri said, and the two men shook hands.

"Please, tell me, Henri, who is this delightful vision of beauty?" Gruber questioned, making the girl feel extremely uncomfortable.

"This is the daughter of my cousin," Henri began, telling the Gestapo officer the same story which he and Yvette had concocted, rehearsed and practised for a couple of hours on the morning after the evening of her arrival.

"Enchanté, my dear," Gruber said, smiling at Yvette, which made her feel even more uneasy.

"She has come from Lille to help us for a couple of months," Henri continued. "You gentlemen are keeping us very busy, so we needed her help."

"You are busy because your bratwursts are too good, Henri," the Nazi laughed. "Have you tried Monsieur DuPont's bratwurst, my dear?" Gruber asked, aiming his question directly at Yvette.

"No, not yet, Sir," she replied as politely as possible.

"Oh, but you must," the Gestapo officer remarked. "They are the best in all of Paris. They are the talk of the town. Madame DuPont, please bring a bratwurst for me, along with one for this delightful girl."

"Oui, Herr Gruber, of course" Nicole said dutifully.

Herr Gruber turned his attention back to Yvette, and with Henri looking on, he asked, "What is your name?"

"My name is Yvette," she told him honestly.

"Yvette, a lovely name for a very pretty young lady," Grubber commented, making her feel even queasier. "Enchanté," he added again.

133

"I am also pleased to meet you," she lied.

Gruber's use of French was not very good, but she could understand what he was trying to say. However, he then totally blew her away.

"Sprichst du Deutsch?" the Nazi officer questioned.

"Nein, ich spreche kein Deutsch," Yvette replied, which made Henri look at the girl in horror. Had she just failed the first test and given herself away?

"But my girl, I just asked you if you speak German, in German," Herr Gruber sneered, "and you answered by telling me that you do not speak German, but you also said this in German! Please explain this to me," he demanded.

"Certainly Herr Gruber, as you wish. When I was a younger girl I went to school," Yvette replied quite sarcastically, maybe too sarcastically than was good for her, whilst reverting to the French language.

"Go on," Gruber commanded.

"In the time I was at school we learned to say things like, 'Sprichst du Deutsch' and, 'Hablas español,' even, 'do you speak English?' We learned to understand and answer these questions, as every child in the world probably does, but we do not know how to speak these languages, and I do not know how to speak, or understand the German language. I'm sorry, Herr Gruber, I hope I have not insulted you." Yvette stopped and looked at Gruber to judge his reaction.

"No, don't apologise my dear, why should you learn to speak the language of the Master Race?" he questioned, also equally sarcastically, but the smile soon returned to his face as he thought, incorrectly, that Yvette was not, and would not be a threat or a problem for him.

"Henri, this young lady is absolutely charming," Gruber disclosed. "I commend you for finding her."

"Merci beaucoup, Herr Gruber," Monsieur DuPont replied in agreement.

"Whenever I come here for my bratwurst mit eggs, brot und café, I want Yvette to serve me," he said, but he said it more like an order than a request.

"Certainly Sir, it would be my pleasure," Henri agreed.

"No Monsieur, the pleasure will be all mine," Gruber laughed, making Yvette feel even sicker.

"You have to be more careful, Yvette," Henri later chastised the girl; still angry by what he thought had been a big mistake.

"Why do I need to be careful, Henri, I knew exactly what I was doing," she revealed with a cheeky smile.

Since that day, now a few weeks ago, every day that Herr Gruber did come to the café to consume his bratwurst for breakfast, Yvette served him as ordered.

Henri and his wife, Nicole, also noticed that Gruber now only came to the café on the mornings when Yvette was on duty. It seemed that Luisa had fallen out of favour with the German, although she never lost any sleep over it!

One good thing to happen because of this was that all the members of the enemy were all extremely polite to the girl. Whether this was out of fear of making Gruber angry or not, she didn't know, but it did make her feel less apprehensive.

"Bonjour Yvette," some said upon entering.

"Bonjour chéri," the braver of the men would say.

"Bonjour belle," the most brave and confident would greet her, although this was never said whenever Herr Gruber was in the café.

However they greeted her, it made her feel somewhat safer to know that because of Herr Gruber she'd won the respect from the officers, which also meant of course that none of them suspected her or anyone else at the Café DuPont of being members of the resistance.

Yvette and Luisa were now living a double life. When in the

serving area of the café they dressed like the beautiful young ladies they were, wearing French waitressing outfits and letting their hair down. When out on the bicycles doing the 'deliveries,' they still dressed looking much younger than their actual ages.

Yvette had even taken to wearing a black wig to cover her shock of wavy blonde hair. She thought this made her look more inconspicuous and less recognisable, should any of the patrons at the 'DuPont' see her out on the bike and wonder what it was she was up to.

She still helped Luisa strap up her ample, but firm breasts with the bandage, although she didn't feel the need to do the same, as her breasts were not yet as plentiful and splendid as her friend's were.

She did worry though when Luisa divulged the real reason for doing this, and it was not to make them look smaller, but to make it easier for her to run away from the enemy if caught at a check-point whilst attempting to smuggle items which she should not have been carrying.

"It's a futile exercise really," she admitted to Yvette. "No matter how much my breasts are bouncing about or not, there is still no way I could outrun a bullet!"

"Don't say that," Yvette pleaded.

"Okay," Luisa agreed, but added, "But it's true!"

Luisa did not choose to wear a wig, instead she put her waist length straight black hair into a bob, and using a long hatpin, she secured it under a hat.

"I could do some damage with that pin if needed," she said to her friend. "I could take someone's eye out with that!"

It never ceased to amaze Yvette that a girl as stunningly beautiful as Luisa Silva, as well as being so soft and gentle natured when in her company, could be such a ruthless resistance member.

During her first week in Paris, she'd asked her new friend if she'd ever actually taken a life. Luisa answered this question by simply raising the brow above her right eye.

A normal and typical day for the girls, well, there were no normal or typical days for the two, but the day began when they were woken by Nicole at seven in the morning. They would then go down to the bakery, where Henri had been hard at work since five. They'd grab themselves a couple of croissants and some bread, both fresh from the ovens, and then make their way to the café area where a selection of cheeses and cold meats were waiting for them on the table.

During breakfast, they'd discuss the day to come. Yvette would discover if she had any messages to send in Morse code from the Hotel Paradiso or not, and if not they would learn what they had to take to the Hotel du Paris, situated close to the Sacré-Coeur in Montmartre.

This hotel was the stop off point for them, and also the beginning of the next 'leg' for the next branch of the resistance. After they'd made the drop, no one knew the destination of where the people they handed it to were going. This way if the Gestapo arrested anyone, no one else could reveal any information, because nobody knew any information, although this prevailing silence would almost definitely result in death by firing squad.

Most days, Yvette and Luisa were taking hand written messages to hand over to the recipient, or recipients, hidden in a secret compartment under the bread in their specially adapted bicycle baskets.

Occasionally they had to carry a far more dangerous cargo, which Philippe Barstrom always delivered. This was because he was well known for being both brave and fearless in the face of the enemy. The reason for this was that he didn't care if he survived this war or not. He didn't care if he lived or died.

Philippe's only ambition was to kill SS officer Herbert Schlesinger, the man whom he'd witnessed killing his brother,

René, by shooting him in the head at close range, and he didn't mind dying in his attempt to assassinate this man!

The girls hated when Philippe knocked on the back entrance door of the bakery, because they always knew that day their mission would be a dangerous one.

Yvette would never forget when during her second week at the Café, she was making her way to Montmartre with Luisa when a member of the French Gendarmerie stopped the girls in the street.

Yvette was extremely apprehensive at first, but she calmed down when she realised the member of the French police actually knew her travelling companion. She was also amazed when she saw Luisa's courageous bravery in action for the very first time.

"Good afternoon Luisa," he greeted with a salute, whilst touching the fingers on his right hand to his cap. "Where are the two of you going?"

"We are delivering bread to a hotel in Montmartre," she answered with honesty.

"And what is in that basket?" he questioned, pointing to the bread.

"Dynamite!" she answered, making both Yvette and the Gendarmerie do a double take.

"Dynamite?" he asked, showing both caution and shock.

"Yes, dynamite," repeated Luisa. "It's baked inside the baguettes."

She grabbed hold of one of the baguettes from the basket and tossed it high into the air. "Quickly, catch it!" she screamed. "Don't let it touch the ground or it will explode!"

The man suddenly had a look of horror on his face as he scrambled so as not to let the bread touch the floor.

At the final moment, realising he was not going to catch it when standing he dived through the air like an international goalkeeper and caught it in mid flight.

"You are an idiot!" Luisa laughed. "Give it here," she demanded. The member of the Gendarmerie walked to the bicycle and handed the bread back to Luisa, to which she immediately took a bite to prove it was just a baguette and nothing more sinister.

"You, Sir, are an idiot!" she repeated again, laughing.

"Get on your way," he ordered angrily, obviously embarrassed by what had just taken place.

As he walked away and before they continued with their journey, Yvette looked at her friend and asked," What IS in the basket? What are we delivering today?"

"Ten sticks of dynamite," Lisa revealed, so matter of factly that it scared Yvette, even though she felt overcome with a feeling of admiration for her beautiful but dangerous friend.

After breakfast, depending on who was working the morning shift, the non working girl would go back to the room to relax for a couple of hours whilst the working girl would serve in the café with Nicole, whilst Henri would pop in and out between the bakery and the café.

Henri was a very clever man as he volunteered to wipe the customer's tables, all the time listening to the conversations between the officers, both Nazi and Gestapo, as they were very confident he did not understand of what they were talking. This is where the resistance learned many details about what the Germans' were planning in the not too distant future.

They opened for business in the morning from nine-thirty until two in the afternoon. They then closed until seven in the evening, and this was the time for Yvette and Luisa to do the dangerous work.

The evening was a much more relaxing time, as all the men were more tranquil after enjoying a few glasses, or bottles of wine. They also took it in turns in singing a song or two, whilst accompanying Nicole on the piano.

As Luisa had told Yvette on her first night of arrival, the two girls, now of course very good friends did indeed have fun working the evening shift. The only thing Yvette hated was the fact that many of the men brought their French girlfriends with them – "Collaborating bitches!" she called them.

Even though the café closed at eleven, two hours after the beginning of the curfew, these French women were safe on the streets as long as they were accompanying a German officer, and this was another reason for Yvette's hatred of them.

"Their day will come," she remarked to Luisa. "You mark my words. Their day will come!"

CHAPTER 15
A PLAN IS HATCHED

Philippe Barstrom stood across the road from the Librairie Rivegauche looking at the bomb blasted shattered body of SS officer Herbert Schlesinger.

As the man stood over the lifeless corpse of his brother, René, all Philippe could think of was taking his revenge on the Nazi bastard who'd murdered not only his brother, but also his mother and father, during the events of what had come to be known as, 'The Massacre of San Eielson.'

Claude Proust had saved the boy's life that day when he physically held him tightly, when all he wanted to do was to run across the street and attack the monster standing over his brother. This however, would have been a suicide mission from which there could be no return. What could an unarmed boy of such tender years do against a building full of heavily armed Nazi officers?

No, Claude Proust had definitely saved the life of Philippe Barstrom that day, just as true as the boy had saved Claude's life on that village green, when he'd decided not to kick the stool away from beneath his feet that day in the village of San Eielson.

After the dust settled, the two made their way back to the sanctuary of Claude's apartment, where luckily the German authorities had no knowledge of its location, being the one question they'd never asked whilst interrogating him, supposedly because they never thought he would still be alive for much longer, certainly not for this length of time.

"We have to get out of here," Claude suggested.

"What, do you mean this apartment?" Philippe questioned.

"No Son, I mean we have to get out of Paris," Proust confirmed. "If they see us, they will arrest us."

"They may arrest you," the boy remarked, "but they do not

know me."

"Well I'll be leaving just as soon as I can," Proust confirmed. "What are you going to do?"

"I am going to stay here in Paris and I'm going to assassinate that Nazi bastard, Herbert Schlesinger," young Barstrom announced, both slowly and cold heartedly.

"I think you will need to wait a long time for that to happen," Claude stated, although sympathetically.

"I don't care how long it takes, one week, one month, or even one year, all I know is, it will happen," Philippe said, his blood running cold.

This all happened some six months or so ago. During that time, Schlesinger had survived two emergency operations to save his life and had been recuperating in a Parisian hospital for four months. At one time the doctors thought he might lose his leg but they fought hard to save it, although he now walked with a permanent limp, which he would suffer for the rest of his life, however long that would be.

Every day, Philippe would return to the scene of his brother's death to witness the progress of the rebuilding of the Librairie Rivegauche, the bookstore situated in the Rue de Livres. He went every day in the hope he might see the return of Schlesinger, but every day was fruitless.

Two weeks after the bombing of the shop, he and Claude received a visit from Jean Renoir and 'Gunter the German.'

"You need to get out of Paris, Son," Jean told the boy, confirming what Proust had said to the lad earlier.

"I am staying put," Philippe argued.

"If that's your decision, we will have to accept it," Renoir agreed, but then questioned the older of the two, "What about you, Claude?"

"I want to get out of here as soon as it's possible," he stated.

"Can you be ready today?" Renoir questioned.

"I am ready to leave now," Proust admitted.

"Me too," Gunter said. "I hate being here in Paris!"

It was true, the German was always scared stiff of being in the capital city for too long, as, although he spoke French very well, he could never lose his broad Munich accent. He was always worried about being caught and arrested for being a deserter, even though this would have been the very least of his problems at the hands of the Nazis.

"But Monsieur Renoir, where will I go?" Claude questioned again, trying to get the conversation back on track and to the point.

"We will take you to join up with the Maquis. You've heard of them of course?" Jean queried.

"Of course," Claude confirmed. "The band of men and women who live in the hills and forests; the organization most feared by the German army."

"Well yes, and now you are one of them," Gunter offered.

"And I am honoured to be joining them," Proust replied.

"What about you, Philippe?" Jean questioned the lad. "Are you coming with us?"

"Yes, come with us, Philippe," Proust pleaded.

"No, I'm staying here," the youngster answered defiantly.

"Then you'll need these, Claude announced, tossing the keys to the apartment in the direction of the boy, which he caught in his right hand.

"Thank you my friend," Philippe smiled.

"I have never seen you smile before," Claude remarked.

It was true, this was the first time Proust had ever seen the boy smile since he'd met him, but then he hadn't had too much to smile about in his short life, especially since his entire family had been slaughtered that day in the village.

"You will see me smile again, on the day I am standing over the dead body of SS officer Herbert Schlesinger," Philippe said boldly, and meant every word.

Before leaving Paris later that day, Jean took Philippe to the Café DuPont and introduced him to Henri and Nicole.

"This young lad is Philippe Barstrom," Jean announced, introducing the two to the boy. "Please take him under your wing and look after him," he begged of the two. The DuPont's agreed to this, but had no idea what they were taking on with this extremely angry and dangerous young man!

Two hours later, Jean Renoir and Gunter the German left the apartment, taking Claude Proust with them on the journey to join up with the Maquis. Suddenly feeling very alone, Philippe had his one and only thought that he might have done the wrong thing. Maybe he should have gone with the three men to the relative safety of the forest, but he soon snapped out of it.

No, his life was here and his mission was here – his mission to kill SS officer Herbert Schlesinger, to stand over him and see all life extinguish from and leave his lifeless body.

Philippe had now been alone in the apartment for six months since the three men had left him. Every day, he made the pilgrimage to the Rue de Livres to check on the progress of the rebuilding of the shop. Well this was one reason for the visit, but the main reason was the hope of seeing his arch enemy, to see if he was also checking on the progress.

Luckily for the Nazi, Schlesinger never appeared, so the pistol which Jean Renoir had obtained for the boy, remained securely locked away in the cabinet inside the living room of Claude's apartment, although on many an evening, Philippe would take it out and sit with it. He loved the feeling of security that it gave him in case any of the enemy came bursting through the door. If this happened he knew he would probably die, but also knew he would take a good number of the occupying soldiers with him!

Finally, the big day arrived, the day of the grand reopening of the Librairie Rivegauche. However, this was the good news for Philippe; the bad news was that the public were no longer allowed to enter the shop under any circumstances.

Whereas before, the shop was still acting as a library and bookstore for the public to borrow or buy books with an area cordoned off for the German officers to congregate, now the entire inside area was designated solely for the use of the Nazi and Gestapo hierarchy.

To emphasise the fact that the public were no longer wanted inside, or allowed entrance to the shop, there was twenty-four hour security in operation at the front entrance. This always consisted of at least two soldiers on guard, heavily armed with machine guns ready to fire at a seconds notice. This of course meant that Philippe's plans to kill Schlesinger at the same spot where he'd killed René were now ruined. He needed to find a different location to carry out the assassination.

He decided he needed to find where Schlesinger was actually living during his stay in Paris. To do this, he followed him on his journey home each night after leaving the Rue de Livres in his enormous black Mercedes-Benz, open top staff car. This was not so easy on his measly bicycle, in fact it was impossible.

What Philippe did was to follow the car as far as he could keep up, and when he could go no further, he made a note of the time and location and returned to that spot the same time the next afternoon. He then waited again for Schlesinger to appear in the Mercedes and followed him again on his journey, until his legs could follow him no more.

He intended doing this for as long as it took to find the Nazi's place of dwelling, but after only four nights, Philippe found what he thought would be the perfect place, when he saw the car turn right into a smaller side street. This would be the spot, because on the journey back to the Librairie Rivegauche the car would have to stop here and wait for a break in the traffic before manoeuvring across the road to get into the right hand lane and continue with the journey. He could be here waiting in hiding, and when he saw SS officer Herbert Schlesinger approaching in the car, he could jump out, surprise him, and end his life.

He knew there was a good chance that he might also be killed, perhaps his own life would end at the same time as Schlesinger's, but this didn't worry Philippe in the slightest. This is what made the boy so exceedingly dangerous!

Over the coming days he returned to this spot at various times of the day to ascertain what time the Nazi normally passed by, making a mental note of the times when he did so. He did not bring the pistol with him on these occasions in case he was discovered acting suspiciously, seen by the German guards and challenged as to what he was doing at the scene. He thought it would be a criminal waste to have the gun discovered before he was able to use it.

A few days later, Philippe woke to see the sun was shining and so decided that this would be the day. It was important for it to be a sunny day because it meant that the roof of Schlesinger's staff car would almost certainly be down, making the kill shot that much easier. If it was raining and the top was up, it would be so much more difficult for the potential assassin.

After first checking the pistol to make sure the bullet clip was full of ammunition, he placed it carefully inside the shoulder bag he would carry. He'd already been awake well into the night, when he'd taken the gun to pieces and cleaned every individual part of it. The last thing he wanted was for it to fail to operate when he had Schlesinger in his sights and pulled the trigger.

Soon he was ready to leave, so took what could be a final look around the apartment. This was the first time he felt nervous, but he said to himself, 'Come on Philippe get a grip. Nerves are for other people, not for you.'

He could have backed down at this moment, because nobody knew of his plan to kill the Nazi on this day but – no –

today was the day. It was now or never!

Leaving the apartment, he closed the door behind him. He was then about to lock the door but instead he looked at the keys in his hand and decided to drop them into the Café DuPont. He could always collect them again later if he survived, or if not, then someone else could make use of the building.

He went to the back door, the bakery door, and without knocking he pushed it open just a little and dropped the key on the floor. He knew that Henri would know what it was and who had left it for him. He also knew that Henri would attempt to talk him out of what he was about to do, if given half the chance.

Eventually he reached the spot of his intended ambush and found a place to hide. It was essential that Schlesinger or his driver did not see him until the final seconds of the attack. He found a spot behind, and in the shade of a tree and waited. Now the butterflies in his stomach were dancing a highland fling!

Philippe Barstrom spotted a black Mercedes-Benz coming towards him. It was now about fifty yards away and the young boy, for that is what he still was, a young boy, took the gun from the bag and threw the bag down on the ground. Holding the gun behind his back, his finger firmly on the trigger, he walked slowly to the curb side and waited for the car to come alongside.

At the last second as the car arrived, both the occupants looked straight at the lad, Schlesinger even offered a smile, but he didn't smile when he spotted the gun in the boy's hand.

"This is for my family, you murdering bastard!" Philippe shouted.

He raised the gun and, unchallenged, he fired two shots into the chest area of Schlesinger, followed quickly by one in the side of the driver's head.

He didn't know where they came from, but suddenly he spotted soldiers coming towards him from every direction, and he quickly found himself surrounded. For a split second, he thought about putting the barrel of the gun into his own mouth and pulling the trigger, but found himself throwing the pistol to the ground and raising his arms in the air.

Instantly Philippe found himself surrounded by German soldiers. Their hands were everywhere as they all wrapped their arms around him to stop any attempt to flee. However, the last thing he wanted to do was to run away. He was overjoyed to have completed his task and now he was just as happy to face the consequences, whatever they may be.

Before the soldiers dragged him away to the Gestapo headquarters, he was able to take a last lingering look at the blood stained corpse of SS officer Herbert Schlesinger.

"Take that, you murdering Nazi bastard!" he shouted defiantly, allowing himself a smile.

CHAPTER 16
WELCOME TO THE WAR - YVETTE

There was a strange atmosphere about the place as Henri and the girls continued with business as normal at the Café DuPont. Nicole was the first to point out that the officers of late had been talking with each other in hushed voices, as though not wanting to be overheard by the DuPont's, Luisa and Yvette, even though they were sure the 'family' could not understand what it was they was discussing.

Henri had his suspicions ever since he found the key on the bakery doorstep three days ago, although until now nothing had been confirmed, which was a good thing.

One thing he was happy about though was the fact that the German officers, customers in the café, had so far shown no animosity towards him, his wife, or the girls, therefore he believed there were no suspicions that the four might be suspected as members of the resistance.

Also, if as Henri believed, Philippe Barstrom had attempted to assassinate the Nazi officer he so hated and been captured and interrogated by the Gestapo, it would seem that he'd not given them, or any other members of the resistance away.

"You have to question Herr Gruber the next time he comes in, Yvette," Henri said to the horrified girl. "We need to know if there's a problem."

"What?" she exclaimed. "Me?"

"Yes Yvette, you," Henri replied. "You are his favourite. He wouldn't hurt you."

"Wouldn't hurt me? I've heard a bullet in the head only hurts for a split second, so you might be right, Henri, he wouldn't hurt me!" she protested.

"Just tell Gruber that you have noticed the officers have been a little subdued of late, and you are wondering if there is a problem you can help with," Monsieur DuPont suggested. "He will love you even more for this."

The very suggestion that Herr Gruber 'loved' Yvette made her feel sick, although it was far better than the Gestapo officer hating the girl.

This entire conversation soon became irrelevant, when two days later there was a tap-tap-tap on the door to the bakery. Henri opened the door and saw a young girl standing there, a pretty girl whom he'd not seen before. Without saying a word, as he looked at her she placed a piece of paper into the palm of his hand, then turned around and left. He looked at the paper and read –

'Philippe Barstrom arrested by the Gestapo – He is being held at the headquarters close to the Notre-Dame Cathedral - Please get a message to Jean Renoir and Madame Chambourcey in the Lorre Valley.'

In the light of this message, it was decided that Yvette should not question Herr Gruber as to what was happening, or what had happened. This was a great relief to the girl, although it meant that she would have to make a visit to the Hotel Paradiso and send the message to Jean Renoir from the radio room on the third floor. This was already making her feel nervous, but it had to be done.

"What should I send?" she asked Henri. "Normally the messages are disguised and cryptic."

"No time for that," Henri admitted. He then looked deep in thought for a few seconds and eventually said, "We have to keep it short and simple. Just send 'Philippe – Boy – Captured."

"So I send, P-H-I-L-I-P-P-E-B-O-Y-C-A-P-T-U-R-E-D?" Yvette asked, writing the message on a fresh piece of paper.

"That'll do," Henri confirmed. "Monsieur Renoir and Madame Chambourcey will know exactly what it means."

"That's good, because I can be in and out in just a few

seconds," said a slightly more relieved Yvette.

Two days later, Yvette and Luisa made their way to the Hotel Paradiso on their trusty bicycles. Being a Thursday afternoon they knew that Madame Chambourcey would be manning her radio at four o'clock, waiting to see if anyone contacted her.

For some reason, even though the girls had made this journey many times before by now, and Yvette had sent many messages from the third floor laundry room, today she felt extra nervous.

As usual they had two baskets full of baguettes, along with half a dozen croissants. Even though it was far too late for staff breakfasts, it was still a good reason and an alibi for them to be there should they be challenged.

"This place has a strange atmosphere today," Luisa said to Yvette, as the pair cycled through the streets of Paris.

"I know what you mean," Yvette replied. "It has a kind of subdued feeling."

"It's too quiet. I don't like it," Luisa commented. "I don't like it. I don't like it at all."

"Me neither, it seems creepy," Yvette agreed. "Let's get this done as quickly as possible, then we can get the hell out of here and get back to the café."

"Agreed," her very attractive companion said.

Twenty minutes later they'd reached the hotel, walked up three flights of stairs to the third floor, given the bread and croissants to the girls in the kitchen, and Yvette was now inside the laundry room whilst Luisa remained outside on lookout duty.

After sending Madame Chambourcey her call sign so the lady knew it was her calling, Yvette began broadcasting the message –

Dot-Dash-Dash-Dot = 'P'
Dot-Dot-Dot-Dot = 'H'

Dot-Dot = 'I'
Dot-Dash-Dot-Dot = 'L'

She did this until the complete message had been sent - Philippe – Boy – Captured – and then began packing the radio and the antenna away. She'd just completed this task when for the first time ever, she heard Luisa knocking three times on the door, the signal for her to say 'someone is on the way.'

Yvette, now in panic mode, quickly laid down on the middle shelf in the corner of the room and pulled the sheets over her, trying to hide her body as best as possible. Seconds later, she heard a man's voice.

"Is there anyone in here?" she heard the man say, with an obvious German accent.

Yvette's heart was pounding so fast that she was sure the man could hear it, and was now becoming really worried for her safety. But her anxiety was eased when she heard the man say, "Come on in, it's empty."

"Are you sure, Claus?" a girl said, with an obvious French accent.

"I'm sure," the German replied.

This was followed by the sound of kisses being exchanged, followed by the noise of extremely passionate love making. Hearing these two going at it, Yvette was no longer scared but she was angry and appalled. Obviously this French girl was not being raped by this soldier, she was with him because she wanted to be with him, and it was obvious that she was there of her own free will. This to Yvette was nothing less than fraternising with the enemy!

She remained under the sheets until she heard the sounds of the love making stop, when the two got dressed and left the room. Half a minute later, from below the sheet she heard the door open again. However, this time she heard a friendly and reassuring voice.

"All clear, Yvette, they've gone," she heard the calm sound of Luisa's voice say.

"My heart is still pounding," Yvette confessed.

"I bet," Luisa smiled.

"Did you see the girl?" Yvette questioned. "Do you know who she is?"

"I know her," Luisa confirmed. "And when the day comes, we will make sure she gets what is coming to her. She will get her just rewards."

"I think she just did," Yvette announced laughing.

As the two girls left the hotel, Yvette was never more grateful to smell fresh air again. It somehow smelled sweeter than it did an hour or so ago and she was overcome with a feeling of relief. However, this feeling would be short lived.

They were cycling through the streets when they turned into a square which was unusually full of people, making it hard work for the girls to pass through. Yvette then spotted the reason for the crowd of people gathering at this spot, for there in the centre of the commotion she saw a boy kneeling down on his knees.

"Luisa, its Philippe!" she stressed to her friend.

"Try to keep calm, Yvette," Luisa advised. "Try not to attract attention," she stressed. The two girls looked around to see an officer addressing the crowd.

"This young man has murdered a German officer," the man in full Nazi uniform announced whilst standing about two yards behind Philippe. This announcement brought a hushed gasp from the crowd of people in attendance.

"We believe this young man is a member of the resistance," the Nazi shouted again, loud enough for everyone to hear.

"Poor bastard," the girls heard a few people close by whisper, although quiet enough NOT to be heard by any of the German soldiers marshalling the crowd.

The Nazi standing behind Philippe began speaking again. "This is what happens to members of the resistance who we catch, so this will be your fate if you belong to the resistance. This is also what happens to people who know members of the resistance but do not inform on them to us, your masters and the Master Race." The arrogance of the man was abhorrent!

As he finished this warning to everyone, he unclipped the holster on his belt and pulled out his pistol. Upon hearing this, poor Philippe knew what was about to happen. He knew what was destined to be his fate.

Brave to the very end, young Philippe Barstrom was determined to have the last word, and before the trigger was pulled, the crowd of voyeurs heard him begin to shout.

"Vive la France," he yelled, flowed by - "Death to Hitler and to all the monsters that follow him!"

Sadly, before Philippe could finish his speech, a loud bang was heard. Yvette, who had turned away when the officer took out his gun, now instinctively turned back. Even though in truth she didn't really like him, she was still devastated to see the boy's lifeless body lying in a pool of blood with half his head missing!

"Come on, Yvette," Luisa said quietly. "Let's go home."

"Go home?" Yvette queried. "I wish I could go home. I still don't know what the hell I'm doing here."

"What do you mean?" Luisa asked.

"I am a medical student in Oxford," Yvette stated, and not for the first tie. "I was learning how to save lives. How the hell did I end up in the resistance in Paris?" This question remained unanswered.

The two girls mounted their bicycles and rode back to the Café DuPont in total silence. They were both stunned by what they'd just witnessed and both girls were apprehensive about revealing the news to Henri and Nicole, although they knew it was something which had to be done.

"Girls, I need you to be extra vigilant," Henri DuPont

instructed an attentive Luisa, Yvette and Nicole, upon hearing the devastating news of the execution of Philippe Barstrom.

Even though Yvette had no great love for the boy, she was still in floods of tears when she and Luisa gave the news of his death to the head of the family.

"We also need to be ready to leave at a moment's notice, should the worst happen," Nicole added, much to the approval of her husband.

This was almost two months ago now and thankfully there had been no change of attitude towards them in the café from their Nazi and Gestapo clients, confirming the fact that Philippe, brave to the end, had met his death without giving his interrogators, or rather his torturers, any information about the French resistance fighters in Paris. For now, Henri and the girls were safe, although poor Yvette never felt safe in Paris again and constantly had nightmares about what she'd seen that day.

Being the first week of October 1943 the nights were now beginning to draw in, becoming darker earlier, as well as now containing a bit more of a chill in the air.

Yvette enjoyed the darker evenings because it made her feel less conspicuous as she cycled through the Parisian streets on her way back from the Hotel Paradiso or Montmartre, or wherever she was coming from or going to.

She also found the city becoming more exciting with the darker evenings, the streets of the city coming alive with all the flashing lights and the neon signs above the entrances to the various cafés, bars and nightclubs, those which were still allowed to remain open during this occupation because their patronage was mainly German.

These days, in the early evenings before beginning her night shift in the café, Yvette often found herself standing at the bedroom window staring at the space where the Eiffel Tower stood. Visible by day, but during the night it was replaced by an area of darkness, a black mass of nothingness.

The reason for this was that Herr Adolph, quite sensibly for a monster, thought it a bad idea to allow this structure to be illuminated at night like a beacon, because it could be used as a guide by any enemy aircraft trying to find places of interest to bomb when flying over the city. Nevertheless, the girl still liked to stare at the dark space, whilst daydreaming about her life back in England.

She was becoming to feel very homesick and was missing her mum and dad in Dorchester. She also missed Peter Collins and Ben Richards, the two young men who'd taught her how to parachute out of an airplane and how to send and receive Morse code. She even admitted to missing the training camp in Kent, where during her time there she considered it to be a place of torture, especially when in the company of the sadistic Mr. Green, the unarmed combat instructor.

Yvette couldn't understand why she was suddenly getting these feelings now, especially the feelings for Peter, but even more so, her feelings for Ben. She had never felt anything romantic towards him when in his company before in Kent, so why had she begun having them now, some six months after she'd last seen him?

This was making the young girl's life very difficult, but if her life was difficult now, it was about to become even more difficult – and also extremely dangerous!

CHAPTER 17
A NIGHT TO REMEMBER

"You girl – Halt!" she heard a voice of authority order. Immediately she stopped where she stood and slowly turned around.

"Me, Sir?" she questioned somewhat timidly.

"Yes, you," the man demanded.

Yvette's heart was pounding so quickly, as she saw the man standing there was in full Gestapo officer uniform. It almost felt like it had fallen out of her stomach and had been sent crashing to the floor!

"Why are you here?" he demanded again. "I see you here many times, but why do you come here so often?"

It was true that Yvette was at the Hotel Paradiso on most days of the week, not always to broadcast, and usually with Luisa Silva by her side, but this was one of the rare occasions when she'd come here solo. She really wished she had her friend with her to give her support.

"I come every day to deliver baguettes and croissants to the girls in the kitchen, and sometimes I deliver cakes," she divulged.

The Gestapo officer looked her up and down, seemingly studying every inch of her voluptuous body.

"And is that the bread in the basket?" he questioned.

"Yes Sir," she returned.

"Let me have one of those baguettes," he almost demanded, but then added, "Please."

Yvette took one of the sticks of bread from the basket and passed it to him.

"Thank you, my dear," he said, surprising the girl. He took a bite of the baguette. "That is very good," he said mid chew, and then continued. "Next time you come here, bring extra for me."

"Certainly Sir," she agreed, even though she had no choice but to agree to his demands.

"You'd better be on your way," he told her. "The girls in the kitchen will be waiting for you and they will be hungry."

"Thank you, Sir," she heard herself say, as if in an out of body experience.

As she walked to the elevator, she could feel the officer's eyes boring holes into the back of her head! She was very happy not to be broadcasting today, as she really was only here on this occasion to deliver the baked goods to the staff, and this was the reason for Luisa's absence.

After making her delivery she took the stairs back to the ground floor, but as she stepped through the door from the stairwell to the entrance, she was shocked to see the Gestapo officer was still standing there. Was he waiting for her?

"Hello again my dear," he began. "Please let me introduce myself. My name is Herr Max von Schtipe of the Gestapo."

He held out his hand to take hers. As she offered her much smaller hand to his, he took it and then kissed the back of it.

"What is your name?" he enquired.

"I am Yvette," she revealed.

"Yvette?" he asked, obviously needing more information.

"Sorry Sir, I am Yvette Colbert," she replied, just about stopping herself from completing the sentence with, 'of the Resistance!'

"Well Yvette Colbert, today is your lucky day," von Schtipe declared, making the girl feel even more anxious. "Have you ever been to the Moulin Rouge, my dear?" he asked, almost sounding human now.

"No Sir, I have never been," she admitted.

"Then I shall take you," he said, shocking the life out of her. "Let me think," he said looking deep in thought. "Today is Thursday, so I will meet you here at the hotel at seven o'clock on Saturday evening. Yes, Saturday will be a good night for us to go."

"But what about the curfew," Yvette questioned.

"It will be okay, Yvette, you will be safe during the curfew because you will be accompanied by me," he confirmed. "I will protect you, my dear. Please do not worry."

Even hearing this man saying her name aloud made her feel physically sick. The sad thing was that she'd always dreamed of going to the world famous 'Moulin Rouge,' but not this way – not in the company of Herr Max von Schtipe of the Gestapo.

"You have to go with him, Yvette. Not to go would be an insult to Herr von Schtipe; therefore it would be as good as suicide. You will never be able to go anywhere in Paris, or even France again!" Henri warned.

"I know this, Henri," she admitted. "But I'm petrified of him. He's an exceptionally scary man to be in the company of."

That night, after putting on a brave face and a fake smile during the evening shift at the café, Yvette went to her bed earlier than normal. She just lay there in the dark and deep in thought, thinking about what was going to happen tomorrow during her evening with von Schtipe. She also couldn't stop thinking about Ben Richards, and how much she was missing him.

The funny thing was that two hundred and seventy-nine miles, seven hundred and four yards and twenty-two inches away from her, in a training camp just outside Maidstone in Kent, a certain young man named Ben Richards was also laying on top of his bed thinking about his affections for a young woman with the real name of, Yvette Jackson. He was also mystified about how much he was missing her.

"Hello my dear," Herr Max von Schtipe of the Gestapo greeted Yvette as she arrived outside the entrance to the Hotel Paradiso. As per usual, the officer took her hand and kissed the back of it, making her feel as though all she wanted to do was go to the bathroom and thoroughly scrub it!

"Good evening Sir," she said, as politely as she possibly could.

"May I say how beautiful you look?" he remarked.

"Thank you," she replied.

She did indeed look very beautiful in the light blue knee length evening dress which Luisa had lent to her, along with a pair of comfortable shoes with a medium sized heal and borrowed from Nicole DuPont.

Nicole had said at the time, "They will be easier to run away in, should the occasion arise." This did nothing to make Yvette feel any more at ease with the current situation.

"You have forgotten two very important things," Luisa told the girl as she was about to leave for her rendezvous with the Gestapo officer.

"What's that?" Yvette queried.

"First of all, you don't have one of these in that dress," her friend said, handing Yvette a cyanide capsule to place in the secret compartment contained within the sleeve of the garment.

"Oh lord! Thank you," Yvette gushed. "And what is the second thing?" she requested.

"What colour was your hair when Schtipe saw you on Thursday?" Luisa questioned with a smile.

"Oh shit!" Yvette almost screamed. "Thank you my friend," she said, as she reached for the wig with the long straight black hair.

"You look stunning," Nicole said as she appeared at the door, "but there is something else missing."

"What, something else, what's that?" Yvette questioned.

"This," Nicole said. As she said this, she produced a beautiful pearl necklace from a black velvet box hidden behind her back. They were beautiful pearls, perfectly formed and graduated in different sizes, all with a lovely creamy white colour.

"My word, they're gorgeous," Luisa said, and quite rightly.

As she put the necklace around Yvette's neck, Nicole said to the girl, "If you are going to dine with the enemy, at least you can dress elegantly."

"Thank you so much," Yvette said thankfully.

"Try not to worry too much," Nicole advised.

"Try to have some fun," Luisa added. "If nothing more, you should have an enjoyable evening at the Moulin Rouge."

"Yes," Yvette agreed. "And if I were going with somebody else, maybe somebody I felt love for, there is no doubt that I would."

"I thought we would take a stroll to the club from here," Herr Max von Schtipe of the Gestapo announced, when he noticed Yvette looking around searching for the car to take them on their way.

"Okay," she replied pleasantly, although inside she was angry. She'd just spent forty-five minutes walking here from the Café DuPont, a journey usually taking her a little more than ten minutes on the bicycle, and now this man wanted her to spend another half an hour or so walking from the hotel to the Moulin Rouge.

As they walked along the streets of Paris, she noticed that all the German soldiers along the way all saluted the man accompanying her. She wondered if this was out of respect, or more likely she thought, out of fear for the man!

"Have you had a pleasant day?" he questioned, trying to make polite small talk.

"Very nice, thank you," she lied.

In truth, she'd spent all day worrying about what was going to happen tonight, and dreading spending time in the company of this Gestapo monster!

"But he might be a very nice man in reality," Luisa had said to her that afternoon, probably in an attempt to calm her nerves.

"Don't be stupid," Nicole had chastised Luisa. "No one in the Gestapo, especially an officer, could possibly be a 'nice man.' It's one of the main requirements when applying for the position. You have to be a bastard!"

"Sorry, Nicole, you are correct f course," Luisa said, now agreeing with the wife of the boss.

"You take care, Yvette, "Nicole continued. "You are correct to be nervous when in the company of this man."

Eventually von Schtipe gave up trying to make polite conversation and they walked together in silence, apart from the occasional "Sieg Heil" shouted from one soldier or another as they walked past, accompanied by the Nazi salute, which the Gestapo officer for the main, ignored.

This actually made Yvette think. Maybe he wasn't as fully committed to the Fuhrer and his Third Reich ideology as his fellow officers believed.

"Nearly there now," Max von Schtipe said, breaking the silence as they entered the Boulevard de Clichy, the street where the Moulin Rouge was positioned.

As per usual, there was a long queue of people waiting to gain entrance to the building. They were all German men in various uniforms, standing alongside Parisian women, all dressed up to the nines in fancy shoes and dresses which their 'boyfriends' had bought for them with, as Yvette thought, their blood money!

Then another thought entered her head. She wondered if these soldiers and their 'harlots' were looking at her and thinking that she was also the loose woman of Herr Max von Schtipe, the 'tart' kept by this monster of the Gestapo.

She kept looking around to see if anyone in the queue was looking at her. However, if they weren't looking at her before they would certainly be looking now, as the Gestapo man took her firmly by the hand and dragged her past everyone who'd been waiting patiently and forced his way to the front door entrance.

"I'm sorry Sir, but we are not quite ready to open yet," a young employee said as they arrived.

"You are open now," von Schtipe ordered forcefully.

The young man, not knowing what to do and looking very worried, turned to one side and opened the door to allow them to gain entrance.

"Thank you," Yvette said to the young man, offering him a smile.

"Do not thank these people, they are pure scum!" her companion for the evening chastised her through gritted teeth, showing an obvious hatred for the French. This made Yvette wonder why he'd chosen to spend this evening with her, a 'French' girl.

Once inside, Yvette took a good look around at the interior of the place. With the lights shining at full power it looked like it could do with some attention, perhaps a little refurbishment. It was much bigger than she thought it would be, with enough tables and chairs to seat eight hundred and fifty people when fully booked, although less than half this number would be here tonight.

Being the first inside, they could have sat in the best seats in the house. However, von Schtipe led the girl by the hand to probably the worst table in the place, furthest away from, and with the most awful view of the stage.

"I do not like to have people sitting behind me whom I cannot see. I like to be able to see everyone in the building, along with anyone who comes through the doors," he later explained to his pretty companion. "I trust no one."

"And does this include me?" Yvette questioned, but her query received no response. Instead, Schtipe raised his arm high in the air, summoning for a waitress to approach.

"Champagne," he demanded from the young girl.

"I am sorry Sir but the............."

"Champagne!" he demanded again, before the poor girl could finish telling him the bar was not yet open, only now he demanded it more forcibly by banging his fist down on the table. If he was trying to impress Yvette with this show of authority, his actions were having completely the reverse effect.

Maybe this kind of bullying worked with the collaborating Parisian whores accompanying most of the men here tonight, but she was finding this man to be a very unpleasant and tedious human being. Compared to this man, Yvette's admirer at the café, Herr Gruber of the Gestapo was as gentle as a pussycat.

As the room filled with the enemy and their floosies, the lights became gradually dimmer. Now the room was darker, the stage became much more prominent. The stage lights were illuminated and Yvette could see the full majesty of the place.

The stage curtains were magnificent, almost as wide as the entire room and from floor to ceiling in height. They were made of what looked like crushed velvet, scarlet red in colour, with a gold trimmed floral pattern running the full width at the base.

Just in front of the stage was a medium sized orchestra pit, where at this moment around twenty or so musicians were tuning up. Yvette thought they were making a heck of a din as they all played different sections of music, but she felt sure they would all sound wonderful at 'curtain up.'

A few minutes after everyone had finished the meal provided, which Yvette thought must have been of better quality when the city was not under the powers of these unwanted invaders and the country was not at war with Germany, the house lights dimmed fully and the stage lights beamed at full power. With a swishing noise, the curtains slowly opened to reveal twenty very beautiful girls with superb bodies, all scantily dressed and using large white feather boas to cover their beautiful torsos.

All the men in the audience let out a huge cheer of approval, with many of them putting two fingers in their mouths and letting out ear shattering whistles, much to the obvious disapproval of Max von Schtipe, who did not look amused. Yvette immediately felt sorry for these female dancers, who probably had to endure this lechery on a nightly basis.

The orchestra began playing some sexy, provocative sounding music, whilst the girls writhed about on the stage moving this way and that, all the time expertly repositioning the feathers and the feather boas to keep their bodies covered from the prying eyes of the audience.

Suddenly the orchestra began playing the music louder and faster, building into a crescendo of noise while the girls began dancing in more and more of a sexy and seductive fashion until the music stopped abruptly and the girls all raised their opened arms, throwing the feathers and the boas high in the air.

Yvette couldn't believe what she was seeing. All the men cheered loudly, including Max von Schtipe, who she noticed was now going crazy at the sight of a stage full of beautiful girls all parading on the stage as naked as the day they were born! All these bevies of beauties were wearing matching silver coloured high heeled shoes, and at this moment, nothing else.

Whilst the men in the audience were all ogling these women, all Yvette could think of was how much she admired these girls for being able to dance so well in these shoes with the ridiculously high heels.

The curtain closed to rapturous applause and then a strange little man came onstage. Yvette was shocked to hear this man speaking in German.

"This man is one of the best comedians in all of Germany," von Schtipe explained as she listened.

This made her almost choke with laughter as she thought to herself, 'The best comedian in Germany. Well there can't be too much competition, can there?'

Soon, all the members of the German army were in fits of laughter, whilst all the women were all wearing the same expressions, those of confusion mixed with boredom, as like Yvette, they couldn't understand a single word he was saying.

Suddenly this man began goose stepping from one side of the stage to the other, all the time ranting and raving and raising his right arm in the air giving the Nazi salute. It was obvious he was making fun of the Fuhrer, Adolph Hitler! Any other man caught doing this would find himself dragged against a wall and shot, but this man had the entire audience in the palms of his hands, and that included Herr Max von Schtipe of the Gestapo.

When this comedian finished his performance, as he left stage left, the curtains opened and the orchestra began playing music again. All the men sat up straight, for they knew what was coming. True enough, as the stage was fully exposed, the dancing girls were back again.

This time there were no feather boas and no feathers, in fact they had nothing at all to cover their modesty. Twenty-five girls this time were all standing onstage wearing only French knickers, which were clearly see through, along with feathery headgear which made them all look at least a foot taller than they actually were. They were all topless, with their young firm breasts exposed for all to see. Every man's eyes were transfixed to the stage as the girls all jiggled about to the music.

When they finished this routine, as the curtain closed again the German comedian returned to the stage. However, this time he only said a few words and pointed to the other side of the stage where another man was seen to come on, this time wearing a dinner jacket and a crisp white shirt with a smart bow tie.

The orchestra broke into music which Yvette and never heard before and the man burst into a song. She had to admit, even though she had no idea what he was singing about, he was very good and had a wonderful voice.

She later learned that normally the Moulin Rouge had top

entertainers from all over the world performing on this famous stage, but with the advent of this war, obviously this was no longer possible. Even the best of the French artists now refused to perform here, hence all these German performers were now in attendance.

She even wondered if the dancing girls were still all French nationals or whether some German women had now been drafted into this group. She wondered if this was the case, but didn't ask this question to von Schtipe. He appeared to be enjoying himself far too much and she didn't wish to spoil his good mood.

Getting close to the end of the show now, as the singer sang his last song and left the stage, to the biggest cheer of the night the curtains opened once again to reveal the girls all standing in a line and ready to perform the Moulin Rouge's grand finale, the 'Can-Can.'

The men went wild as the girls went through this dance for the thousandth time in their careers, whooping and screaming whilst throwing themselves around the stage, leaping high into the air and landing with a bang and dong the splits. Even the women, by now all suitably drunk, looked on and seemed quite impressed.

When the girls finished the routine, again to rapturous applause and wolf whistles, the house lights again came back on.

Yvette looked around and saw more than two hundred sweaty men, along with many of the women accompanying them, were now in various states of undress. Obviously the men had been having a bit of a fumble in the dark with these French, collaborating whores whilst the show had been going on.

"Come, my dear, it's time to go home," von Schtipe stipulated. This was the time Yvette had been dreading all night, and finally that time had arrived.

As she stood, he took her coat from the back of her seat and draped it around her shoulders, just as any gentleman would. However, being a gentleman was the last thing she thought described Maxwell von Schtipe!

As they left the Moulin Rouge, Yvette turned to the left to head back in the direction they'd come from, but was surprised when von Schtipe turned to the right.

"This way, young lady," he announced, causing the girl a little trepidation.

"Where are we going?" she questioned.

"Home, of course," was his reply.

"But I thought you lived at the Hotel Paradiso?" she queried.

"No, young lady," he returned, beginning to laugh aloud. "Surely you don't think an officer of my standing would live in a scheisse place like that?"

"But the Paradiso was one of the finest hotels in all of Paris," she stated, but then added, "Before the occupation."

"Maybe it was and maybe it still is," he replied, clearly ignoring the girl's last remark. "But it's certainly not a good enough place for me to live."

"So where do you live?" she asked.

"You'll see," he commented. "It's very close, only ten minutes from here."

This put the girl into a state of panic. She'd incorrectly thought this man would be putting her into a car after the show and returning her to the Café DuPont. This was obviously not the case.

By now it was almost midnight and the streets had an eerie feeling to them, being empty, dark and ghostlike. The only people on the streets were the guards on duty at the checkpoints, of which there was one positioned at the beginning and end of every street. She noticed that Herr Max von Schtipe of the Gestapo was never challenged by these men, curiously neither was she, as she kept her head down so as not to be seen.

It swiftly dawned on her that the realisation of this situation was that she was being forced to stay with him tonight, as there was no way she could get home alone during the hours of the curfew. She presumed to her horror that he was probably expecting to receive sex from her as payment for the evening.

This was a serious situation. She was still a virgin and did not want to lose this precious gift to this Gestapo monster, or indeed to any man whom she did not love.

"Here we are, my dear," he announced as they arrived outside an extremely grand looking building. "Come." He held out his hand to guide her, but she ignored it and walked unaided.

Upon entering the building, if the outside looked grand then the interior would be described as lavish. Yvette had to agree with the man accompanying her, this place really was far better that he Hotel Paradiso.

There was a young man sitting behind a desk in the foyer who Yvette thought must be the doorman. She estimated him to be about eighteen years of age and at this moment she thought he'd just woken from a deep sleep. He looked shocked to see the officer had entered the building and quickly jumped to attention.

"Guten Abend, Herr Schtipe," he addressed the officer in German, but with a broad French accent.

"Guten Nacht," Max von Schtipe corrected. Yvette looked away and raised her hand, not wanting her face seen by this young man.

"Come, my dear," von Schtipe said whilst leading Yvette towards the old, almost antiquated lift positioned in the corner of the reception area.

He pulled back the sliding gate, invited her inside and duly followed her, pulling the gate closed behind him. She watched him press button six, the highest button available, which made her think they must be going to the top floor.

"I hope this thing will get us there," she remarked making a joke, at which he let out a small snigger.

When they reached the top floor, the lift came to a shudder and stopped. It did not offer the most elegant of arrivals for a building of this quality and grandeur, but at least it had taken them there safely.

"Come, my dear," he said again. She noted he did like using this phrase.

She followed him along a corridor until they came to a rather fine looking entrance door, where emblazoned upon it in gold lettering were the words, 'Penthouse Suite.' Yvette considered if this sign had been added after the present occupier had stolen it, or whether the original 'legal' owner had placed it there before the occupation.

Max von Schtipe put the key in the lock, turned it anti-clockwise and pushed the heavy door open.

"Please, come in," he invited, to which she did as was requested.

Once inside the apartment, Yvette was able to take a good look around the place. What she saw both shocked and amazed her in equal measures. The first thing she noticed was the quality of the carpet. It seemed to wrap itself around her feet as she glided over it, sinking into her as she moved around feeling its luxury.

As she studied the apartment, taking in more detail she noticed four large patches covering the walls. She surmised these patches were once paintings, works of art which had been stolen by the authorities and were now part of a collection somewhere, probably never to be seen again by the Parisian public.

This made Yvette really angry. What right did the enemy authorities have for doing this to people whose only crime was to be born under the Jewish faith? This apartment was obviously once owned by people who had worked hard all their lives to provide them and their families with a good standard of living, only to have had it all stolen away from them.

These poor souls were more than likely now rotting away in a German prison, or worse, they could have suffered death at the hands of these monsters on the inside of a prisoner of war gas chamber!

How she hated these Nazis, and how she despised Max von Schtipe for having the audacity to now be living in the luxury afforded to him by these innocent people.

Continuing her search of the apartment, Yvette looked at the beautiful furnishings, high quality leather armchairs finished with a huge ten seated, very beautiful oak table, where she imagined the previous occupants enjoyed many social gatherings with their friends before the occupation. She now thought that most, if not all these friends, were now no longer with us.

She noticed that Schtipe had appeared from the kitchen carrying two large glasses of wine.

"Here you are my dear," she heard him announce.

"Thank you," she replied politely, all the time thinking about how she could get away from this man.

"What do you think about my apartment?" he questioned. "Do you like it?"

'Your apartment?' she thought to herself without actually saying the words. Instead she heard herself say, "It's very beautiful."

This made him smile. "Yes, it is," she heard him reply.

"Do you live here alone?" she questioned.

"Yes I do," he replied suspiciously. "Why do you want to know this?"

"I'm just curious," she lied. What she really wanted to know was whether it was likely or not that they would be disturbed during the next hour or so.

Suddenly, his demeanour changed. "Take off your clothes!" he demanded.

"What?" She was shocked. "What do you mean?"

"I mean, take off your clothes and get naked!" Schtipe demanded again.

Yvette's mind went into overdrive. How was she going to get herself out of this dilemma? She instantly thought about Madame Chambourcey and her stories of her own adventures during the last war.

"Remember my dear, these men are bored with their lives," Madame Chambourcey had begun, before continuing. "They are so fed up with everyone taking orders from them and no one giving orders to them that I used to boss these men around and they loved it! If you get the chance, you should give it a go."

Although Yvette agreed with everything that Madame Chambourcey advised the girl, she did think that 'giving it a go' might not be too wise a recommendation for her during these proceedings!

"Take off your clothes and bend over the table," Schtipe commanded.

"You take your clothes off and bend over the table," Yvette replied defiantly. She was angry now and he knew it, although he did very quickly become really excited.

"My dear, what are you trying to do to me?" he questioned with a wry smile.

"You met me straight from the Hotel Paradiso," Yvette divulged. "You came with me to the Moulin Rouge and now you're trying to get amorous with me. I'm not having this."

He looked gobsmacked as she continued. "The very least you need is to freshen up and have a good wash."

"Why don't you join me?" he questioned hopefully. "We can bathe together."

"No," she replied. "You go and have a good wash whilst I prepare some more drinks for us. We can relax for a while and get to know each other a little better."

Like a dutiful dog, Schtipe made his way to the bathroom. While he did so, Yvette collected their glasses and gave them a thoroughly good scrubbing. She then took them to the kitchen and fetched a good bottle of Bordeaux from the cupboard.

Having to work fast before the monster returned, she quickly opened the bottle and poured two small glasses of the strong tasting liquid into the two drinking vessels. She then felt for the sleeve of her blouse and was reassured to feel the cyanide capsule still inserted inside. Taking out the capsule, she unscrewed the top and poured the liquid inside one of the glasses, making doubly sure to select the glass only intended for Schtipe to consume. She then placed the two glasses on the table and waited for his return.

"Now, where were we?" he questioned upon returning from the bathroom, his body still glistening with the excess water.

"We were about to get naked," Yvette claimed, building his excitement into a crescendo.

"So come on girl, let's get to it," he stressed. She could almost see his manhood, now throbbing from below his dressing gown.

"Calm down, Herr Schtipe," Yvette ordered. "Let's you and me have a little drink first."

As she said this, she raised her glass and gestured for Schtipe to do the same, hoping that he would not take a small sip, but down the drink 'in one.'

"Prost," she declared, raising her glass and aiming it towards him.

"Prost," he replied.

Herr Max van Schtipe of the Gestapo then picked up the glass and like a good German, he downed it. Instantly he grabbed at his throat and began gasping for air. He looked horrified, and in his last dying seconds he looked at Yvette accusingly.

"Yes, you Nazi bastard," she said. "You have just been murdered by Yvette Jackson of the French Resistance!"

She watched as Schtipe's body fell completely limp. The life drained from his eyes and he slumped into a chair in the corner of the room. The miserable Nazi bastard was dead!

CHAPTER 18
A NEW DAY DAWNS

Yvette looked at the large clock on the mantelpiece and noticed the time. It was just after one o'clock in the morning and she realised she still had to wait almost four hours before the end of the curfew. She had no choice but to sit it out and wait for the nightly blackout to come to an end. Attempting to leave the building any earlier would surely result in her suicide.

She suddenly had a thought. Even though Schtipe had told her he had solo occupancy of this apartment, could she be sure of this? Could she risk her life assuming that he did? Was Max von Schtipe living alone in this luxury, or was he sharing this apartment with another Nazi officer who might come home at any minute? She had no choice but to take hold of his gun and sit in the darkness, waiting in silence in case anyone came crashing through the door.

The night seemed to be never ending, with Yvette listening to every creak and cracking sounds of the building, as it echoed through the rooms.

Without letting go of Schtipe's pistol, after her eyes had adjusted themselves to the darkness she made her way to the balcony to take a better look at the surrounding area which she'd temporarily inhabited.

Slowly and as quietly as possible, she slid open the French windows and found herself outside on a large balcony overlooking the River Seine. More importantly, not too far in the distance, even though it was no longer illuminated during the hours of the curfew, she could clearly see the outline of the Eiffel Tower and knew she was close to the Café DuPont and so hopefully, relative safety.

As her eyes adjusted even more to the light she could just about make out the silhouette of another large dining table, this one almost as grand as the one inside the apartment, where Yvette imagined the previous occupants enjoying even more lavish dinner parties and having fun with their friends and relatives, before all this dangerous stupidity began.

The area outside the apartment block was deathly quiet with no sound coming from this side of the building, although Yvette had no idea what was happening on the other side. However, she was sure that as the morning went on, the amount of troops gathering in the streets below would have been gaining momentum.

Back inside the apartment now, she looked at the body of Schtipe lying limp and slumped on the seat. She knew she had to do something about this, knowing that she couldn't just leave him here in this state.

Making her way to the bathroom where the officer had been only an hour or so earlier, she looked around in the cupboards to see what she might find. Although she found nothing belonging to Schtipe she came across a bottle of pills with the name 'Cohen' emblazoned upon it. Giving the bottle of pills a reassuring shake, she returned to the living area and sprinkled the tablets around the arm of the sofa, also placing a few inside the Nazis mouth, although she had no idea of why this man would have attempted to commit suicide, but this was not her problem.

Finally, after listening to the sound of the large mantelpiece clock slowly ticking the night away, it was time for her to make her departure back into the streets below.

After first checking to make sure there were no signs of her ever being inside the apartment, she made her way down the stairs. Avoiding the lift, she walked down the six flights of stairs to make sure nobody would intercept her on the journey. However, she was angry with herself when she eventually found herself back in the reception area, after hoping there might be a different exit to use.

Just about to leave through the reception area, she was

interrupted by the same young man who'd spoken with Herr Max von Schtipe when he'd entered the building a few hours earlier.

"Good morning Madam," the young man announced. He'd clearly just woken from his slumber. Yvette tried to ignore him but he persevered. "I hope you had a good evening?" he questioned. She didn't know what to do, but knew she had to do something.

"What is your name?" she asked the young man.

"My name is Alain," he replied curiously but courteously.

"Well Alain, if you were to look inside the Penthouse Suite on the sixth floor, then you would find the dead body of Herr Max von Schtipe of the Gestapo."

As she revealed this, she pulled out the gun from the bag she was carrying and pointed it towards the young man's head.

"He's dead?" Alain questioned incredulously before seeing the gun, which was now pointed in his direction.

"Yes, Alain, he's dead," she confirmed. "Now, I do not want to kill you, but I will if I have to. Do I have to kill you, Alain?" she asked, trying to sound as calm as she possibly could.

"I really hope not," he replied, by now physically shaking.

"Okay, then here's what we can do," Yvette began. "You do nothing."

"Nothing?" he gasped.

"Nothing," she confirmed. "You wait until someone complains about the smell coming from the apartment. This should take at least three to four days. Can you do this?"

"Yes Madame," Alain replied.

"Are you sure you can do this?" Yvette queried sternly.

"Yes Madame," Alain repeated, but this time with total honesty.

"Good," Yvette stated, but then continued. "If you don't do this and you choose to call the authorities as soon as I leave this building, then believe me when I tell you that you will be dead before this day is through! Do you understand this?"

"Yes Madame," he agreed again, but then what could he say?

"Then I will not kill you at this time," she stated, placing the pistol back inside her bag. "But please be warned!"

"Thank you," the relieved young man said.

By now she was shaking almost as much as Alain, although trying her best not to show it.

This was not Yvette, she was not this person! Only a few months ago she was having fun at the University in England with her big bosomed friend, Jennifer Rumsey, partying the nights away and having fun with the boys. Now she was here in Paris, threatening to kill innocent people like Alain, and this after leaving the dead body of Herr Max von Schtipe of the Gestapo rotting away in the Penthouse Suite.

How had this happened? This was never supposed to have happened to her. She hated this war so much and no longer wanted to be a part of it. Yet here she was, stuck in the middle of all this craziness and seemingly with no way out.

"Now, show me how I can get to the river bank from here," Yvette requested of Alain.

The young man, after taking a good look around and checking to make sure there were no German troops milling about close to the building, pointed the girl in the direction she needed to go in order to get down to the banks of the river.

"Thank you," she said, still feeling guilty about scaring the young man half to death and probably scarring him forever.

After reaching the banks of the Seine, Yvette immediately began feeling more self conscious about the way she was looking. The long evening dress, which she'd borrowed from Nicole DuPont the evening before, now looked far too long and far too dressy. Looking around to confirm she was alone, she hitched up the dress and tied it so it hung just above the knee length coat she wore. She was really thankful she'd worn this coat, firstly it was nice and warm on this cold November evening, and secondly because it was rather drab and plain, so practically unnoticeable by any Nazis she might encounter along the way.

After walking for a further fifteen minutes she found a bushy area on the bank, a thick patch of grass which she thought could be a good place for losing the wig. Despite really hoping that the young man she'd met earlier, Alain, might keep his word and not report her to the authorities, she still felt it would be a good idea to lose the long, straight black hair which Herr Schtipe knew her for, and to replace it with her own natural curly blonde locks.

As soon as she was able to do this, she breathed a sigh of relief. She was no longer Yvette of the Hotel Paradiso, now she was Yvette Colbert of the Café DuPont, even though she considered this would not be a position held for much longer.

After ditching the wig she had another dilemma, and this was a major one – what to do with the pistol? Should she hang on to it in case questioned by one of the guards? If this happened, she would either have to kill or be killed. My word, how she hated this game!

In the end she decided to keep the pistol nestled inside the bag she was carrying and just try to get back to the DuPont as fast as her legs would carry her. This seemed more difficult than she first thought. It was like an optical illusion for the girl, as the more she walked towards the Eiffel Tower, the further away it seemed to become. Eventually however, before reaching the structure, she recognised the area where the café could be found and headed towards it.

Now the butterflies really did begin to dance a merry jig. With every step made closer to the Café DuPont, it was a step closer to seeing Henri. How on earth was she going to tell him that she'd just killed a man – and a Nazi at that?

Finally, after reaching the back entrance of the building, the entrance to the bakery, Yvette pushed the door open and stepped inside.

After slowly opening the door to the bakery, she was hit by the intense heat coming from the oven. Henri was standing there having just removed a plate of croissants and placing them on the shelf to cool before replacing them for a third time that morning to bake even more. He was shocked to see Yvette come through the door, still dressed in the same clothes which she'd worn the night before.

"Yvette, I thought you were upstairs with Luisa. Where have you been all night?" he asked suspiciously.

"Oh, Henri," she cried, trying hard not to break down.

As he looked at the girl, Henri DuPont witnessed the sight of her collapsing into a heap as she burst into tears. She was totally inconsolable.

"What on earth has happened, child?" he queried, throwing his arms around her to comfort the girl.

After removing her from the heat of the kitchen and leading her into the relative coolness of the café, Henri listened intently as Yvette told him everything. She thought he would be angry, but no. "Nazi bastard!" was all he said.

They were soon joined by both Nicole and Luisa, who had come to discover what all the commotion was about. The two listened in shock and horror as the story was repeated for their benefit.

"One thing's for sure," Nicole began after receiving all the information about what had happened during the previous evening, "you can never return to the Hotel Paradiso, not ever again."

Yvette woke a couple of hours later. Although she didn't think she would be able to, she'd fallen into a deep sleep within seconds of her head hitting the pillow.

Still in a deep state of drowsiness, as she looked through the window at the blue skies of Paris, she thought about the night before. Had it all been a dream? Had it really happened? Was Schtipe really dead or had she imagined it?

"Morning sleepy," she heard a voice say. It was Luisa.

"Good morning. How long have I been sleeping for?" Yvette questioned.

"It's now ten-thirty, so I guess around three hours," Luisa replied.

"Shit!" Yvette cried out. "I should be at work now in the café."

"Don't worry, it's been taken care of. Henri decided you needed to sleep more than you needed to work," Luisa instructed.

"How is he? Is he angry?" Yvette questioned, concerned to discover the answer.

"On the contrary, far from it," Luisa disclosed. "He is very angry, but not with you."

"Angry with whom then, Luisa, I have just killed a man." As she said this, she started to shake. "My God, I have just killed a man!" she repeated, as the reality of what she'd done finally hit home.

"But he deserved it," Luisa sympathised. "That man, Schtipe, was a Nazi and a monster!"

Luisa put her arm around Yvette as the girl curled up cat like into a ball, lay on the bed and began sobbing. The poor girl was inconsolable.

Yvette was left to her own devices for another couple of days. She knew the situation could not stay like this for too much longer, but she still couldn't lift this depression which was still hanging over her. She had to get back to work in the café, both for Nicole and Henri's sake, but also more importantly for the resistance and the cause.

Early the next morning she rose from her bed, dressed in her uniform, and was just about to leave for the café when Nicole came rushing into the room.

"Stay here Yvette," the older woman pleaded.

"Is there a problem?" Luisa questioned with caution.

"Yes, is there a problem, Nicole?" Yvette asked nervously.

"Not really a problem, but Herr Gruber has come to the café," Nicole confirmed. "You know how he is with you, Yvette, so it might be a good idea to keep away from him for a while."

"How he is with me?" the girl queried. "Whatever do you mean?"

"Oh come on child, are you really that naive?" Nicole interrogated.

"What do you mean?" Yvette questioned again.

"You must know that Gruber fancies you," Nicole stated.

"Fancies me?" Yvette pleaded.

"Of course he fancies you," Nicole confirmed. "You can see the way he looks at you and that he would love to take you to his bed and make mad passionate love to you."

"Ooooohhhhh," Yvette could only make a noise, disgusted by the thought of what she'd just heard.

"As you have just been forced to kill one Nazi, it might be a good idea not to be put into the position where you have to kill another high ranking officer of the Gestapo!" Nicole said, somewhat sarcastically.

Yvette did not answer but just removed her uniform and prepared to go back to sleep, whilst Luisa and Nicole made their way back down the wooden stairs to the café.

When they arrived, Nicole was slightly concerned to see Herr Gruber deep in conversation with Henri. She strained her neck to try to better hear what they were talking about, but could only catch little snippets of the dialogue.

"Monsieur DuPont, I haven't seen Yvette for a day or two," Herr Gruber remarked to Henri. "I trust she's in good health?"

"Yes Sir," Henri replied. "She is fine, Herr Gruber, but she's taken a couple of days away from the café as she is worried about her mother."

"Her mother," Gruber questioned. "What is the problem with her mother?"

"I'm not sure exactly, but I do know that she is not very well and Yvette is worried about her," Henri lied, whilst quickly thinking on his feet.

"Well, please give her my best wishes," the man of the Gestapo offered.

"Thank you I will, Herr Gruber," Henri commented.

"And please offer my best wishes for the health of Yvette's mother, should you see her," were Gruber's final words on the matter as he returned to his table and to his freshly prepared bratwurst.

Henri made a mental note to speak to the girl as soon as possible and to make it known to her as to what he and Herr Gruber had been speaking about.

"So what am I going to do?" Yvette questioned Henri a little later, after he'd come to talk with her. "If you think I should disappear, then that is what I must do. But go where? Where will I go?"

Henri looked deep in thought, contemplating what he should do. Then inspiration suddenly came to him when he said," You must go to the apartment where Philippe Barstrom stayed," Monsieur DuPont announced. "You can stay there."

"How long should I stay there?"Yvette asked.

"You must stay for a few days, maybe a week," Henri told the girl.

"But will I be safe there?" Yvette questioned. "I still remember Philippe being executed at the hands of that Nazi monster," she stated. "I will never forget the look in his eyes as he looked straight at me at his point of execution. That is something I will never forget."

"I agree that must have been harrowing for you, but you must forget it now," Henri demanded. "Yu must go to the apartment owned by Claude Proust. I will have Luisa take you there as soon as we can organise it."

That was the end of the conversation. Yvette watched as Henri DuPont left her room and returned to take his place in the bakery, ready to continue with baking his bread, cakes, his tasty croissants and of course, his very tasty Bratwurst sausage.

CHAPTER 19
SIX DAYS AND SIX LONG NIGHTS

Yvette felt extremely nervous as she walked through the streets of Paris. This was the first time since she'd arrived at the Gare du Nord train station in the Rue de Maubeuge that she'd not been disguised in her long black wig. Now she was making her way along the road 'naked' in her natural blonde curly hair. Because of this, she felt strangely vulnerable.

She kept looking to the girl on her left hand side for some kind of reassurance and was very glad to have the beautiful Luisa Silva by her side, guiding her and keeping her company. Even so, she still felt like every German soldier on the street that day was staring at her and scrutinizing her every move with great suspicion.

"Try to relax, Yvette," Luisa pleaded, seeing her friend's obvious uneasiness.

"How can I relax when I know that every man here wants to kill me?" Yvette claimed.

"Don't be silly," Luisa demanded. "Why would they think that?"

"Because I killed one of them," Yvette pointed out. "I murdered that man, Schtipe."

"He was not a man he was a Nazi, and a murdering bastard monster at that!" Luisa retaliated.

"But I still killed him," Yvette argued, feeling a little sorry for herself.

After a further forty-five minutes walk, after reaching a cobbled side street the two girls arrived at a rather shabby, depressing and dilapidated looking building, situated in an area known as, 'Louvre.'

"Come on, let's get inside," Luisa instructed.

Yvette meekly followed her friend inside the dark, dank and

dismal interior. Her first observation was the smell. It stank to high heaven!

"What is that stench?" Yvette questioned, turning up her nose as if to exaggerate the foul, odorous pong.

Luisa had to admit that during the past couple of years of the enemy occupation, this building was no longer the pleasant place to live as it had once been. It now contained a musty smell, which Yvette claimed was like the 'stench of death!' One of the good things about this however, was the fact that not even the lowest ranked of the German soldiers wanted to live here. It really was that bad.

"No, it smells more like dog piss!" said Luisa, making the observation. This made Yvette laugh.

"Oh Luisa, you are so funny sometimes," she remarked.

"That's better," Luisa gestured. "It's good to see you laughing again."

"I'll remember that when they put me up against a wall and shoot me," Yvette said sarcastically.

"Oh my friend, please pull yourself together," Luisa demanded. "I hate to think of you like this."

They walked up the three flights of a very unsafe staircase until reaching an even shabbier looking front door, the entrance of the apartment which was still owned by Claude Proust and last occupied by the young, and now very much deceased, Philippe Barstrom.

"What a shithole!" Yvette expressed after they'd first pushed the door open and stepped through the entrance.

"I have to agree with you my friend, but we can clean it and make it more respectable," Luisa advised.

"Yes we can, but we will not be able to clean that paint off the table," Yvette stressed.

She was correct. Practically every work surface was covered, not in paint, but what Yvette would later discover was printing ink, the very ink which Claude Proust had used to print his 'Adolph Hitler' propaganda posters which very nearly cost him his life, but also indirectly cost the lives of the two young brothers, Philippe Barstrom and his older brother, René.

"Open the window, Yvette," Luisa requested.

"Do you think we should," her friend queried.

Luisa walked to the window and moved the curtains slightly, not too much, but just enough to be able to see the street below. She could make out that the positioning of this apartment was not at the front of the building where they'd arrived, but was at the back.

On the ground level there was a shop selling fruit and vegetables, although mainly to the enemy troops who could afford to buy them. Above this shop there was an awning, which when the shop was open, was fully extended and completely covered any view of the third floor apartment. However, when the shop closed later in the evening, this window which Luisa was staring through would be clearly visible for anyone in the street below to see, should they wish to look up to discover if anyone was in occupancy, if they wished to do so.

"I will make sure to keep the curtains closed at night," Yvette promised.

"There will be no point in that," Luisa instructed.

"Why?" Yvette questioned.

"There is no electric, so the only light you will have will be the light of a candle," Luisa informed her friend.

"Bloody Hell, it's like living back in the dark ages!" Yvette exclaimed, which made Luisa laugh out loud.

Yvette moved from the living room area where the dining table was found, and went to explore the rest of the apartment. The first thing she noticed was the size of this place. She thought about that fateful night with Herr Schtipe and surmised that the entirety of this apartment would have easily fitted inside the bathroom of that place known as 'The Penthouse Suite.' Compared to that dwelling, this place was smaller than tiny!

Reaching the bedroom, she fell backwards onto the bed. The mattress was surprisingly comfy, with absolutely no springs poking through. Yvette considered this to be a bonus.

The bathroom was adequate, although she decided it did warrant at least one full day of cleaning to make it even the slightest bit hospitable for the girl.

"So what do you think?" Luisa asked her friend when she re-entered the living room.

"It will be okay for a few days, but I don't want to stay here for too much longer than that," Yvette replied, to which Luisa made no comment. She knew her friend might well have to stay here in hiding for a lot longer than, 'a few days.'

Luisa watched as Yvette unpacked a few things from her bag, but was shocked when one item was removed.

"What the.......?" she began, but was too shocked to continue with her question, as she noticed Yvette had removed a gun from her bag.

"This is my insurance," Yvette revealed.

"But it's a gun!"

"I know."

"But where did you get it?" Luisa asked, eager for information.

"I took it from Herr Schtipe and carried it home in my bag that morning, just to make sure," Yvette told her attentive friend.

"But Yvette, what would have happened should we have been stopped on the streets?" Luisa asked, angry now to think that her friend had put her in great danger without her prior knowledge.

"I would have walked away from you and disassociated myself from you my friend," Yvette replied with honesty. "I would never have put you in danger."

"But what about now, what do you intend to do with that gun now?" Luisa questioned.

"I will sit here all day and all night, waiting for German

soldiers to burst through this door and apprehend me," Yvette stated. "I have only six bullets available, so should the worst happen, I can kill five of the invaders and use the sixth bullet on myself."

"What do you mean?" a worried Luisa asked.

"Suicide," was the shocking reply.

"You cannot do that," Luisa begged.

"I can, and I will," Yvette stated.

She remembered that day at the training camp when she believed she'd been captured by the Gestapo, tortured and eventually taken outside and stood against a post waiting to be executed.

She clearly recollected how she'd heard the Gestapo officer order the firing squad to take aim and then fire, only to hear the sound of seven rifles being shot but receiving no pain, as the guns all contained blanks and it was all part of a training exercise which she'd passed 'with flying colours.'

"Believe me, Luisa, if the enemy come here and attempt to capture me, they will not take me alive! They will NEVER take me alive!" Yvette stated, whilst Luisa listened.

Every day, Luisa went about her normal routine. Each morning she rose early, dressed in her waitress uniform and went down to work in the café, where she spent five or six hours being pleasant to the German patrons, men she wouldn't spit on even if they were on fire!

How she hated these monsters. She despised the way they 'accidentally' brushed the back of their hands against her ass as she passed them whilst carrying their food. However, she had to be nice to them and smile politely at heir indiscretions, whilst really wanting to pick up a large kitchen knife and drive it straight through their hearts!

When the café closed for a few hours in the afternoon, after resting for half an hour or so, she made her way back down to the kitchen and helped herself to a few freshly baked items from the oven and made Yvette some tasty cheese and ham baguettes. She then loaded them into the bread basket of her bicycle to take to Claude Proust's apartment, currently being used by her friend.

All the time whist Yvette waited for Luisa and the food to arrive; she sat on in a chair and continuously stared at the back of the entrance door, listening for any unwanted sounds she might hear coming from the corridor outside.

All the time she waited, the pistol was never further than an arm's length away. She was ready for any occurrence that might happen.

She was alerted by a gentle tap on the door but ignored it. She heard it again. Tap-Tap–Tap she noticed. She then heard the welcome, soothing and gentle sound of Luisa calling to her.

"Yvette, let me in," her friend requested.

"Are you alone?" Yvette questioned.

"Of course I am," Luisa confirmed as she heard the click of the lock turning, followed by the door being opened just enough for her friend to look through the crack to check to see if Luisa was indeed alone or not. She was.

"Please, come in," Yvette requested, and Luisa entered the room.

Immediately, Yvette returned to, and took her place back in the armchair where she'd spent the night and continued to nurse the firearm placed within easy reach on the table to her right hand side.

"You still have the gun then," Luisa stated obviously.

"Of course," Yvette replied. "It's my insurance."

"Have you been sitting here all night?" Luisa questioned.

"Yes, apart from using the bathroom, I haven't moved a muscle," Yvette replied.

"You need to sleep," Luisa instructed.

"How can I sleep?" Yvette pleaded. "The street outside was very noisy last night. There must be a bar close by and it sounded like it was full of drunk German soldiers partying the night away."

"Did you get any sleep?" a concerned Luisa questioned.

"I think I must have dosed off at some point throughout the night, but the people walking up and down the hallway corridor kept interrupting me," Yvette divulged. "I don't know who they were, but they come really close to me shooting them. I was ready!"

"Don't do that for heaven sake, they are only normal people who live here," Luisa pointed out to her friend.

"What d you mean?" questioned Yvette. "You mean other people live here?"

"Of course," her friend confirmed.

"Germans?" she questioned.

"No, French people also live here," Luisa revealed. "They are mainly elderly couples or middle aged single women."

"Where are their husbands?" Yvette queried.

"Either dead, or they have been taken away to work in the factories in Germany," Luisa answered.

"Bastards," Yvette motioned. "So no Germans are living here?"

"Germans," Luisa remarked. "Why would German troops choose to live in this shithole when they are living in the comfort of places like the Hotel Paradiso?"

"The Paradiso, I'd almost forgotten about that place," Yvette reminisced.

"Anyway, I have brought food for you," Luisa told her friend, presenting her with a basket containing a couple of croissants, a few baguettes and some cakes, all of which, Yvette was eternally grateful for.

"Thank you, Luisa," she said.

Luisa stayed with her companion for an hour or so whilst Yvette devoured the food, although she saved some for later that day.

"I will return tomorrow," she told her friend in hiding, as she walked towards the door.

After checking that the coast was clear, when she was sure, she smiled at Yvette in an attempt to reassure her that everything would be okay and then left, with Yvette closing the door firmly behind her and resuming her position in the armchair, with gun in hand.

Luisa came downstairs to begin the morning shift at the café as usual, something she had to do on a daily basis now that Yvette was no longer available to perform her work. As she entered the dining room, an unusual sight greeted her.

"What's going on?" she asked her boss.

"I'm not sure," Nicole replied. "But they don't look happy."

Luisa could see at least eight high ranking officers were all crowding around the table currently being occupied by Herr Gruber of the Gestapo, and as Nicole had stated, he was indeed not looking happy.

"Try and get a little closer and see if you can hear what they are talking about," Nicole requested of the younger girl.

Luisa, doing as was asked of her, picked up a cloth and began wiping the tables around her, slowly edging towards the eight angry men now huddled together in a group, all in deep and heated discussion.

Suddenly, she heard the word 'Suicide' mentioned and she heard Gruber banging his fist angrily down on the table. She decided to return to the relative safety of Nicole, who immediately went to the bakery and called to her husband.

"What is it?" Henri asked his wife with a curious expression on his face.

"You should speak with your friend, Gruber," Nicole requested, and Henri made his way to the dining area of the café.

"Is there a problem, Herr Gruber?" Henri questioned, after tentatively approaching the normally gentle, polite (with Henri) and well spoken officer.

"What?" Gruber demanded angrily.

"I'm sorry, Herr Gruber. Sorry to interrupt you, but I'm just wondering if there is something wrong with your food or the service here today," Henri stressed, whilst lying through his teeth.

"Not at all, Henri," Gruber stated and then continued to say, "I am sorry my friend, it's just that I have received some bad news this morning."

"I'm sorry to hear this, Sir, is there anything I can do to help?" Henri questioned.

"Nothing for you to worry about," Gruber stressed. "I have just been informed that one of my men has been found dead in his department."

"I'm sorry to hear this. Did he suffer a heart attack?" Henri asked.

"No, but why do you ask that?" Gruber returned, a little confused by the question.

"Because all your men stationed here in Paris are extremely young and fit, so why else would one of them die if not caused by a heart attack?" Henri replied, very happy to have paid the Nazi a complement, although not at all meaning it.

"Not a heart attack, Henri, more serious than that" Gruber confirmed. "It was suicide."

"Suicide," Henri said, making Luisa's ears prick up.

"Yes, suicide," Gruber repeated. "He took the cowards way out and took his own life."

"What happened," Henri questioned, instantly wondering if he was correct to do so, or maybe pushing his luck a little too far, although Herr Gruber seemed happy to answer is query.

"He was found in his apartment by a couple of residents complaining about the smell, and was discovered with an empty bottle of wine lying by his side. He stank of the stuff. He also had a mouthful of tablets which he never even finished swallowing." Gruber looked at Henri and tried to give him a smile but was unable to.

"What a terrible way to go," was all Henri could offer.

"It was a coward's way to go," Herr Gruber shouted, bringing his fist forcibly down on the table again, as the anger returned to his voice.

"But we have arrested a suspect," another of the officers announced, instantly regretting saying this as Gruber gave him a blood curdling stare.

"Yes," Gruber said, giving the confirmation. "When the neighbours complained about the smell coming from the apartment, there was a young man working on the reception desk and he went to take a look. Obviously, when he arrived and used his pass key to gain entrance to the apartment, he found Herr Schtipe was now long deceased and had been so for at least four days."

When Luisa heard the name 'Schtipe' being bandied about, she immediately thought of Yvette and her involvement in the death of the Nazi, so strained to better hear what Herr Gruber was saying.

"When the Gestapo arrived with the doctor who pronounced Schtipe as dead, they noticed something was missing," Gruber revealed.

"What was missing?" Henri queried, again instantly regretting his line of questioning.

"His gun was missing," Gruber stated. "And there is no way he would not have had his gun with him."

So, what happened to it?" Henri asked, even though one or two of the other officers were by now looking at him with suspicion, as well as disdain.

"The young man on reception must have stolen it. That's the only explanation possible," Gruber replied. "He pleaded his innocence of course, but was arrested and taken away to Gestapo headquarters for further interrogation."

"And what happened to him?" questioned the café owner.

"He is either on a train bound for Germany, probably to work in the munitions factory in Düsseldorf as slave labour; or my guess is that he is more likely dead, taken into the woods and shot by firing squad," Gruber said this with a wry smile, before continuing. "Wherever he is, we are all well rid of the thieving bastard!"

As Luisa listened to this she thought about Yvette. She couldn't wait to tell her friend all about these revelations. As soon as the café closed and her shift was over, she made her way to the apartment in Louvre to deliver this news.

"Alain," Yvette said. "His name was Alain."

"Whose name was Alain?" Luisa asked of her still beautiful, but by now slightly smelly friend.

It was obvious that Yvette had not washed now for at least six days and was smelling quite ripe! Six days was also the amount of time she'd spent sitting in the armchair without sleeping in a bed. The poor girl was exhausted, almost to the point of tears.

"Alain was the name of the young man the Nazis arrested and took away for interrogation," Yvette explained. "The poor man never had a chance. I have the gun he was protesting his innocence about, I have it here." As she said this, she moved her right arm towards the gun, as if to prove its existence.

"There was nothing you could do," Luisa offered.

"Of course there was. I killed him as sure as my pointing the gun at his head and pulling the trigger," Yvette stressed.

"Rather him than you," Luisa returned.

"Why? What had he done to deserve dying for?" Yvette questioned. "All he ever did was open the door for Schtipe to let him into the building, and now he's dead. I killed him!" she repeated.

"But he might not be dead," Luisa interrupted. "Herr Gruber told Henri that he was maybe taken away and transported to

Germany to work as slave labour in a factory there."

"Maybe! – Maybe! – Maybe!" Yvette stressed. "There is no maybe about it. I know, and you know that Alain is dead and it's my fault."

"Would you rather it was you who the Nazis shot?" Luisa demanded.

"Yes," Yvette replied, shocking her friend.

"Yvette," Luisa pleaded, but was forced to listen as she continued.

"I hate this bloody war. I hate everything about it. I should not be here. I should be at my university studying medicine, not here in Paris killing Germans and causing the death of innocent young Parisian men!"

"So what is it you want to do?" Luisa questioned.

"I want to go home," said Yvette

"Go home to England?" Luisa asked.

"Yes," Yvette confirmed.

"Well, my beautiful friend, there are only two ways for you to be able to return to England," Luisa stipulated. "One way is in a body bag."

"And what is the second way?" Yvette questioned.

"You have to knuckle down, take the resistance seriously and fight for them against the enemy, kick these Nazis out of France amd win this bloody war," Luisa raged, losing her temper now. "Then and only then will you be able to return to England and resume your life back there."

As she said this, Yvette could see how angry she now was. She also knew that what she was saying made a lot of sense.

"Then that is what I have to do," she admitted to Luisa. "I will fight for my freedom and we will win this bloody war."

CHAPTER 20
A FAREWELL TO PARIS

The train began to pick up momentum as it gathered speed. Yvette felt as though she was able to breathe again as she left the outskirts of the city and approached the countryside, leaving the streets, smells and hopefully the problems of occupied Paris behind.

She'd been accompanied by Luisa, as the two now inseparable friends both made their way to the Gare du Nord, the main train station at the Rue de Maubeuge.

As she arrived at the station, once again surrounded by many German soldiers of the enemy wandering about the place, she remembered and thought about Philippe Barstrom, the young boy whom had met her from the train that day when she'd arrived in Paris all those many months ago.

She remembered that fateful day when she saw him in the street, down on his knees and about to be executed. Even though she didn't really like Philippe, or even got on with him, she still strongly admired his bravery. He'd faced death that day as a man, even though he was still just a young boy of only fifteen years of age.

Yvette looked up at the overhead luggage compartment and smiled when she saw the small suitcase she carried. She was happy, in fact she was overjoyed to see that this time it only contained her clothes and not the 'guns' she thought it contained on her previous journey to Paris, that day when the Nazi officer had assisted by picking the case up for her, carrying it onboard the train and depositing it in the overhead luggage compartment.

She smiled again when she recollected how what she suspected were four guns being transported in the case, turned out to be a completely innocent set of 'French Boules,' placed inside the suitcase to make her think they were guns and so testing her nerve with the extra weight.

She smiled as she thought there would be no problems for her today. This should be a far more leisurely trip, with nothing for her to worry about. On this journey she carried only legal papers, prepared and supplied by the men and women at the offices of 'The Department of Fish & Fisheries,' albeit in the name of Yvette Colbert and not that of her real name, Yvette Jackson. These papers gave her permission to travel from the German occupied zone and through the Demarcation Line and into the Vichy area of the country, known as the 'Free Zone.'

Although she was on this train bound for Lyon, in reality she would be disembarking at a station called, Grouville, a station about fifty miles past the Demarcation Line and around fifty miles short of the beautiful city of Lyon. Although not as far as journeys end, it was still a good seven hours from Paris, so she was able to relax, settle down and enjoy a nice sleep.

"When you arrive at Grouville, you will be meeting a man named Patrice Bauton," Henri DuPont had announced previously to the girl. "When you leave the train, you will leave the platform and make your way to the exit. When there, Patrice will look for the pretty girl with the blonde hair and he will find you."

"But what if he's not there waiting for me?" Yvette questioned.

"He will be. Don't worry," Henri reassured the girl.

"Okay," Yvette answered with caution.

"From there, he will take you to the village," Henri told her.

"The village," Yvette repeated, and then begged the question. "What village?"

"Never you mind, my girl," Henri remarked. "You just be ready."

At that time, Yvette thought that Henri appeared to be a little angry with her for all that had happened in her life since her arrival in Paris, but what more could she have done? She'd been sent there to be a radio operator and nothing more, and as far as she was concerned, she'd completed that task and done all that had been asked of her.

It wasn't her fault that that bastard Nazi, Herr Schtipe had felt a lust for her and could not control his sexual urges. What was she supposed to do, lay back and think of England whilst allowing him to rape her? No, that would never have happened. She would never have allowed that, and she hadn't!

When it came to the final day before her leaving Paris, Henri and Nicole DuPont both closed the café after the morning shift and came to visit Yvette at the apartment in Louvre. They had both offered emotional goodbyes, Nicole with tears in her eyes, whilst even Henri had to bite his lip to control his feelings, feelings he thought he would never have had for her.

"Take care of yourself, Yvette," Henri told the girl, whom he now considered to be more like a daughter to him and his wife.

"Please stay safe and don't do anything stupid to get you into trouble," Nicole pleaded. "Hopefully this war will end soon and we will all be able to meet again."

"I truly hope so," Yvette replied, to which both Nicole and her husband, Henri, smiled and hugged her.

"Are you Yvette?" a tall, good looking man asked.

"Yes that's me," Yvette replied. "Is that you, Monsieur Bauton?"

"At your service, Madame," the new arrival smiled and then added. "But please, my name is Patrice."

"Patrice," Yvette repeated, as if needing conformation. "I'm very pleased to meet you, Patrice."

"Likewise," the extremely attractive man replied. "Now come with me please."

Yvette dutifully followed Patrice out to the small car park, where she spotted a battered and bruised, beat up old looking 'Citroen Traction Avant,' a car which she'd never seen before.

She imagined that when it was new it looked rather majestic, a beautiful car that she considered to look similar to the vastly more expensive German built Mercedes-Benz. She also imagined it to be driven by many Nazi officers whilst stationed in occupied France, whereas in reality it was also a favourite vehicle used by members of the French Resistance.

However, it was sad to think that many of these 'Tractions' were commandeered by the Gestapo and put the fear of God into the French locals, as they were spotted being slowly driven along the streets close to where they lived, with many men and women disappearing into the night after being arrested and taken away in the back of one, never to be seen again.

"You like the car?" Patrice questioned after seeing Yvette's apparent admiration.

"Yes, but it looks like it has seen better days," she joked.

"But looks can be deceiving," the Frenchman stated.

"What do you mean?" a curious Yvette questioned.

"The car is actually quite new and mechanically in very good condition," Patrice told her. "When the Nazis invaded our country, a few of us got together and kicked the shit out of it! We put dents in the bodywork and threw paint stripper over the paintwork, so if the Gestapo wanted to commandeer one of these, they wouldn't touch this one with a bargepole!"

"Clever," Yvette commented, whilst looking at him and liking what she saw.

Patrice Bauton, she thought was about twenty-eight years of age and very good looking. He was quite a tall man, being around six feet in height and of slim build. Today he was sporting a three day old beard, a look which Yvette considered as being rather attractive.

Before the German invasion and occupation of France, Patrice Bauton had been a Parisian school teacher, teaching both boys and girls from the ages of twelve to sixteen. Sadly, many of these young pupils he'd taught had been of the Jewish faith and had been taken away to work camps in the beginning, but he now feared that many would have lost their lives in one or more of the notorious death camps dotted around Germany and Poland. This was one of his main reasons for his leaving the teaching profession, albeit hopefully temporarily, and joining fellow members of the Resistance to fight against the Nazis and rid them from his country.

"Are you ready for a road trip?" Patrice questioned.

"Are we going on a road trip to Grouville?" Yvette asked.

"No, we are already in Grouville," Patrice laughed.

"So where are we going now?" she asked of the good looking Frenchman.

"I'm taking you to the village," Patrice began to explain. "It's a small village called, Tourant, and it is just two miles this side of the Demarcation Line."

"How far is that from here?" the girl queried.

"It's around fifty miles," Patrice Bauton stated.

"Will we be safe driving there?" a cautious Yvette asked and Patrice looked deep in thought.

"It will be quite safe driving there at the moment, because as we are still in the safe zone there will not be too many troops hanging around, and those that are should be no bother for us. However, as we get closer to the Demarcation Line, well let's just say that things could get a little but messy!"

"I don't like the sound of that," Yvette stressed, sounding a lot less confident about her situation now.

They drove mostly in silence, with the girl becoming more and more nervous and agitated as they came closer to the destination.

They finally left the main road and were driving along a narrow country lane when Patrice made the announcement, "We're here."

"Where are we?" Yvette asked the man with the piercing blue eyes. "I can't see anything."

"That's the point," Patrice replied. "If you cannot see

anything, then the Germans can't see anything either. Do you see that small tree stump over there?" he asked the girl, whilst pointing slightly up a short hill.

"Yes, but what about it?" she replied.

"That is the entrance to Tourant," he stated.

"But it's just a forest clearing," Yvette claimed. "It's nothing but trees and vegetation."

"Exactly," Patrice beamed triumphantly. "The enemy troops would pass by here without ever noticing the village up on the hillside."

He slowly drove the car twenty-five yards up the short incline and then stopped. Leaving the Citroen Traction Avant, Patrice walked for a few steps to stand by the tree stump and then moved a large bush to the left hand side of it, revealing a small passageway just big enough to squeeze the car through. He then got back into the car and after driving just far enough past the tree stump, he got out again and pulled the bush back into position before driving on up the hill.

"Here we are, home sweet home," Patrice remarked whilst smiling at his young passenger.

"How far is it to the village," Yvette queried a little nervously.

"Very close," Patrice returned, "maybe half a mile, just a little further up the hill."

As they drove on, the road widened slightly and they came to a sharp right hand turn. Right on the bend they spotted a man sitting on his backside and holding an expensive looking pair of binoculars.

"Buenos tardes, Herminio," Patrice said to the man sitting there. "Is everything okay?"

"Si Señor, todo bien," the man answered.

"He's speaking Spanish," Yvette said, surprised to be hearing the man talk in a foreign tongue, at least, foreign to the French language.

"But of course," Patrice confirmed to the girl. "Herminio is from the Spanish city of Madrid. We also have Italians, Greeks, Portuguese and even Germans living amongst us here in the village of Tourant."

"Herminio Crespo, Madame," the older man said whilst directing his introduction to the girl, to which she smiled before turning back to Patrice.

"I met a German when I first arrived at the Loire Valley," Yvette stated. "He was working in Paris when Hitler's army invaded the city and he got the hell out of there."

"Is his name, Gunter?" Patrice questioned.

"Yes, but how do you know him?" the girl asked.

"I've never met him in person, but I have spoken with him many times on the radio, he and another man called, Renoir."

"That will be Jean Renoir," Yvette pointed out to the Frenchman. "I stayed with them for the first few days when I arrived here in France from England. I was with Gunter, Jean, and a lady named Madame Chambourcey. Do you know of her?"

"Yes, I have heard of her and her wartime exploits," Patrice confirmed smiling. "Apparently she is a lovely lady now, but was a very dangerous young woman to be around during her time."

Yvette laughed at him saying this. She had also heard the stories of Madame Chambourcey in her younger days, along with her dalliances with the young German soldiers, often resulting in deadly consequences!

As she thought about the Madame now, the only 'dalliances' she imagined her having these days would perhaps be a little hanky-panky when alone with a certain Monsieur Jean Renoir.

Again, she enjoyed having a little chuckle at the prospect of her having this thought.

"See you later, Herminio," Patrice said politely to the man sitting there on the floor and still clutching the binoculars.

"Hasta pronto, mi amigo," the man remarked.

As they were about to drive further up the hill, before they did so, Yvette looked at Patrice and begged the question, "What is that Herminio is holding in his right hand?"

"That'll be his bell," the Frenchman laughed.

"His bell," Yvette exclaimed.

"I'll show you," Patrice said.

Having said this, he turned off the car engine and invited Yvette to leave the car and join him.

"Herminio, this is Yvette," he announced again to the man from Spain, properly introducing the new girl. "She's asking about your bell."

"My bell, she wants to know about my bell?" the Spaniard questioned gruffly. "I can tell you that it's a much valued piece of equipment." Yvette smiled when hearing this.

"Let me show you," Patrice offered, taking over the conversation before the Spaniard could further get involved. "Come," he invited.

He led her by the hand until by Herminio's side. "You see what he has in his hand?" he questioned.

"That's not a bell," she scoffed.

"No, it's a leather strap tied to a rope which is attached to a bell at the other end of the rope," the good looking Frenchman informed her. "Come," he said again, and led her a few yards up the hill. "You see?" he queried, pointing to the grass bank.

"See what," she replied. "All I can see is a length of thick string."

"Exactly," he said.

Patrice held her hand and dragged her slowly up the hill. Every ten yards or so, he pointed to a butcher's meat hook with a rounded end that had been hammered into the ground.

What the resistance members had done then was to hammer these meat hooks, similar to tent pegs, into the ground on that side of the road, and then they'd painstakingly threaded a thick piece of string (or a small rope) through the eye of each meat hook. As the string was not long enough to reach all the way to where Herminio was now sitting, they'd tied several pieces together.

"But what is it for?" Yvette asked Patrice.

It's for our safety," he replied. "Herminio, or whoever is on lookout duty at the time, will ring the bell exactly on the half hour and again on the hour, just once, to let us know that he is still with us and there are no problems."

"That's clever," Yvette said, now quite impressed.

"Yes it is," Patrice agreed, "but if the bell is rung twice, that means he has seen something of interest and maybe wants us to take a better look. If he rings it continuously, then there's a major problem and he needs all of us to come to his aid, all armed to the teeth and ready for action!"

"Let's hope that doesn't happen," Yvette remarked.

"It will," Patrice observed, "and probably sooner and more often than you'd think."

Yvette climbed back inside the car and the two of them continued on with their short journey to reach the top of the hill. After only a couple of minutes, they reached a small collection of ten wooden chalet type buildings, along with one much bigger brick built dwelling.

"What the hell is this place?" a disappointed Yvette questioned. "Where is the village?"

"This is it, home sweet home," Patrice said, but seeing her mixture of anger and disappointment, he elaborated. "Believe it or not, this place used to be a luxury holiday park where the rich and famous came every year to spend their holidays, although some people actually lived here all the year round."

"So what happened to the place?" the girl questioned.

"When the war broke out, all these people became uneasy. And when word got out about the Nazis preparing to enter Paris and occupy the city, the residents here decided to cut their losses and get the hell out of France, so they just upped sticks and deserted the place, leaving it like the ghost town it is now."

"So who lives here now, apart from Herminio I mean?" she asked curiously.

"You will meet them all very soon," Patrice remarked. "Come on, come with me."

Yvette collected her small suitcase from the back seat of the Citroen Traction Avant and dutifully followed her new host as he guided her towards the biggest of the buildings. Once inside, she was very surprised to see quite a few people there, all seemingly waiting for her arrival.

"Who are all these people?" Yvette asked.

"These people are your new family for the foreseeable future," Patrice stated. "There are too many to mention right now, but you will get to know them all very quickly."

As Patrice said this, Yvette heard the bell ring above the door. It was louder than she'd imagined.

"That must be Herminio," she remarked. "And it sounds like he's right on time," she said, beginning to laugh.

"You may be laughing now," a fellow Frenchman confided. "But the noise of that bleeding bell will get on your fecking nerves before very long!"

"Yvette, this is André," Patrice announced, making the first introduction of the new girl's new life.

"Pleased to meet you, Monsieur," she smiled.

"Likewise," André said, also returning the smile.

She looked around the building. This first room was the largest of all, but she noticed corridors going off in four different directions, she thought to separate rooms. There were roughly a dozen men milling about the place, with around half a dozen women and a handful of children, all between the ages of two to five years. Yvette was confused.

"Are all these people living here together in this building?" she asked Patrice.

"They are now," he replied. "They all live in the separate wooden chalets in the summer, but when the weather gets cold, like it is now; it's easier for them all to keep warm by sharing this accommodation."

"That must be cosy," Yvette claimed.

"That's not the word I would use," a man said in a German accent.

"Yvette, please let me introduce you to my friend. This is Helmut," Patrice announced.

"Helmut Schön," the man said, smiling in her direction. "I am very pleased to meet you, my dear."

"Likewise," Yvette returned.

The conversation was interrupted by the ringing of the bell, again smack on time.

"That effing bell," André pleaded. "I swear that one day I am gonna take that bell, present it to Herminio, and shove it right up there where the sun don't shine!"

"Don't knock it, André," Patrice laughed. "One day that bell might just save your life."

CHAPTER 21
EMBRACE THE MUSIC OF THE WIND

During the coming days, Yvette became acclimatised to her new surroundings and got to know the people she would be sharing her life with for, well, she didn't really know exactly how long for, but supposed it would be until all this silliness was over.

She explored the area of what she now knew was the holiday village named, 'Tourant,' and this was where all the wooden chalets could be found. She went inside all these dwellings and deduced that they must have been very pleasant places to live in, before the Nazis interrupted the previous occupants' pleasure.

All the time she explored these surroundings she aired on the side of caution, remembering what Patrice had constantly reminded her.

"Yvette, don't you go too far and get lost in the forest," he warned. "It would be dangerous for you to do so."

A few days after her arrival the snow began to fall, and it would continue to snow for the next two and a half months. Two and a half long, tedious months, eleven to twelve weeks of total boredom! The good thing about this was that, as Patrice told her, with the snow being as deep as it now was; there was absolutely no chance of any enemy invasion forthcoming. Everyone could relax and enjoy each other's company as much as they could.

Yvette had to admit that she enjoyed the company of the men far more than she did that of the women. However, the company she enjoyed the most was that of the children. Over the coming days and weeks the children had grown attached to her, even beginning to call her, 'Aunty.'

She in turn loved being in their company, playing games with them and having fun playing in the snow. Little Marta always had great fun and laughed incessantly when she covered her 'Aunty' in the white stuff whilst enjoying a snowball fight.

Marta was only four years of age and had only ever known life as a war child. She'd never known what freedom was like, to live a normal life and go to school with other boys and girls of her own age.

For this, Yvette was angry. How dare that Hitler monster put these children in danger and ruin their young lives by being the silly little man that he was. He was pure evil, and she hated him with a vengeance!

The weeks passed by slowly, with not much ever happening. The highlight of the day was when one of the men relieved Herminio from his stint at his lookout post whilst waiting at the end of the bell. He would come into the room almost blue with cold and everyone would cover him with extra blankets to warm him.

However, the best event to occur during that cold winter happened when everyone was sleeping soundly one night. Suddenly the Spaniard, Jacques Santiago, jumped up from his mattress on the floor and shouted loudly, "Wake up, wake up everyone!"

"What the flip," remarked Maurice Lazlo, trying really hard not to swear in front of the now wakening children.

"Yes Jacques, what the hell is the matter with you?" Patrice demanded.

"Don't you know what day it is?" the Spaniard questioned.

"No!" everyone answered in unison.

"Why. It has just gone past midnight, so Happy New Year everybody," Jacques announced. "Welcome to nineteen forty-four."

"Bloody hell, he's right," Patrice agreed. "Happy New Year everyone," he repeated to anyone still awake. "Let's all hope that this year will be a good one. But above all, let us pray that this will be the final year of this God forsaken war!"

This was followed by a group hug, which Yvette really enjoyed. However, she particularly enjoyed being in the strong arms of a certain, Monsieur Patrice Bauton.

Two weeks later, Yvette was sleeping soundly when she was woken by two of the children, Marta and Maisie.

"Can we get into bed with you," they asked.

"Of course you can, but why?" Yvette asked the two.

"We're scared," they admitted.

"Scared? What are you scared of," she queried.

"It's so noisy outside," Marta said.

"We think the Germans' are coming for us," Maisie admitted, almost with tears in her pretty blue eyes. Yvette could see the children were petrified.

"Get in," she said, and hugged the two until they felt better and far less worried. "Don't worry it's not the Germans coming. You're safe."

"What is it then, why is it so noisy outside?" little Marta begged the question.

"Well children, the sound you can hear is the noise of the wind rushing through the trees. The wind is so strong that the trees are bending in its path and trying to get out of the way."

Yvette stopped to look at the two to see if they were still awake. They were wide eyed and both still paying attention, so she continued.

"The trees are now fighting so hard to get away from the wind's path that the only thing they can do is sing to each other."

"Sing to each other?" Marta remarked, butting in to the story.

"Yes, the trees sing to each other," Yvette stressed. "But we humans cannot hear the trees singing to each other. To us, it just sounds like the noise of the wind tearing through their branches, but to the trees, it sounds like the most beautiful music that anyone has ever heard. It's like a choir of angels and we must embrace it."

Yvette looked down at the children again. She could see that they were both relaxed now and no longer in fear, so she ended the story by saying, "Marta, Maisie, whatever happens you must always embrace the music of the wind."

She looked down again, but this time the children were both sleeping soundly.

By the end of January the snow started to melt, as the land finally began to warm up. By the end of the second week of February 1944, the snow had completely disappeared.

This worried Patrice Bauton a little, as he'd heard rumblings on the radio concerning German troop activity on the other side of the Demarcation Line, the imaginary line situated only a few miles from the 'village' of Tourant and found in the 'occupied zone.

"Okay everyone, we have to keep our wits about us once again. The Nazis are back and playtime is well and truly over," he stressed, as he gathered the resistance members together for a meeting.

True enough, his prediction came to fruition only a couple of days later, and with severe and deadly consequences!

Herminio Crespo had taken up his usual position and was holding the bell firmly in his hand, which was now an automatic action for him. He was sitting on the cushion which he'd started using for a little extra comfort.

Taking out his binoculars, he was perusing his 'kingdom' when he spotted a man in the distance, a man he didn't recognise, who at this moment was walking along the road and looking as though he didn't have a care in the world.

It was true that since the beginning of this particularly cold and snowy winter there had not been any evidence of German troops on the ground, and because of this, this past winter had been an uneventful and relatively quiet one.

Although the Spaniard could just about make out the figure of the man in the distance, even through these high powered looking glasses he could not make out any of the man's features, but he stayed concentrating on the gentleman's progress as he sauntered along the country lane about half a mile in the distance.

Herminio watched as the man walking ahead turned, raised both hands into the air and dropped to his knees as if in surrender. The Spaniard panned around to the right to better see what was happening. He was shocked when he spotted a handful of German troops approaching, with the gun barrel of an armoured tank looming into view.

His mouth opened wide with the shock of what he was witnessing, so much so that the rolled up cigarette, which was normally permanently attached to his bottom lip, instantly dropped to the ground! Immediately he rang the bell, and continued to ring it constantly.

The first man to arrive was fellow countryman, Jacques Santiago. "Que pasa amigo?" he questioned. His question was answered by his Spanish friend pointing to the murderous scene ahead of them.

"Holy shit," Jacques simply exclaimed.

There was nothing the pair could do but watch, as they waited for the rest of the gang to arrive. They watched as the turret of the tank slowly turned towards the man. My God, were they about to shoot him with a high powered missile, a large bullet usually reserved for the battlefield? The two men watched transfixed, as more troops appeared from behind the tank.

"Where are the rest of the guys?" Herminio asked his friend.

"Yo no se," Señor Santiago stressed, "but I'm sure they are on the way."

A few seconds after Jacques had said this, a dozen or more

of the men arrived, including the main man, Patrice Bauton. Patrice followed Herminio's arm, which now pointed in the direction of where a major war crime was about to take place.

"Come on, let's go," demanded one of the arrivals, German compatriot, Helmut Schön.

Helmut was one of the men whom Patrice had told Yvette about, shortly after she'd arrived from Paris. He'd been involved in Hitler's army since the war began in 1939, but just after he'd arrived in Paris and seen what they were doing to the Jews, the severe way they were treating them, with regular beatings in the streets and mass evacuations to the camps, he'd deserted.

He ran away to join the French Resistance, the very same people who were fighting against the people he had once stood by and represented. This act of desertion alone would mean instant execution for Helmut, should he ever be captured by the Nazis.

"No Helmut," Patrice snapped, bringing the angry man back to his senses. "There is nothing we can do from here. We are too far away to be able to help this poor man now, but we'll get the bastards later!"

All the men watched in a mixture of shock and horror as a Nazi officer approached the man, who at his moment was still down on his knees. They watched the man stand, obviously upon the order of the officer. They then watched as the officer removed his pistol from his gun belt and shot the man in both knees, sending him crashing back to the floor in agony.

"What the freaking hell are we watching here?" an astonished, André Gastard questioned angrily.

"We are witnessing one man torturing another man, just for the sheer fun of it!" Herminio Crespo stated, whilst still seated at his lookout post, his rolled up cigarette now reunited with his bottom lip.

However, the situation became increasingly worse when the group of resistance members spotted the Nazi officer order two of his men to grab a hold of the man by his ankles and drag him into the center of the pathway.

"Good God, no!" was all Patrice Bauton could say, as he heard the noise of the tank engine increase amd watched as it manoeuvred slowly towards the innocent, helpless, waiting man.

"Surely not," Helmut Schön gasped, as the realization of what was about to occur became a reality.

As the enormous tank edged slowly towards the victim, even though the group of onlookers were not able to see his face, they all imagined what he was thinking as the tank finally arrived by his side.

"Surely not," Helmut Schön gasped again.

They continued to watch in the hope that the Nazi officer would not go through with his threat, but he showed no mercy. All the men grimaced as the tank continued towards the victim and did not stop. They saw his body completely disappear below the massive machine and could only imagine the pain he must have suffered. Mercifully, it was only for a split second and then it was all over.

As the tank travelled a few more yards, all they could see was the dirt track road, the body was no longer in view.

"What the feck!" André Gastard gasped in disbelief.

"His body's probably still under the tank," Patrice observed.

"Or liquidized and stuck to the road," Herminio offered.

As the men looked on from their vantage point, they all agreed that the victim must have suffered such agony that he surely must have screamed for mercy, but no mercy came, and from that distance, no scream was heard!

"Poor bastard," Yvette gasped, as Patrice noticed she was standing there with the rest of the men.

"Go back to the house please," he requested.

"No, I'm okay," she replied.

"Yvette," Patrice said, a little more sternly now.

"I'm okay, I promise," she said again.

"Maybe you are, but I need you to go back and get on the radio to ask for help. We need backup," Patrice stressed.

Hearing him say this, there were no more arguments from the girl. She turned around immediately and obediently made her way back up the hill to call for the help which Patrice desired.

"Okay men, what are we waiting for?" Helmut questioned. "Come on, let's go."

"Wait," Patrice interrupted his German friend.

"Wait, wait for what?" Helmut questioned indignantly.

"If we leave now, by the time we get down there they will be long gone," Patrice pointed out to Helmut and the rest of the gang.

"So what should we do?" Helmut queried.

"What we do is wait a few minutes and see where they go to next, and in which direction they head. Then we can anticipate where they are going and we can get there before them."

"We can ambush the bastards," André Gastard suggested.

"Yes," Patrice remarked. "Yes we can."

The men did as suggested and stood almost to attention as they watched the German party preparing to leave the scene. However, they were shocked when they realized there were more members of the enemy than they thought, when they saw more troops appearing in jeeps from further along the dirt track road.

"Bloody hell," Jacques Santiago gasped. "How many of the enemy are there?"

"I can see around twenty," Patrice returned, "plus two or maybe three more inside the tank."

"But there are only twelve of us," Jacques pointed out to the rest of the resistance members.

"Only twelve of us, but we have the hearts of one hundred men!" Helmut said boldly. "Plus we can ambush and surprise them."

"They will not know what hit them!" Jacques Santiago said with a sinister smile. "We will scare the shit out of them!"

Seconds later, they watched as the German troops moved off in the direction they'd been going in when the innocent man had been spotted earlier.

"We will leave the Citroens' here and go through the forest on foot. Let's go that way," Patrice said, as he pointed in the distance to the required direction needed. "If we leave now, we should be ready and waiting for them."

"Okay guys, what are we waiting for?" Helmut said defiantly. "Let's go and kill us some Nazis!" which was more than a little ironic, as five years earlier, he'd been one!

All the men picked up their arms and ammunition, which in Jacques Santiago's case included a couple of sticks of dynamite, and after throwing their rifles over their shoulders, they began the trek down through the forest to intercept the enemy in their tracks.

In the beginning they raced through the trees in excitement, but this excitement soon turned to feelings of both fear and trepidation as they continued to proceed down the hill.

They had to admit that it had been a long time since they'd taken part in a battle situation, in fact for some of them this would be the first time they'd ever confronted, or been confronted by the enemy. By the time they all reached the roadside, every one of them was now feeling extremely nervous.

"I feel like I'm having an out of body experience," Maurice Lazlo whispered to his Spanish friend, Enrique Leron.

"You will be okay," Enrique told Maurice, in an attempt to reassure him. "You just keep your head down and remember why it is we're doing this."

"Everyone take cover and be as quiet as you can," Patrice gave the order. All the men spread out a little and found trees with good thick trunks to hide behind.

"Can you hear anything yet?" Helmut questioned the leader, but as quietly as he could.

"Not yet, but I think I will hear them before I see them," the

Frenchman admitted to the German.

"Well you keep watching," Helmut advised.

"Helmut, go back and tell the men to spread out so they are not in each other's way. Tell them to wait until they see the whites of these Bastard's eyes before they shoot," Patrice instructed before continuing. "And tell them not to waste any bullets by firing into thin air."

The men were all like statues as they waited in silence for the enemy to arrive. Even though the snow had all but disappeared completely from the ground and the temperature was still freezing, André Gastard had beads of sweat glistening on his brow.

"I can't stand this waiting around," Gastard confessed. "I just want to get at the Bastards!"

"Keep cool my friend," Helmut told him, although in this weather, it might not have been the best choice of words to have used.

"Okay, I hear them," Patrice suddenly announced. "They are maybe one hundred yards away. Everyone get down, take cover, and wait for my signal."

"Good luck everyone," Helmut offered, before everyone fell silent.

As the men waited, Jacques Santiago took out the dynamite from within his bag and inserted a short fuse into each. He figured if he cut the wire short enough, it would give him four or five seconds to light the fuse and throw the sticks in the direction of the tank.

He took out his trusty 'Drago' lighter from his pocket and gave it a flick to check that it was working correctly. It was, and the smell of petrol that greeted his nostrils was strangely reassuring.

The procession came closer and the first thing they heard was the putt-putt-putt of the tank's engine, as it trundled slowly along the road.

"Here we bloody go," Jacques whispered to himself. "Keep calm, Jacques," he repeated quietly, over and over again.

The men were happy that with the trees and the long grass to use as cover, they were in the ideal position to carry out the ambush successfully and without being seen. They lay down on the wet grass and made their rifles and pistols ready for the battle. The men then waited for Patrice to give the order to attack.

By now, the tank was almost upon them. Patrice looked around at the men and gave a signal for them to wait just a few seconds longer. When it had almost reached him, he turned to Jacques and moved his finger to give him the signal to release the dynamite.

With the Drago lighter now almost greasy with sweat, he opened the lid and flicked the metal wheel to spark the gasoline and then held it to the fuse wire. The end of the fuse immediately caught fire and became like a firework sparkler. Jacques knew he had to act quickly. He stood momentarily for a second and threw the dynamite towards the tank, in a motion similar to that of throwing a discus, or that of skimming stones at the beach as a youngster. The dynamite stopped in the road just two yards in front of the oncoming tank.

"Take that, you Nazi Bastards!" Jacques shouted triumphantly.

With one second to go, the tank took another revolution and ended up directly above the explosive. If Señor Santiago had tried this manoeuvre a hundred times, it could not have gone any better. A huge explosion followed, shattering the peace and quiet of the surrounding scene as the tank lifted into the air. From the outside there appeared to be little or no damage to the machine, but it stopped moving, so Jacques afforded himself a little smile of victory. However, almost instantly, German troops appeared from everywhere.

As he prepared to launch phase two of the attack, Jacques

spotted five jeeps carrying around twenty men, and these men, maybe suffering from shock, left the relative safety of the jeeps and ran like headless chickens towards the tank. This was a huge mistake.

The Spaniard once again used his trusty lighter and sparked the second stick. This time he launched it towards as many Nazis as he could reach. He did this using an over arm action, with all the expertise of a championship cricketer bowling at Lords. The dynamite landed smack in the middle of the troops, instantly killing eight of them and throwing their bodies into the air. Patrice gave the order to "FIRE!" and all hell broke loose.

The entire battle was a blood bath. Before the German troops could even reach for their rifles they were cut down by a barrage of bullets. Within a second they all lay dead and piled in a heap.

Helmut went to check to see if any had survived. As he was amongst them, he saw one man climb to his feet and put his arms up in surrender.

"What should I do, Patrice?" he questioned his French colleague.

"We cannot take any prisoners," Patrice replied. "Anyway, my friend, what would they have done if they'd captured you? They would have executed you without any hesitation."

Hearing Patrice saying this, Helmut raised his pistol and shot the German between the eyes. It was a clean and painless kill.

"What about him?" the men then heard as André Gastard queried, whilst pointing to the last jeep in the group.

The men all looked in the direction to which André was pointing and were amazed to see an officer, dressed in full Nazi uniform. He was just sitting there, defiantly alone in the jeep and nonchalantly smoking a 'Sturm' cigarette.

"What the F....?" Patrice gasped.

"Good afternoon, gentlemen," the Nazi said to the

disbelieving gathering, as though he didn't have a care in the world.

"What the.......?" Patrice said again, "and who the hell do you think you are?" the Frenchman questioned.

"He's a dead man, that's who he is," proclaimed fellow Frenchman, Maurice Lazlo.

"Please allow me to introduce myself," the Nazi said smiling. "My name is Herr Otto Sherman of Herr Hitler's SS, and I have diplomatic immunity."

"Immunity from who?" questioned Patrice Bauton.

"Adolph Hitler himself," the captured man said, once again smiling broadly.

"Do you remember the man you murdered an hour ago by driving a tank over his poor, broken body?" Patrice demanded.

"He had diplomatic immunity also," Jacques Santiago butted in on the conversation. "He had diplomatic immunity from us, the French Resistance. So wipe that stupid smile off your face!"

"Just shoot the bastard," Helmut Schön insisted.

"You, man! Why are you speaking with a German accent?" Sherman interrogated.

"Because I AM a German, you piece of Nazi scheisse idiot!" Helmut replied.

"So why are you not fighting for the German army?" the Nazi cross-examined angrily, ignoring the insult. "Why are you not being faithful to the Fuhrer?"

"I was fighting for your, so called army, until you invaded France and began killing all those many innocent Jewish men, women, and worst of all, children," Helmut began and then continued. "How could you look a blameless child in the face and then have them transported to their deaths?"

By now, Helmut was raging. He looked at Otto Sherman, but in return, could see no reaction and certainly saw no remorse.

"What do you want us to do with him, Helmut," Patrice asked his angry friend.

"If that tank is still working, I can drive it," Helmut stated.

"Really?" Patrice questioned.

"Yes, I drove tanks in nineteen thirty-nine," Helmut revealed. "Let me try and fire it up."

"And then what?" Enrique Leron enquired.

"I will drive it over the Bastard like he did to that man earlier," Helmut reiterated.

"You cannot do that," Herr Sherman pleaded, as the brave look on his face was replaced by that of fear. "Herr Hitler would not allow you to do that."

"Can you see him?" Helmut asked sinisterly. "Can anyone see Adolph Hitler standing here beside this asshole?"

"No," everyone joined in saying.

"Pin him down, men," Helmut was heard to say.

He then jumped onto the tank and was about to climb inside when two gunshots rang out.

"Two more for you in here, Sherman," Helmut laughed. "You can add them to the tally."

Seconds later the tank engine was heard to start up successfully and Helmut's face was seen coming out of the entrance of the tank. By now the men had grabbed hold of the Nazi and were holding him down in the road in readiness for Helmut to drive the tank over him, as he had done to that poor, innocent French victim earlier.

"Please, don't do this," Otto Sherman screamed, as he begged for his life. As the tank sprang into life and came closer to him, the Nazi pissed himself!

The tank was now only inches away from reaching him when Patrice Bauton let out a loud, shrill whistle and the tank stopped in its tracks.

"He's all yours, Helmut," Patrice said to his German friend as he jumped athletically out of the tank.

"Lift him to his knees," Helmut instructed the men, who did as ordered without question. "This is a message from all the Jews you murdered," he said. "Please give this message to Hitler on the day you see him, the day when he also arrives in hell!"

Helmut had to admit to admiring the defiant look of bravery on the face of Herr Otto Sherman, as he gripped the pistol in his right hand. When he raised his right arm, the Nazi did not avert his gaze or even flinch as he continued to stare in the face of Helmut Schön. The German squeezed on the trigger and finally sent the Nazi to his death.

The men then spent the rest of the day burying the bodies as best they could and cleaning up the scene. Helmut climbed back inside the tank and began driving it to the right hand side of the road and was able to jump out at the last second, just as it careered down a steep slope to be hidden from view.

Within three hours, any passing enemy troops would never have known that anything untoward had ever happened.

The men eventually completed the task, and as they began the hike back to the village, Patrice decided to gather them.

"Men, I think that for the next few days we have to be extremely vigilant," he said to the gathering. "I think it would be a good idea for us all to come here every day and keep a lookout, just in case any of the enemy comes in search of the men they lost today."

"And don't forget that they lost the tank," Jacques Santiago joked, at which everyone laughed.

Patrice agreed that it was good to see the men in such high spirits and it made him happy, but he knew they had to be on high alert, at least until such times as they could be sure that all danger had been eliminated from the area.

When they arrived back at Tourant, Patrice walked down the hill to see Herminio Crespo. He advised him of the events of the day and confirmed the warning for him also to be extra vigilant and keep his eyes and his binoculars primed and ready at all times, keeping an eye out for any unusual and unwanted visitors who may appear on the horizon.

Two days after the Nazi ambush, whilst the rest of the men were out searching for more evidence of the enemy, Yvette was in the forest looking for logs to use with the wood burning stove in the kitchen of the community area.

As she made her way back through the forest to the village, the girl was shocked to see a few of the villagers currently being held at gunpoint by just one lone gunman wearing a lowly German Army uniform.

If she could have seen his face, she would have witnessed just how petrified this young man looked. However, she couldn't see his face, as all she could see were the faces of the wives and children of the resistance members all standing to attention, as he pointed his rifle at them.

She wasn't even sure whether the gun was loaded or not, and if it was, she had no clue as to how many bullets were contained within it. All she knew was that this young man must have been wandering aimlessly around the forest for at least two days. He would be tired, hungry and desperate at having lost the rest of his comrades. Indeed, he may even have thought of himself as a deserter, a crime punishable by death.

She was ten paces behind him now, and a couple of the women in the line-up spotted her. Yvette put her finger to her lips, signalling to them not to give her away.

She gently put the bag containing the logs down on the floor and looked around for a good sized rock with a sharp, jagged edge. When she found one, she placed it within the palm of her right hand and slowly crept towards the young soldier. She looked at the woman who was still glancing in her direction and Yvette mouthed to her, 'Make some noise.'

"Please Sir, don't shoot us, we are not your enemy," the woman shouted.

Realising what was happening, the rest of the people all joined in by shouting, "Please don't shoot - Please don't shoot -

Please don't shoot!" This affected the soldier's attention and gave Yvette enough cover to come up behind him without him noticing her.

Suddenly, everything Mr. Green had taught her in his unarmed combat training at the camp clicked into her memory. Without thinking and without any fear or hesitation, she ran the final five paces towards the young man. Swinging her right arm as fast as she could, she struck the man with the jagged edge of the rock as hard as possible, connecting with his body right at the base of his spine. The soldier let out a loud, blood curdling scream, dropped his rifle and fell instantly to his knees.

Yvette, without thinking, automatically folded her arms around his neck and head and twisted it to the right as far as it would go, and then a little bit more. A loud cracking noise was heard to echo through the trees, as the young man's neck snapped. Immediately his body became limp, and as she released it, it fell to the floor.

Yvette looked at the young man's now lifeless body, for that's what a he was, still a very young man, probably younger than her. The girl felt no sense of achievement, no sense of pride, all she felt now was immense sorrow amd a feeling of deep sadness.

Everyone crowded around her, patting her on the back and thanking her for saving his or her life, but all Yvette could think of was the fact that she'd just killed a mother's son, a brother, possibly a young woman's sweetheart, or even a fiancé.

She thought about the mother receiving that knock on the door, when two men in military uniforms were standing there and telling her how her son had lost his life in battle, how he'd saved the lives of his fellow soldiers and how he'd died as a hero. However, Yvette knew the truth, and she would carry it with her for the rest of her life.

This young man would never marry, never have children, and never live a normal life. He would never grow old, and she'd deprived him of all these things which most people would take for granted.

"Fuck!" she shouted loudly in desperation.

She then walked away from everyone, found a secluded spot where she could be alone, sat down on a large rock, and not for the first time in this bloody war, she covered her face and cried like a baby.

CHAPTER 22
THE END OF AN ERA

Two hundred and seventy-nine miles, seven hundred and four yards away from Paris, back in Maidstone, Kent, it was the end of an era.

On the orders of the man himself, Prime Minister Winston Churchill,, the order came through that the training camp was to close during the March of 1944 and everyone who'd been involved in the preparation of the many men and women (although mainly women) to join the 'Special Operations Executive' were to be disbanded and ordered to join the regular army, and to prepare themselves to participate in the war effort, hopefully for one final push.

"Well you have to admit, we've had a good run," Ben Richards announced to his friend. "But all good things must eventually come to an end."

"Let's hope this bloody war comes to an end soon," his friend, Peter Collins remarked.

"I have a funny feeling that it will," Ben offered.

The pair, along with everyone else involved in the running of the training camp had been given their orders to disband and then to report to 'The Department of Fish & Fisheries' to present their official call up papers, just as soon as they possibly could.

Messer's Black and Blue were both deemed too old to fight for 'King and Country,' so both were drafted into the offices to personally work alongside Churchill, with the two being given employment in an advisory capacity.

Mr. Green, the unarmed combat instructor at the training camp, was deemed to be "not too old for service" and was ordered to accompany Ben Richards and Peter Collins, along with the remainder of the staff at the camp and report to the Department, situated at 5A Great Portland Street.

As they departed the camp for one final time, several questions were asked, the main one being, "What is your real name?"

This was answered by Mr. Green, the big, tough, unarmed combat instructor when he finally admitted, "my name is Malcolm Boothby."

"He doesn't look like a Malcolm," Ben Richards remarked to his friend, Peter.

"No he doesn't," agreed Peter Collins. "But I'll tell you what he DOES look like!"

"Behave yourself!" Ben joked, at which both friends laughed raucously.

As they'd all signed the 'Official Secrets Act' at the beginning of the war they were all ordered to attend a meeting, about what, they didn't really know, but they knew it had to be important and probably top secret.

Later at this meeting, officially they'd been informed that 'something was in the air,' but they were not allowed to speak about it. Unofficially, they'd been told by the 'War Cabinet' to prepare themselves for the final push.

They'd been sworn to secrecy by Churchill himself, and the word was that there was talk of an invasion on French soil involving the British Army, alongside American and possibly Canadian troops.

"There will be a final push to get to Berlin," Churchill had announced in secrecy, whilst smiling broadly and puffing on the biggest cigar that Pater Collins had ever seen.

"We must ready our troops and prepare them to erase Hitler's army of tyranny, his fanatical Nazi lunatics, and wipe them off the face of this earth," Churchill had continued to say.

"This is all brave talk and all well and good," Ben Richards said to Peter Collins as they chatted a little later in private. "But whilst Mister Churchill is safe and warm, drinking his glass of brandy and dishing out his commands, how many of his brave men are going to lose their lives by following his orders?"

"Yes exactly, and you and me included," Peter Collins replied to his good friend. This comment was received with a pair of crooked smiles.

During the April of 1944, Henri was going about his business at The Café DuPont when Herr Bogdan Gruber of the Gestapo entered the premises. Normally this would have been a stressful occasion for Monsieur DuPont, but during the past few months, Henri had noticed that Gruber's demeanour had mellowed considerably, so much so that when in Monsieur DuPont's company, he could be positively pleasant. However today, Herr Gruber seemed sadly melancholic.

"How are you, Herr Gruber?" Henri questioned, knowing that if he'd asked the Nazi this question even only a few months ago, he would have been in serious danger and fearing for his life.

"Henri, I am sick of this war," Gruber replied, shocking the Frenchman with his honesty. "I just wish it would end so we could all go home and get back to our lives."

Henri took great comfort in hearing the man saying this, for if this was how he genuinely felt, it gave him hope that this war may indeed end soon.

"Have you heard anything, Herr Gruber?" Henri asked the Nazi, instantly regretting this dangerous line of questioning, thinking that he'd maybe pushed his luck a little bit too far. However, Herr Gruber's reply shocked him even more.

"Henri, I am going to take my officer hat off now and talk with you as a man and as a friend," the Nazi commented. "Would that be okay with you?"

"Of course, Her Gruber," Henri replied, trying hard to hide his excitement, whilst also wondering just what information this man was about to divulge.

"Henri, I will ask you again, but please remember, if you

agree and I tell you, if you speak to anyone about any of this, I will be forced to have you shot. Do you understand?"

"Yes, Herr Gruber, I fully understand," Henri agreed, excited now that he might hear something from this Nazi that he could pass along to the resistance.

"My men are all deflated. We have all been here in Paris far too long," Gruber began.

"I'm very sorry," Henri commented ironically, immediately regretting his sarcasm.

"It's not your fault, my friend," Gruber laughed.

He then did something which Henri felt was strange when he touched the back of his hand. Was this a mark of affection, or even respect? The Frenchman listened as the German continued.

"As I say, Henri, we have all been in your beautiful city far too long and have been stagnating, bored by all this inactivity," Gruber sighed before continuing. "Also my friend, when we first came here in nineteen-forty, there were more than two hundred thousand of our troops in the city. We now have less than thirty thousand."

Henri's ears pricked up when he heard this revelation. "What happened to all these men? That is a lot of men lost, one way or another," he questioned.

"One name, Henri, Adolph Hitler, this is what happened to them," Bogdan Gruber stated angrily. "Over the past four years that man has sent so many of our young men to their deaths, and now we are on our knees. If we were to be invaded by the British now, I don't think we would survive for very long, not very long at all."

Henri DuPont's lack of any response to Gruber's comments made the German reiterate his warning. "Don't forget my friend, if you repeat any of this to anyone, I will have no choice but to have you executed!"

Even though Gruber smiled when saying this, Henri knew that he meant every word. Although mellowing recently, he was still an extremely dangerous man.

However, the ironic thing about this talk was the fact that Herr Bogdan Gruber of the Gestapo still had no idea of Henri's allegiance, involvement, and loyalty to the resistance. The only thing he knew for sure was that Henri cooked an extremely tasty bratwurst.

The main thing which Henri did take away from the Nazi during this conversation however, was the fact that Herr Gruber of the Gestapo had revealed to him that only thirty thousand men still remained in occupied Paris, and this was a fact that surely HAD to be passed on to the French Resistance.

CHAPTER 23
INTO THE UNKNOWN

As the amphibious landing craft was fast approaching the beach, Ben Richards turned around to look at the men accompanying him on this dangerous journey into the unknown. These men, who last night were all full of bravado, were now making no noise whatsoever. They just huddled together as silent as new born lambs.

The evening before, these same men were all bellowing boisterously, shouting things like – "We're coming for you, Adolph" – "Prepare to meet your maker, Hitler," or more blatantly, "You Nazi Bastards, fuck the lot of you," – as well as shouting many other anti-Nazi taunts.

"Just look at this lot," Ben said to his friend and travelling companion, Peter Collins. "They couldn't fight their way out of a paper bag!"

It was true. For many of these men it was the first time they would see combat, as well as being the first time they would face the enemy or even leave the shores of Britain and stand on foreign soil. Sadly, for the majority of them, it would also be the last day of their short lives.

Many of these men had been drafted into the army at short notice by Winston Churchill and his War Cabinet, recruited by him and his men to be used as cannon fodder, target practise for the German troops, the enemy consisting of well trained soldiers who would be lying in wait in much better positions on the cliffs and in the sand dunes, just waiting for these poor souls to arrive and perish whilst facing their makers.

"Poor bastards," Peter Collins said to his friend, Ben, as he also turned around the scan the faces of these young men.

As the two looked at these boys, for that's what they were – boys – they could see the extreme fear in their eyes. Some of these young men had still been attending college only a few months earlier. In fact, Ben and Peer believed that a few of them had, bravely or stupidly, volunteered to join up for the army whilst being underage. One thing was for certain, in spite of last night's bravado, not one of them now wanted to be here today.

"Are you okay, son?" Peter enquired of one young man. The boy looked at him and tried his best to raise a smile, although he was failing miserably.

"What's that you're holding?" Ben asked the same lad.

"It's a picture of my girl," the young man returned, flipping the photo to show both Ben amd Peter.

"She's beautiful," Ben told the youngster.

"Yes she is," the young man replied.

Ben could see that the lad now had tears streaming down his face, but he didn't know if they were tears of fear at what he was about to do, or tears because he knew what he was about to lose.

"You're going to be okay, son," Ben advised.

"Thank you, Sir," the youngster said whilst still clutching the photograph and now holding it close to his heart.

"What is our name, my friend?" Peter Collins asked the boy, trying to make him as calm as possible.

"My name is Thomas, Sir," he replied.

"Well, Thomas," Peter began. "Take another look at the picture of 'your girl' and remind yourself that she is the reason why you're here. You are doing this for her. You are fighting to protect her and to keep her safe."

"But I don't want to die," was all that Thomas could say before breaking down and almost collapsing. Immediately, his entire body began to shake with fear.

"Come on, son," Peter Collins pleaded, as he threw his arms around the lad to support him.

"He should not be here," Ben Richards stated.

"None of them should be here!" Peter said angrily, looking around at the faces of all the young men in the group.

"Agreed," said Ben, but he continued to say. "In fact, none of us should be here, and that includes you and me!"

The date was the 6th of June 1944 and Churchill and his War Cabinet had been planning this attack, in secret, since the beginning of May.

This day, Tuesday the 6th of June was a perfect day for the invasion, being beautifully hot and sunny and with not a cloud in the bluest of blue skies, unlike the day before.

Originally, this invasion had been planned for the previous day, but Monday the 5th of June 1944 had been a day of torrential rain and high seas, making it frustratingly impossible for the plan to go ahead, even for Churchill and his merry band of cronies. However, now the day was here, it had finally arrived and nothing was going to hold the invasion back.

All along the length of the beach they could hear the shrill sound of whistles being blown, announcing the arrival of the landing parties.

"Good luck, my friend," Ben said, vigorously shaking Peter by the hand.

"Good luck to you too," Peter smiled. "See you on the other side."

"Ben was just about to ask his friend what he meant by, "see you on the other side," when the front of the landing craft was lowered into the sea and they caught their first glimpse of 'Sword Beach' stretching out before them. All hell broke loose as pandemonium set in.

The men, not realising that the landing crafts had deposited them short of the beach, all jumped into the sea to find it was almost four foot in depth in some places. For some, this was fatal! More than one young man tripped as they entered the waves, shocked by the deepness of the water. Some of these young men could not swim, with the result being that after only a few seconds, Ben and Peter could see bodies floating on the surface of the water, although far worse was yet to come.

As they ran like hysterical chickens onto the sand they stopped in their tracks, for there was no noise – no sound whatsoever.

"Where are they? Have we survived?" Ben questioned his friend.

His query was answered by a sudden crescendo of noise, as hundreds of German troops opened fire on the men in front of Peter and Ben, cutting them down like the sitting dicks at a funfair that they were.

"Get down!" Ben ordered, with the pair leaping onto the sand and taking cover, both lying as flat as possible.

As they lay there, they were surprised to hear gunfire coming from behind the German stronghold. What had happened was that the night before, just after midnight, hundreds of commandos' had been parachuted behind the enemy lines, dropped from silent gliders.

All night long they had been busily destroying bridges and roads, thus blocking any German retreat or stopping more troops from arriving in the area to fortify the soldiers already here.

This resulted in this battle, which began at 07-25 in the morning and had all but ended by 08-00, with far less casualties occurring than was first expected. Even so, of the twenty-nine thousand British soldiers who landed that day on Sword Beach, there were still six hundred and ninety men who gave their lives, although the German casualties were far greater.

It would later be confirmed that the total number of allied troops who died in that one day of battle on the combined beaches of Normandy would be Four thousand four hundred and fourteen men. This did not include the German casualties.

After the commotion seemed to have died down, Ben Richards dared to lift his head to see what was happening. Twenty yards ahead of them, he could see there were dead bodies piled up two or three deep. Looking around he could see many more bodies were now floating on top of the waves, although now in a sea of blood. This was a heartbreaking sight to see.

"Come on, my friend, time to go," he whispered to Peter Collins, but there was no response.

"Come on, Peter," he said again, a little louder this time. Again there was no response.

"Peter!" he demanded, louder still and poking his friend in the back, but his friend did not move.

Ben then spotted the hole in his best friend's head and realised that his friend and companion for the past three years whilst at the training camp, was now dead!

"Hitler, you Nazi bastard!" he yelled as loudly as he could. Even though nobody heard him, he was still distraught and raging with a mixture of sadness but mainly anger. His best friend had died, and for what?

Ben Richards found himself in a state of extreme shock. Heartbroken for his loss, he suddenly felt very alone and distressingly helpless.

Immediately, as he looked down at the limp and lifeless body of his colleague Peter for the last time, his thoughts turned to a certain young blonde girl, a girl with a mass of beautiful, long flowing curly hair. A girl named, Yvette.

"I have to find her," he said quietly to himself. "I need to find her. I must find her – I just have to find Yvette," he despaired.

CHAPTER 24
THE SAVIOUR OF PARIS

Since that fateful day when she'd been forced kill the young German soldier, life for Yvette in Tourant had become pretty sedentary, as well as being very boring.

She became angry with Patrice, because even though she'd proved herself to the rest of the men in the gang by protecting the women and children of the village, he was still reluctant to allow her to go with them when on missions of destruction.

With plenty of time on her hands the young woman had spent many hours talking with fellow resistance members on the radio, as well as receiving messages broadcast in 'Morse Code' and sent by the authorities in Britain.

During one of these broadcasts, one coded message sent in secret, told of the forthcoming invasion of the beaches in Normandy involving the combined British, American and Canadian armies.

This message was also intercepted by members of the Maquis, who in turn, contacted as many members of the resistance as they possibly could, instructing them to organise raids and attacks on the German enemy, blowing up railway lines and road bridges, so as to stop the flow of the Nazis from travelling to and reaching the beaches on the coast, to intercept the invaders and to stop them in their tracks.

The Maquis were the largest of all the resistance groups in France and were known as the 'French Forces of the Interior.' (FFI) They lived in the mountains and were made up of German deserters and Spanish compatriots, although they mainly consisted of French men and women in hiding from the enemy.

The Maquis particularly hated a man who was the leader of the Gestapo at that time, a man named, Klaus Barbie of the SS, christening him 'The Butcher of Lyon.' He in turn also hated them and everything they stood for, and dedicated his life to hunting them down and killing as many of their members as possible.

During his time working in the area known as 'Vichy France,' Barbie made it his duty to torture as many prisoners as he could, especially those being of the Jewish faith along with members of the resistance, or better still, both!

The leader of the Maquis was a man named Georges Guingouin. During one of his broadcasts listened to by Yvette, Patrice and the rest of the men in Tourant, he ordered that one of the resistance members, "Must kill Barbie." It was said that whoever achieved this would be given a 'very good bonus.'

"That's it then," Patrice had stressed to his men. "We have to find Barbie and kill the bastard. The man has to die." This statement was met with a huge cheer by all the men.

Yvette did not react in this way, as during her short time based here in France, she'd seen enough death to last a lifetime and she didn't wish to see any more.

For the next few months, every evening the men gathered to listen to the 'British Broadcasting World Service' broadcasting from London and giving details about the British and American advances into France, and eventually into Paris.

"We've got those Nazi bastards on the run," Patrice smiled while the rest of his men agreed.

"It will not be long now," Helmut Schön claimed.

Yvette always found it strange how the German could be so happy about his fellow countrymen suffering in this way.

"They'll soon be there now," Jacques Santiago stated.

Jacques was correct in his assumptions, as British, American and Canadian troops, after sweeping their way through the villages and towns of France, reached the outskirts of Paris by the middle of August.

Upon hearing the news of the allied troops good progress, on the 15th of August the Paris police force all went on strike, resulting in German troops facing an uprising and losing control of many public buildings.

The resistance became highly active when they blocked many roads and damaged German vehicles, so much so that a ceasefire was called. However, this ceasefire was ignored by the resistance and many skirmishes continued into the next day.

"Time to go," announced Patrice Bauton.

"And about time too," Maurice Lazlo declared. "Let's go and kill us some Nazi bastards!"

They all piled inside the three Citroen Traction Avant cars, which by now had all been painted with the sign of the French flag on the side panels and roof of each car for safety, and began the journey into Paris.

As she stared up at the entrance of the Hotel Paradiso, all the memories came flooding back to Yvette. She reminisced about her time spent there with her beautiful friend, Luisa Silva.

She thought of the occasions spent inside the laundry room close to the kitchen, and all the nervousness she'd felt when sending and receiving messages on the radio which was very well hidden there, all the time with Luisa being 'on guard' whilst waiting outside in the corridor.

"Are you ready, Yvette?" Patrice questioned the girl, becoming very aware of her impending trepidation.

"I'm ready," she replied.

The girl stepped inside the once beautiful hotel and was surprised to see how quiet it now was. Gone were the hoards of troops traipsing about the place, many of them being rude to the girls who still worked there, with some of them making sexual advances to these young ladies. Even though the younger soldiers had been ordered not to do this, well, as they say, 'boys will be boys!'

Glad of the company of Patrice, alongside André Gastard,

Jacques Santiago, Helmut Schön, Enrique Leron, Maurice Lazlo and the rest of the group of resistance men, Yvette made her way slowly along the corridor, remaining diligent at all times.

She stopped in her tracks when she heard the sound of the lift door sliding open, and froze when she spotted a young girl walk into the reception area. The young girl also froze when she suddenly saw twelve men pointing rifles at her, standing beside one girl whom she thought she recognised.

She looked at Yvette and screwed up her face, contorting it as she racked her brain to think where she recognised her from.

"I used to have long black hair when I came here regularly," Yvette admitted, helping the girl with her memory.

"I remember you now," the girl stated. "Do you remember me – Maisie? But your hair.....?"

"It was a wig," Yvette told the girl before asking, "Maisie, where are all the German soldiers? Are they in hiding here?"

"No, they all left last week," Maisie replied, happy now that the men had all lowered their rifles and were no longer a threat to her.

Yvette was just about to say something to the girl, but Maisie suddenly revealed, "There is still one young German staying here. He is a very nice young man named, Wolfgang."

"Wolfgang," Patrice repeated almost choking.

"Yes Wolfgang," Maisie stipulated. "And he IS a very nice man," she stressed. "When the troops all evacuated, Wolfgang went into hiding for two days. All that time he was hiding in the laundry room."

When she heard this, Yvette equally almost choked. She thought about her time operating the radio from that very room and wondered whether the radio equipment was still there, or if it had been discovered by now and destroyed.

"Where is young Wolfgang now?" Yvette asked Maisie.

"He is sitting all alone on the top floor of the hotel. He's in room seven-twenty-three," Maisie divulged.

"Come," Patrice said, instructing Yvette and the rest of the men to follow.

"Please don't hurt him," Maisie pleaded as they began to leave. Yvette gave her a reassuring smile.

A few minutes later they all stood outside the door of room seven-twenty-three. "Wolfgang," Yvette shouted. "Are you there?"

"Allo, yes, I'm here," a voice from inside the room nervously replied.

"Is it safe for me to come inside?" the girl questioned.

"Of course," the German replied. "I am no danger to you."

As Yvette was about to enter, Patrice stopped her. "Let me go first," he said.

"Okay Patrice, but please don't hurt him," Yvette said gently.

Patrice took three steps inside the room with his rifle held high and ready for action, but as there was no danger for either him or his men, he nodded to Yvette for her to enter the room.

"I surrender," Wolfgang said, whilst raising both arms into the air as Yvette entered.

She looked at, and felt sorry for the lad. He looked about nineteen years of age and was sitting on the edge of the bed looking like a little lost soul. After removing his German uniform, he'd placed his rifle and firearm neatly in the corner of the room and in plain sight.

"You can put your arms down now," Yvette instructed.

"But I surrender," he repeated.

"Yes, we got all that, but Wolfgang, everyone has surrendered," she revealed. "All your men have surrendered. For you, the war is now over." Hearing this brought a massive smile to young Wolfgang's face.

"I never even fired my rifle," he stated, still smiling broadly. "I promise you, I never hurt anyone, and I definitely did not kill anybody."

"Come with us, Wolfgang," Yvette said in a soft and friendly voice. "I promise that you will be okay. We will all keep you safe."

The next day, Friday August the 25th 1944 was a day that history was made when all the dignitaries came together in the Hotel Maurice, situated on the Rue de Rivoli, a hotel which had been set up as the headquarters of the General de Infanterie on the 8th of August 1944. This was a very regal hotel and not too far from the Hotel Paradiso, where it had all began for Yvette, so many months ago.

Although the occupying troops surrendered on the 24th of August, the next day was the day when Germany officially surrendered the city of Paris and all the lands of France. All the troops still left in the city were taken prisoner, although there were not too many of them left, and those who were left were a sorry sight, being mostly unmotivated conscripts who had no interest in being there.

The surrender was made to the 'Free French Forces' by a man named, General Dietrich Hugo Hermann von Choltitz, who was officially known as the last commander of Nazi occupied Paris.

Two days earlier, on the 23rd of August 1944, the Fuhrer, Adolph Hitler, had sent Choltitz a personal telegram ordering him to destroy the city before surrendering to the 'enemy.'

"Paris must not pass into the enemy's hands, except as a field of ruins," Hitler had stated in his order.

However, this was an order that Choltitz had refused to obey, stating that Paris was too important and far too beautiful a city to destroy at the hands of Hitler.

When later questioned about these actions, he also stated that another reason for his refusal to carry out such an act of carnage was because he strongly believed that Hitler, by now, was totally insane!

Because Hitler's directive was not carried out, Choltitz was forever after known as the 'Saviour of Paris.'

Along with other senior German officers he was escorted to England, where he spent the rest of the war at a place called Trent Park, based in London. No charges were ever brought against Choltitz and he was released in 1947.

The threat by the Maquis to hunt down and execute Klaus Barbie, 'The Butcher of Lyon,' never came to fruition.

After France was liberated, Barbie disappeared and went into hiding. It would be thirty-eight years before he was caught and convicted of war crimes. He was never executed and died at seventy-seven years of age, after living for many years in Bolivia.

The 25th of August 1944 was also an historic day for a certain young and beautiful blonde girl, because for Yvette Colbert, or Yvette Jackson to give her real name, her war and her adventures in France were finally over.

CHAPTER 25
LIFE GOES ON

That night, at the end of the day of the official surrender, Patrice Bauton and his merry band of resistance members chose to spend the night at The Hotel Paradiso. It seemed a fitting end to stay in the same place as where the enemy had been residing for most of the past four years since the occupation.

Yvette was made to feel very welcome by the girls who'd been working there for all that time, waiting hand and foot on the soldiers of the enemy. They gave her the best room in the hotel to stay in, also using the finest linen to spread over the mattress of the freshly made bed for her to sleep on, all taken from the laundry room where she'd been broadcasting from when she'd first arrived in the city.

That night, even though she could hear the constant noise of people partying in the streets of Paris, the second she lay her head down upon the extremely comfortable pillow, she drifted into a deep, luxurious sleep.

It gave her great comfort to know that for the first time in many, many months, she actually had a key to the door of this room and was able to lock herself away, confident in the knowledge that she could sleep soundly with no interruptions and no danger of being woken by enemy soldiers in the dead of night, whilst on the end of a machine gun and bursting through the door!

The next morning, Yvette woke bright and early. She was excited about the prospect of visiting her friends at the Café DuPont, but Patrice gave her a warning.

"You're not going there on your own," he told her.

"But why?" she questioned. "I should be safe now. The occupation is over."

"Yes, it may be over, but there may still be a few disgruntled

Germans wandering about the place, willing to extract revenge on anyone unlucky enough to get in the way," Patrice pointed out to the girl, and then as if to emphasise the point, said, "And that could include you!"

But I want to see Henri and Nicole," Yvette stressed. "And I really want to see my friend, Luisa."

"I know you do, but it's not safe at the moment," the Frenchman stated. "But we will come with you. We will take you," he suggested.

"What, all of you?" Yvette said, asking for clarity.

"Of course," Patrice confirmed. "Anyway, it will be nice to meet your friends."

And so, a little later in the day, Yvette, surrounded by her twelve 'bodyguards' left the hotel Paradiso to begin the forty-five minute trek to the café. Along the way they could see that the celebrations, which had started the previous night, were still in full swing. If anything, it seemed even more boisterous than the night before, with far more of the young allied troops joining in with the festivities.

The young Parisian ladies were now loving all this attention, with some of them being far more amorous and, it must be said, 'generous,' than they'd bargained for.

"I believe there could be a large population explosion in nine months from now," Yvette joked, to which all the men laughed. They all observed how nice it was to see the girl looking happy again.

The reality of this was that many of these women partying away and giving their bodies to these young British, American and Canadian men were the same women who would have been giving their bodies to the Germans, only a few weeks earlier.

The fact was that many of these women were later discovered as living with high ranking Nazi officers for the complete duration of the four years of occupation. When these collaborators were caught, they were dragged kicking and screaming to very public spaces, where in plain view of all in attendance, they were being shown no mercy and had their heads shaved down to the scalp. This way, when they were seen out in public, everyone knew they were collaborators of the enemy for many months to come.

This happened to at least twenty thousand of these 'scum' women, although it would be far worse for the six hundred or so who blatantly lived full time as 'kept women' with these Nazis and paid for it with their lives, being publicly executed for their indiscretions!

As Yvette approached the café, this time approaching for the first time at the front entrance and not the bakery door, she was surprised and a little sad to see the premises were not open. She tapped on the glass fronted entrance and waited.

Sure enough, after two or three minutes, she spotted the large figure of Monsieur DuPont looming towards her. He stopped to slightly move the curtains aside to better see whom it was disturbing him, but when he noticed Yvette standing there, in his excitement he almost tore the door from its hinges in his desire to get it open.

Yvette, I cannot believe it's you," he shouted, making no attempt to hide his extreme pleasure at seeing the girl standing before him. "Come in, child," he invited, but was surprised when she was followed inside by the twelve men who'd accompanied her.

After throwing her arms around him and kissing him on both cheeks, Parisian style, she introduced him individually to the men, finally telling him, "And this is my very good friend, Patrice Bauton, the man who has taken very good care of me for all this time."

"It's very good to finally meet you," Henri said to Patrice. "I have heard you spoken about many times by our mutual friend, Jean Renoir, but it is an honour to finally put a face to the name."

"The pleasure is all mine, Monsieur, I can assure you," Patrice replied smiling.

"Henri," Yvette said. "Is Luisa still here?" She asked this question but was nervous about the answer, as she didn't know if anything might have happened to her wonderful friend.

"She is upstairs, still sleeping," Henri revealed. Instantly seeing the look of relief on the young girl's face, he said. "Go up and see her."

Yvette almost skipped up the rickety staircase until she reached the top floor and the attic room. There before her, she could make out the beautiful shape of Luisa Silva's body slowly moving up and down as she snored whilst under the cover of the blanket.

"Luisa," Yvette whispered. "Luisa," she said a little louder. The body began to stir. "Luisa," she repeated again, a little louder still this time.

She saw the body begin to slowly move and then noticed the head turning towards her. She spotted the eyes beginning to blink, so as to adjust to the light coming through the sloping window, where Yvette had spent many hours craning her neck to look at the Eiffel Tower.

"Yvette?" Luisa questioned, as her tiredness seemed to evaporate. "Yvette?" she said again. "Yvette, is that really you?"

"Yes it is," Yvette replied, and waited for the excitement to explode.

"Yvette!" Luisa screamed, as she leapt from the bed in all her glory, reaching for a blanket to cover her naked body.

The two friends met in the middle of the room and threw their arms around each other. They then hugged and laughed – hugged and cried – hugged, and hugged, and hugged, almost squeezing the life out of each other, whilst screaming with delight at being in each other's company again.

"Yvette, you made it. You survived," Luisa finally blurted out with great emotion.

"No, my friend, we survived," Yvette replied with equal passion. "We have both survived."

Over the next few days whilst life returned to some kind of normality, Henri, Nicole, and of course, Luisa sat down with Yvette and filled her in with what had been happening during her absence.

She was shocked when she heard how Herr Gruber of the Gestapo had more or less confessed his love for her that day when speaking with Henri, but she was even more shocked to discover that two days before the surrender, not wishing to live with the guilt of what he, as a Nazi officer, had been forced to have taken part in, in the peace and quiet of his office he'd taken out his service revolver, put the gun to his head, and had blown his brains out!

A few weeks later, Yvette had a surprise visit from Jean Renoir accompanied by Madame Chambourcey. He had some devastatingly bad news for the girl.

He told her that he'd been contacted by Mr. Black, formerly of 'The Department of Fish & Fisheries' and during this conversation, when the talk had turned to that of Yvette, he informed Jean that her friend, Peter Collins, had died on the beach during that day of the Normandy landings.

"What about Ben Richards?" Yvette had asked tearfully when hearing the news of Peter's death.

"No news as of yet," Jean responded to the tearful girl.

Although this was true at the time, within the next year or so, Yvette would discover that Ben Richards had also been killed in action, this time during the final push into Berlin and only days before the end of the conflict. Upon hearing the confirmation of this news, the girl was naturally devastated.

At the end of the war, in June of 1945, Yvette returned to the shores of England and took up her previous post at the medical college, which she'd left after having that fateful meeting with Messer's Black and Blue at 'The Department of Fish & Fisheries' in Great Portland Street, London.

However, after only a few months at the college, with Jennifer Rumsey no longer in attendance she was bored with this life, so gave up her medical training. She had to admit that she was hankering for her old life in Paris.

After a tearful farewell to her parents, she returned to Paris in the December of that year and walked through the door of the Café DuPont on Christmas Eve 1945, where she was welcomed back with open arms by Henri and Nicole DuPont, along with the very beautiful, Luisa Silva.

The two girls worked alongside each other for many years, and when Henri and Nicole eventually retired, they were happy to hand the business over to the two, still firm friends.

After years of hard work, Yvette and Luisa were able to change the business from a humble café into a modern and very swanky restaurant, which they renamed, "Le Maison DuPont."

There was one thing that never changed however; the menu forever contained one item – "Henri's German Bratwurst."

Even though they had come close over the years, neither girl ever married. They were not sad about this and always said to each other, "We'll always have Paris," usually said at the bottom of the Eiffel Tower on a boozy ladies night out. Whatever happened in the future, they would always have their memories, but one of them would always be known as –

Yvette of the S.O.E
(Winston Churchill's Special Operations Executive.)

Thank you for reading her story.

THE END

Also by this author

RETURN TO AUSCHWITZ
By
Kevin Paul Woodrow

A sixteen year old boy notices a beautiful sixteen year old girl across a crowded room. Their eyes meet and an instant attraction is formed. They fall madly in love, but there is a problem – They are both prisoners in Auschwitz.

This is the story of Peter Florea, a young Jewish boy who makes a terrible mistake when in 1943 he volunteers to be sent from Hungary to a 'work camp.' He arrives to find he is in the notorious, Auschwitz Birkenau, the death camp in Southern Poland.

Whilst there he meets and falls madly in love with a beautiful Polish girl, Margo Koval, but will their love survive?

Two days before Auschwitz is liberated by the Russian army, Peter watches in horror as Margo is marched out of the camp. Has she been executed? Is she lying in a mass grave somewhere in the forest? He will spend the rest of his life trying to discover the truth - and find her.

This is the romantic story of holocaust survival, a tale of a love that spans many decades. Beautiful but heartbreaking, this is a story that will leave you breathless.

THE SECRET JEW
OF MUNICH

A beautiful story of wartime survival, this is the romantic love story about a young Austrian Jewish girl who survives WWII by hiding from the Nazis whilst living amongst them in Hitler's Munich.

There was a knock on the door of the apartment. She looked through the spyglass to see two Gestapo officers standing there. What did they want, had they come for her? Had she been discovered after all this time? Was she about to lose everything, including her life?

Rebecca was a beautiful teenager with many friends who loved her. However, for her, life as a young Austrian woman would change dramatically when her country was invaded by the Nazis, resulting in Austria being annexed on the 11th of March 1938.

The problem for Rebecca was that even though her family were not at all religious, her papers contained the word "Juden." This word alone was enough to make her life impossible, for in the eyes of the Nazis, as a Jew she was the enemy.

Her friends rallied, all wanting to help. Her best friend was an artist and he made fake papers for her by copying those of another friend, but the two girls could not live in the same city, Vienna.

For this reason, Rebecca moves to live with her friend's relations, in of all places, Munich, the birth place of the Nazis. Here she will spend the entire war years hiding from the Nazis by living amongst them whilst working and socialising with them – all the time hiding in plain sight.

Both Books Are

Available from your local Amazon site

In eBook and Paperback

Printed in Great Britain
by Amazon